HELL BIRD

The Fourth Anna Harris Novel

A V IAIN

8.35:00

D ARKNESS DOMINATES EVERYTHING.
   Walls on every side of me.
No room to even stretch out my limbs.
Hardly able to even shift a fingernail.
I lie in a coffin. A simple wooden box.
My feet face the cockpit.
My head is lolled back.
As if I'm about to compete in some sort of reverse luge competition.
Outside, but seemingly right inside my skull, the aeroplane engines hum.
High-pitched.
Almost *impossibly* loud.
They rise to a *screech*.
Vibration takes hold of everything.
It feels as if the whole plane might break apart.
Feels as if it'll break *me* apart.

The whole baggage area stinks of kerosene.

As if someone holds a rag soaked with it over my mouth and nostrils.

I try to take shallow breaths.

But know I have to breathe deeply sometime.

Now.

The plane rockets forwards. Drags me along.

Its unwilling passenger.

I feel the box shifting a little.

Then the elasticated straps I heard the baggage handlers working on stretch tight, pin the box down to the base of the plane. Keep it from shifting off its spot. Keeping the box—*me inside*—from sliding off into the side of the baggage area.

Shattering open.

Breaking every bone in my body.

Right as the vibrations, as the *screech* of the engines, become almost too much to bear, I reach down to my side. Feel for my teddy bear. For the .45 strapped to my ankle. I slip my hand over the top, feel its sturdy shape, feel its chill up against my skin.

Whoever said guns are evil?

There's a long moment where I feel the plane wheels rooted to the runway, surely not going to lift off. Perhaps we'll end up in a field, the plane pitching forwards onto its nose.

And I know that I'll die.

And I wonder if I'll care.

But the speed hits a harder note still, and then, with that gut-lurching moment of weightlessness, I feel the plane lifting off.

Lifting its *passengers* up . . . along with its hidden human cargo.

Even though the darkness surrounding me is complete, I clench my eyes shut. Then I reach down for my wrist with my free hand—the one which doesn't grip my gun.

God, I *hate* flying.

Almost as much as I hate Brian Mathewson and his rancid enterprise: Mathewson Media.

. . . If only I didn't need the two of them so badly.

I find my wristwatch, the familiar button there, and I squeeze it.

Set off the timer.

Give or take eight and a half hours to get this done with.

Eight and a half hours to kill.

8.34:59

N EVER ONE to trust my own judgement, I lever open an eye, illuminate the display of my watch and see that, indeed, the countdown has begun.

Eight hours, thirty-five minutes, and fifty-nine seconds.

Said like that, it sounds an awfully long time.

But, I know, in reality, that there's a lot to get done.

And it's not like there's going to be anything necessarily pleasant awaiting me at the finish line, either.

I've heard, here and there, that plane hijackers aren't much in vogue these days.

I can feel the plane climbing steeply, and already I can feel sweat trickle up from my lower back to my shoulders. Perhaps, if I choose to fly this way again, I'll be sure to slap a sticker on the side of my coffin, indicating that my head should be laid in the direction of travel.

I loosen my shoulders, still feeling the forces of the rising plane in all the wrong places on my body. I feel my abdomen tighten, and I'm glad that I went for comfortable clothes—as is advisable on any sort of long-distance plane journey:

All-weather, waterproof trousers.

A light-weight, zip-up fleece.

And a sleeveless vest underneath.

All of them black, of course, but that goes without saying.

Now that the plane's lifted up some way, the pressurised cabin is beginning to get the best of me. Already, I can feel it robbing me of my sense of smell as efficiently as someone jabbing a bundled-up hanky in each of my nostrils.

I guess that even in *executive* travel they cut back on the air con.

As I hear the engines lower their tone a little, I become aware of another sound around me. A sort of *scratching* sound. I swallow hard, trying to regain my hearing. It doesn't work first time, or the second. Third time, though, is a charm.

Yes, sure enough, I can hear scrabbling around.

The unmistakable sound of wood cranking against wood.

Time?

Is it time already?

To be honest, I can't quite recall the plan, if there was ever a plan at all.

That's the thing with last-minute jobs, everything's in the air . . . if you'll excuse the pun.

Deciding that it's *definitely* the sound of scratching, I reach about, remembering how to let myself out of this coffin. There, sure enough, are the little fluorescent tabs, one for each of my hands. I reach out, take hold of them both, and *yank*.

Nothing happens.

I try again.

Once more, *nothing*.

The plane banks sharply to one side.

The coffin encasing me shifts a little.

My gut goes in all sorts of unnatural directions.

In my mind's eye, I picture the plane, only a couple of metres above the surface of the earth—or, God forbid, the *ocean*—and ready to topple right over.

To *explode*.

I breathe in again, willing the plane to level out.

And maybe someone *is* looking out for me, because the plane does just that.

I relax my shoulders.

Lay them back.

Tell myself that I'll be getting off soon.

Be getting off in just a few hours.

Just a little more than a normal working day.

A nine-to-five job.

Once more, I reach up, take hold of those fluorescent tabs, and pull them as hard as I dare. Just like that, and maybe I over-cook it a touch, the lid of the coffin flies upwards.

Away from me.

It clatters to the floor of the cargo hold.

And, just like that, I rise from the dead.

8.19:32

A S I SIT UP in my coffin, I feel a jab of pain in my chest. I cracked some ribs a few weeks ago, and I'm not exactly one-hundred-per-cent.

Not that I was going to let on that fact to my employer, Brian Mathewson.

Darkness continues to surround me.

And then a bright—*too bright*—light blinks on.

As the painful, prickling sensation in my chest fades, I hear, off to the side, "I've got painkillers if you'd like some, Anna."

I jerk my head around, holding up my forearm to shield against the glare of the light. The sound of the plane engines obscures the voice somewhat, but, still, it's clear as day.

Of course it is.

Adam Alderknot—AKA 'AA'—stands beside his own coffin, the lid, just like mine, lying on the floor, disposed of.

He holds a bright torch in his hand.

And I wonder why *I* didn't get one.

My eyes, just on instinct, really, drift down to AA's thigh, see the gun he has holstered there. Like mine, a .45. And I can't help wondering if it's *Hotflush* . . . AA's weapon of choice.

Yes, *surely* it is—AA would only bring his very best friends along on *this* job.

And, yes, my gun has a name too:

Punisher.

Not *too* compensatory, is it?

AA has on the same clothes as me. A light-weight, zip-up fleece. A vest of his own underneath.

Back in the hotel room we shared last night, I couldn't help but make a comment on how his biceps were looking a little 'weathered'.

To say that AA got antsy with me is an understatement, and I can tell, from the way that he's keeping that zip-up fleece very much *on* that he's somewhat self-conscious.

Like my opinion matters at all.

As if any *woman's* opinion matters to AA.

I'm glad to see that AA's usually perfect, slicked-back black hair has come a cropper during take-off. During our little adventure in our respective coffins.

AA paces over to me, offers me his hand.

I think a long while about it, resting my elbows on the sides of the coffin, and then I accept.

There's no point in us playing macho games here, we're on level-pegging: allies on this job, at the very least.

I feel somewhat less steady on my feet when I eventually get there, and I feel a slight blush rise in my cheeks as AA takes a hold of my forearm firmly, to stop me from slipping over.

From falling on my arse.

When he meets my eye again, I see there's none of that joviality there from when he offered me those pills a couple of moments ago. "You okay?" he says.

I shake off his hold, give him a nod. "Yeah," I say, "just fine."

Without AA's help, I step out over the side of the coffin.

Stand nice and firm on the floor of the cargo bay.

He hands me the torch. "Keep it shining on me, okay?" he says, turning his attention downwards, to his trouser pockets.

I'm pleasantly surprised—not to mention *suspicious*—that the plane is flying so neatly, so *smoothly*. I've learned to trust that planes and turbulence just can't be separated, no matter how much this nervous flyer would like them to be.

So I'm wary in the knowledge that turbulence is *never* too far away.

Even as he goes through the cargo pockets of his trousers, I can't help but notice that AA's still slipping me sidelong glances. A couple of times, I get the pleasure of seeing him give a wince.

I actually smile when I see it happen.

Around the time that I cracked my ribs, AA went and got himself shot . . . in fact, he seems to be getting himself shot so often now that it's almost become something of a joke between the two of us.

Assassins' humour.

I glance about what will be our new home for the coming hours.

Getting a decent look at it from the light which seeps out from the torch into our surroundings.

I don't know quite what I was expecting from the cargo bay of an executive jet liner, but I'm surprised to see that it's fairly sparse. That there're these elasticated, sludge-green coloured nets all about the place; at our feet, covering other luggage.

AA slips out this device that looks, to me, something like a barcode scanner. He taps away at the buttons, scowling at himself in a way which makes him look like a Neanderthal. I don't say anything, of course. I know I'm on thin ice as it is, following that remark of mine about his biceps the night before.

Male confidence is a very fragile thing.

Finally, AA seems to make something of a breakthrough.

He holds the device up to the torchlight, showing me a series of numbers on the green-backed screen. "We're good to go," he says.

"Are we?" I say, not really following what just happened, and instead deciding to do my best in my de facto role of *torchbearer*.

I hang onto AA's heels as he trudges across the cargo hold, and over to the door which, apparently, leads out into the main section of the plane.

As I stand at his shoulders, the plane lurches a little to the left.

I brace myself just as hard as if we'd been hit by a cruise missile.

AA, not missing a beat, says, "You know, the best thing about flying is that if something does go wrong then we're all most likely dead." Turning his attention away from that *device* in his hand for a few seconds, and to the locking mechanism on the beige, flight door, he adds, "It'll be over"—he clicks his fingers —"just like that."

I suck in a long, deep breath.

Then blow it out.

What've I got myself into this time?

7.56:10

WHEN I GLANCE BACK at my watch, I see that a
good amount of time has gone by.

Returning to day-job think, I imagine myself in a nice, smart
trouser suit, just having turned up to the office, just having sat
down at my desk to check my email, cup of black coffee steaming
away before me, bringing me around from my dozy state.

Readying my brain for another workday.

"*Shit!*" AA says.

"What?" I reply, turning back to AA, and seeing that he's *still*
busy with the door, and—more specifically—the locking mechanism. "You can't do it?"

"No," AA says, "it's not that I can't *do it* it's just that I'm not
sure whether I've brought along the right tools for the job."

I get in a quick roll of my eyes.

If there's something about men—and *problems*—it's that they
won't *ever* admit that they're beaten.

I just keep on shining my light down on the hands of the

ever-more frustrated AA, doing my best to make sympathetic noises, because, truly, what I know about locks on planes could fill the back of a box of matches.

AA finally reaches the end of his wick, though, letting out a parting, "*Bugger!*" while dropping the metal tool he was working with. He kicks the door *hard* and I sort of hope that no member of the cabin crew happen to be lurking at this end of the plane at this particular moment.

I listen to the tool tinkle about on the floor and—just as if it was some enormous whale angered by AA's lack of reverence for its insides—the plane banks to the right sharply.

Bounces once.

Then again.

I lose my footing.

AA loses his.

The two of us take a tumble.

I cling on tight to the torch, some sort of ragged determination stopping me from loosening my grip on it. I hit the side of the plane *hard* with my shoulder and come to a sudden stop.

I blink away my daze, trying to get a handle on what just happened.

I glance up, about the cargo area, only figuring out that I still cling to the sole light source after a second or so of staring into the gloom.

When I breathe in this time, I feel a flash of pain through my ribs.

I can't help but give a slight *whine*.

When I finally get my breath back, I shine the torch about the cargo hold, trying to catch sight of AA again. But the best that I can make of our surroundings is a whole landscape of *lumps* . . . of luggage, and *packages*, all being carted along to our destination.

"AA?" I say, out into the darkness.

No reply.

I brace myself for AA to pop up from any side—it would be his idea of a joke to do that.

Still feeling the plane wobbling about on turbulence, I ease myself back up onto my two feet. I'm glad I decided to go with a pair of well-worn-in trainers—*also black*—for this particular job. It means that when my feet swell up, as they *always* do on flights, I have some more wriggle room than in the standard ankle boots.

I take a step forwards, well aware that the plane might bank in a direction of its choosing at any moment. Or it might be buffeted by a fresh wave of turbulence.

I trust mechanical engineering just about as much as I trust nature . . . which is to say not at all.

As I go along, I focus on keeping my torch shining on the path before me, on the elasticated netting which drapes over everything and which acts as a sort of man-made foliage, just tempting me to shove a foot in its embrace and trip me over.

I step over several suitcases, feel the plane give a slight shudder, then level out.

I stand with my legs a shoulders-width apart, already with a *far* greater appreciation for the job flight crews do—and all while wrangling shopping carts on wheels and dealing with troublesome passengers.

I shine my torch about the cargo area, trying to catch sight of AA, and—*finally*—I do.

He's lying flat on the ground, on his front, his arms resting down at his sides, as if he's simply decided to drift off to sleep.

As I get closer to him, I'm *sure* that he's trying to pull my leg in some way, but, if he is, then he's making a good fist of playing dead.

"AA?" I say again, sure that he's about to bounce up, like the proverbial spaniel.

But, no.

It's only when I get down beside him, in a crouch, shine the torch in his eyes, that I get some sort of a response. I watch on as his eyelids flicker and a half moon of eyeball swivels about in its socket. I reach out, take hold of AA's shoulder. "Come on," I say, my voice much lighter than the tension I feel growing in my throat, "time's a wasting."

AA crunches his eyes shut, obviously in pain, and then, with a shudder which seems to pass along his entire body, he folds himself, arriving—*unconvincingly*—back onto his knees. As he rubs at his head, the part where, apparently, he hit the side of the cargo area, I notice his fleece has ridden up to expose his abdomen.

Although I know it's *rude*, I can't help but stare.

Stare at AA's side.

See the skin there, even in the uneven, bright torchlight I hold, has got a greenish hue to it. A little bruising, sure, but there's something about the way the bullet hole—where he was shot—has turned black around the edges, that makes my stomach sink.

I look back to AA. "Tell me you've seen a doctor about that."

7.44:44

IN THAT MACHO WAY men do, AA fobs me off.

He simply pulls his top back down to conceal the bullet wound.

I wonder if he's going to drawl something along the lines of 'don't worry about it' out of the corner of his mouth, to complete the image of the hardened, solitary cowboy he's trying hard to project.

I wonder if I should tell him that there *weren't* any English cowboys.

Not as far as I know, anyway . . .

Realising that AA's not in the mood to speak about his injury, I decide to turn my attention back to the job at hand. Our mission, quite simply, is to retrieve a memory stick from a passenger on the plane: the memory stick which our employer, Brian Mathewson, is being blackmailed with.

The one with *our*—mine and AA's—details etched onto it.

Although Brian's paying us to go through with this job, and

has been the one to mastermind our *unique* entrance onto the plane, we know that each of us is on the line here. And not just me, AA, and Brian are implicated. Every 'respectable figure' who has been forced to use an assassin, or another somewhat under-hand employee, stands to lose everything.

Brian can usually deal with such threats with a barrage of bad press for the individual in question—having friends on the senior editorial staff of just about every single media outlet in the western world has its benefits—but the people implicated by the information on the memory stick might get just a *touch* twitchy to (a) discover such a database exists, and (b) to find out that their names are on it.

And the people on the memory stick are the sorts who make it their business to know all about themselves, where they appear and—*more importantly*—where they *don't*.

Simply put, if me and AA fail to recover the memory stick then it's not only Brian's goose that's cooked, but ours too . . . and when some valiant do-gooder goes public with the contents of the memory stick, with the revelation that Brian Mathewson and his—extremely exclusive, and *celebrity*—clientele are involved with murder, and worse; well, then I suppose that these Great British Isles are going to get a really nasty shock.

Perhaps we aren't so different from those third-world dictator-ships we like to look down our noses at.

That revelation would *really* hurt on a national—if not *international*—scale.

So, in other words—or maybe I just say it to make myself feel better—the world's on the line right here.

On this plane.

And Brian, never one to skimp on the theatrical, dubbed this job Hell Bird.

Good, old Brian.

I wonder if—one of these days—he'll deign to get his own hands dirty.

Or if he'll be just as content passing out dirty money.

Money which ends up in *my* account.

AA shifts away. Making a show of turning his back to me, he heads for the door once again. This time he doesn't have the tool, so I have no idea exactly how he's planning on making inroads.

A couple of moments later, he enlightens me.

AA begins to shoulder barge the door.

When he goes for his third try, I grab him by the elbow and hold him back.

I don't like to show off my superior strength too often.

I like it when men underestimate me.

When they don't realise that a whole bunch of muscles are coiled—*ripped*—beneath this diminutive interior.

Ready to *spring*.

"What're you doing?" I say, hardly able to keep the outrage from my voice.

Already, my ear is half listening for any sound on the other side of the door, in case an overcurious member of the cabin crew might be on their way to come and check out the sound.

I wonder if the pilots, among all those glittering lights and polished-up metal levers, have some kind of means of checking sound levels throughout the aircraft.

To note disturbances such as somebody smashing into the cargo bay door.

Right as I feel AA getting away from me again, the plane dips long and hard. This time I'm ready for it, though. I drop down into a crouch and snatch hold of one of the elasticated belts which keep luggage in place.

I cling tightly onto it.

AA doesn't have the same instinct, but at least he doesn't take another tumble.

I guess getting bumped on the head hard teaches you something.

When I turn the torchlight onto AA, I see that he latches hold of a pipe sticking out from the side of the plane.

He stares back at me, lean and cold.

And *injured*.

"Your pride's showing," I say.

AA just glares at me some more, and then, after another few bounces of the plane, he turns his attention back to the door. "How're we going to get through there?"

It's a good question, and one which I have no idea how to answer.

Until, the torch clasped in my hand, my gaze drifts upwards.

To the hatch just above our heads.

7.37:22

I T'S ALMOST as if we've got one of those telepathic connections twins are often claimed to have. As I point the torch upwards, at the hatch, I observe AA—standing on a pair of vaguely square-shaped suitcases we salvaged from beneath the elastic belts—reaching up and working at the clasp on the hatch.

I *did* offer to do the physical work for him, but AA—*bless his soul*—seemed intent on showing off his manliness.

Guess his male pride really *is* showing now.

I actually quite like having something meaningful to do; what with the shining the torch upwards, at the hatch, it takes my mind off the constant movements of the plane; those tiny adjustments which, I'm sure, are critical to keep this plane in the sky.

As I observe AA, I notice, towards the fringes of my torch-light, that there're several stacked cardboard boxes, with a single, felt tip-written message: *Chicken Pasta*.

For several moments, I forget the sheer grimness of airline food, how it's over-salted, and undercooked, too moist, and how, particularly on a longer flight like this one, it swells my colon up like a balloon.

Yeah, maybe too much information . . .

My stomach grumbles.

AA glances down at me, apparently having heard the disturbance over the plane engines. "You all right down there, or do you want me to get you some peanuts?"

"How's it going?" I say, the circle of light from my torch still shining on the clasp of the hatch, and, I can't help noticing—just a bit smugly—that it remains very much locked.

AA shakes his head, and then he writhes his hands, as if he's been toiling beneath a car, like a mechanic on one of those skateboard things they use. "No good," he says, "it's on too tight."

I shine the torch on the pair of suitcases piled on top of one another, making sure, like the careful mother I am, that he gets back down to the floor of the cargo area safe and sound.

"So," I say, "what now?"

AA gives a shake of his head, then a slight sigh. He places his hands on his hips, and is almost caught off guard by the sudden movement of the plane.

He catches himself, though—*just*.

I can't help looking at AA and picturing a giraffe on roller blades in my mind's eye.

Some people have natural balance, and others don't.

When AA turns his head back towards the ill-fated door he first tried to pick the lock of, and then, rather rashly, attempted to barge right off its hinges, I give a sigh of my own, shove the torch into AA's chest, and clamber up onto the suitcases.

"A woman's work is never done," I say, quite pleased with myself as I reach for the hatch's clasp.

I turn it—*hard*—and get it open.

Smug doesn't quite cover it as I lie on my belly, staring down at AA from my place up in the hatch. I can just about make out the wires surrounding me from the glimmer of AA's torchlight below.

With a smile, I can't help saying, "You look *really* small from up here."

"Yeah?" AA says, almost spitting the word through his teeth.

I glance about the cargo bay, seeing it from a whole different perspective.

I see our coffins; both of them still open, and looking just as they are . . . a pair of people come back from the dead, risen up here in this most unlikely of places.

AA looks to the suitcases, and then, without a word, he hurls the torch upwards.

I just about manage to catch it before it conks me right on the chin.

Before it knocks a tooth or two out.

I take hold of it and shine the light down on AA as he clambers up onto the top of the suitcases.

With a wry smile, I stretch my free hand, the one which doesn't grasp the torch, down to him.

He either doesn't see my hand, or chooses to ignore it.

I can't help thinking that it's the latter.

Somewhat annoyingly, he takes hold of the opened hatch, and drags himself up first time. I thought, what with his slightly doughy shape these days—having had to cut back on his strenuous exercise regime while he recovers from that gunshot wound —that he would at least be out of puff by the time he got up with me.

But, no.

AA draws in a quick breath, then he glances along the duct,

taking in the wires, and surely—with his infinitely superior *male* brain—noticing things which I could only ever dream of.

As he lies down on his belly, begins to slither his way along, he utters, "Let's get cracking."

I estimate that we've been slithering about on our bellies for about five minutes when AA brings an abrupt halt to our proceedings.

Lying on his side—there's not enough room to so much as crouch in this duct—he withdraws that device I noticed from earlier, the one which looks something like a barcode scanner.

The backlit green screen illuminates AA in a nuclear glow.

His eyes flicker back and forth across the readings displayed there.

Then he glances to me.

"What?" I say, in a voice close to a whisper, not wanting anybody to potentially overhear me. "What's the matter?"

"We're descending," he says.

7.22:53

"WE'RE *WHAT*?" I say, hardly able to believe the words which've just tumbled out through AA's lips.

AA's attention, though, is turned back to the backlit green screen, apparently busy with all his *man* stuff once more.

I can feel my heart throbbing away in my chest, and the blood pumping hard up to my temples. I just *know* that I'm going to be contending with a headache before too long.

And that's not going to be pretty.

Not even with those *painkillers* of AA's.

"How far have we gone down?" I say.

AA sucks at his teeth.

His features look somewhat eerie with the combination of the half-light from the torch I lug along. He blinks rapidly several times, then adds, "Down to three thousand feet, more or less. And still dropping."

I screw up my features. "I don't understand," I say. "Where

do you think we are? I mean, we can't be out of the UK yet, can we?"

AA looks away from the screen, and then back along the duct. "Probably just about," he says, and then glances back at me. "Unless they decided to double back."

"And why'd they do that?"

AA hunches his shoulders, doesn't say anything for several moments.

"You think they know we're on board?" I say, already feeling the rage begin to seethe through me, that bitter *anger* that AA might've given the whole job away what with his chimp act back on the cargo area door.

Realising that AA's not responding, I reach out, take hold of his fleece, grip it tight.

Drag him back to me.

"I want you to know that if they've discovered us then it's *all* your fault, okay?"

AA looks back at me with sad eyes, and then a slight smile tweaks his lips. "Could be a technical fault."

"Yeah," I say, flashing my eyes. "*Right.*"

"I don't think they've discovered us."

"*Then* what?" I say.

"I think that we're picking somebody up."

For several moments I'm rendered speechless.

Maybe it's my fear of flying that's got me a little riled—that's got me jumping to conclusions without thinking the whole matter through.

I shake my head. "And how'd that idea come to you?"

"Dunno," AA says, glancing back down at the screen, "it's just a hunch." Then he turns the device towards me, but it might as well be in Double Dutch.

There's a whole bunch of—*seemingly*—constantly changing figures.

I shake my head and glare at AA. "You're going to have to explain it like you would to one of my kids."

"Really," he says, "an assassin, and you've never managed to get your head around coordinates?"

"Call me crazy," I say, "but *no* . . . my mobile's always served me quite well."

AA pouts, turns back to the screen. "Well," he says, "all you need to know is that we're somewhere in the region of the Isle of Wight."

"Wow," I say, with just a *touch* of fake enthusiasm, "that *is* off course."

AA continues to study the screen.

"What now?" I say. "What should we do?"

AA taps one of the buttons, doing God *knows* what. "Let's get back to the cargo area."

7.08:21

W HEN AA TOLD ME to go back to the cargo area, I thought we were going to drop back down and box ourselves back up.

But that's not at all what AA has in mind.

First things first, we ensure that the hatch we busted through to get up to the duct is out of sight, that we keep it up there with us. Once that's done, AA turns his attention back to his device. "We're close to landing," he says.

But *I* could've told him that.

Already, I can hear the reverse thrusters.

The mechanical *groan* of the flaps.

The wheels whirring into place.

"All right," AA says, slipping me a sidelong glance, "brace yourself."

I have to admit, whenever I've been sitting in a passenger seat, in economy class, which is the way in which I'm *accustomed* to travelling, I don't often see the point of the seatbelt.

That's one of those things that I'm actually *with* AA on.

If something goes wrong with the plane, as far as I'm concerned, I'm *dead*.

Here, though, I make a point of grabbing hold of one of the struts within the duct, and 'bracing myself', as AA suggests.

We touch down a few moments later and, thinking quickly, I reach out and tap the button on the side of my wristwatch. I bring the countdown to a halt for now.

Stuck at just over seven hours.

I wonder just how much the countdown will matter now that we've made this—*seemingly*—unscheduled stop.

Still, something tells me that Brian knew all about this stop.

Knew all about the precise flight time he told me to tap into my watch.

The toughest part of the whole landing experience comes when the wheels touch tarmac and everything seems to fire in the opposite direction.

Seems to push me into AA.

But he puts up with it like a trooper, and the two of us remain there, both of us *braced*, holding on for dear life.

As the plane taxies, I push myself back up into a sitting position.

And then, because I haven't done so since I was woken from my coffin, I reach down for my gun, slip it out of its holster. Give it a quick once-over.

Everything looks fine.

When I glance to AA, he gives me a smirk. "That fed up of me, huh?"

As I slip my gun back in its holster, I reply, "Never hurts to be prepared."

———

It's strange to be back down on the ground and to know that we're not getting off.

Everything within me seems to scream out for me to get *off* this plane.

I suppose that's just something hardwired—something to do with *survival.*

Because, and let's be clear about this, humans are *not* naturally designed to fly.

If it was up to me, I'd probably just leave it for the birds.

Me and AA remain where we are, in the duct above the cargo area.

I become aware of the rising heat, feel it glowing out from my cheeks.

We just sit tight there.

Waiting.

To see what's going to happen.

We've been parked up for what seems like a very long time when there's a mechanical *whirring* coming from down below. I only just catch myself—AA doesn't remind me, the *idiot*—and I flip off the torch.

We're only in darkness for moments.

Daylight streams in.

With AA slumped on his belly beside me, we watch on as a pair of technicians—baggage attendants, whatever—stride up into the cargo bay.

They both wear light-grey overalls, baseball caps snugly down on their balding scalps.

Although they speak to one another, I can't quite make out what they're saying.

As they tread onwards, into the cargo area, a tingle runs down my spine. A spark flashes through my blood. The two of them notice the coffins.

Of *course* they do.

And they see that the lids of both are open.

I half expect the men to retreat out of some sort of neo-gothic horror.

But neither of them does.

On the contrary, I hear the two of them exchange a chuckle —something about *Dracula?*—and they toss the lid into each coffin, then drag them out of the cargo area.

Outside, I can hear the *beep-beep-beep* of some vehicle backing up.

Since the door to the cargo area is open now, I catch a whiff of the fresh, *outside* air.

It feels good to breathe it again.

To not have to be breathing kerosene.

While the baggage handlers are out of the cargo area, I look to AA. "You think they suspect anything?"

AA shakes his head. "Nah, you saw how they acted when they saw the coffins—thought it was some sort of a joke, *high jinks*."

"But what if they chat with someone, with the pilot, with somebody on board? Somebody who won't think that it's a joke at all?"

AA shrugs. "Cross that bridge when we come to it, I guess."

The baggage handlers appear again, this time with a large wooden crate held between them. I glance over the labels—the various stickers smoothed on all over. I try to pick out some sort of a *clue* . . . a *logo*, perhaps, but it seems that the crate will forever remain a mystery to me.

The baggage handlers spend a good amount of time securing the wooden crate, making sure that it's nicely put in place. Once they're done, the two of them, laughing and joking again, in the way of two friends on the job, head back out of the cargo area.

With a heavy *slam* the cargo area door shuts.

And darkness reigns once again.

The plane has hardly shuttled back off along the runway, become airborne once more, when AA turns to me and says, "Want to take a look?"

_____

LIKE A PAIR of uncaged panthers, me and AA circle the wooden crate.

I shine the light.

"What'd you reckon?" AA says.

I feel the throb of the aeroplane's engine through the floor, creeping up through the soles of my trainers, and sending vibrations right to my bones.

I have to say that I *didn't* miss the nuances of air travel at all while we were stationed on the ground.

In fact, I can clearly say that I would've been *far* happier if we could've somehow arranged to get the job done on the Isle of Wight.

But here we go again.

I glance about the edge of the wooden crate, give a shrug, a pout, look back at AA.

He sighs at me. "No imagination, huh?" He looks over the

crate in a way that tells me he has a Very Active Imagination Indeed. "Nuclear bomb," he says.

"Yeah, I hear that they truck them about the globe constantly."

"Not *truck*, Anna," AA says, thrusting a finger in the air, and swooping down on some detail of the crate. "*Fly*."

I roll my eyes at that, already wearying of AA's company. "So," I say, "how'd you reckon we get this thing open?"

AA stops his prowling, then stares long and hard at me. "Really?" he says. "You're asking me? The guy who couldn't even get that stupid door open?"

He's apparently so riled by this failure that he only gives a vague wave off in the direction of the door he failed to get open.

"Look," I say, "I don't think this crate falls under our remit."

The plane banks hard to the left, but this time, already with my very best *stewardess's* legs, I keep myself standing on my two feet—not even needing to grab hold of anything.

AA, too, keeps himself rooted pretty steadily.

When the plane levels out, I see the twinkle in AA's eye, and I know that there's *no way* we're getting out of here without him getting into this crate.

7.04:21

"WELL," I SAY, standing before the remnants of the crate —we've torn it down so that all four sides, what were *previously* the sides, now lie on the floor of the cargo area. "I guess we've gone and done it now, huh?"

AA holds his hand clenched at his chin, his head slightly tilted to one side, as if he's examining some piece of abstract art:

A sculpture.

"Yes," he says.

I look over the object which sits in the centre of the unpacked box another time.

Transparent plastic wrapping.

Lots of that Styrofoam stuff.

And within sits a Jacuzzi bathtub.

"Don't reckon," I go on, "that us hoping to sit quiet—not be discovered—is going to work anymore."

"No," AA replies.

There's a long pause, and then I put in, "Why'd you think somebody's taking a Jacuzzi along?"

AA shakes his head. "Suppose where we're going—*wherever* that is—somebody has ordered a Jacuzzi." He glances back towards the door that he failed to get open. "Or maybe somebody on board wanted to stop on the way to pick this up."

I look to the mess we've made with the wooden crate, then look back to AA. "You think we should box this thing up again— you know, in case somebody comes snooping around during the flight?"

AA shakes his head, fixes his gaze back up above, to the hatch. "Nah, we've wasted enough time with this, let's get back to the job at hand."

And—*somehow*—AA steals the thought right out of my own mind.

6.46:13

ONCE WE GET BACK UP into the duct, back to the place we were sitting pretty before AA informed me that the plane was about to land, we sit there, plotting our next move.

AA, as always, is in favour of us smashing right through the hatch to our left, busting right in on the passenger cabin. And, no doubt, firing off shots.

I manage to swing him around from that course of action with the argument that neither of us—*really*—has any clue what might happen in a pressurised cabin if we go along shooting. I suppose, for all AA's apparent smugness at being comfortable stupid quantities of distance above sea level, he's actually secretly afraid of flying.

Just as afraid as I am.

Or, at the very least, he's afraid of *dying* in a plane crash.

In the end, we decide to be a little more subtle.

To try and scope out the area before making any rash decision, though that's easier said than done seeing as the hatch beside us has no window to it—and there're no cracks in the duct large enough to peer down into the passenger cabin.

I argue that the main thing we want to keep in mind is that the pilot has the ability to turn us around, or to divert to some other airport.

He has the power to keep on flying.

Or dive us into the sea.

And despite all the hype leading up to this job, I can't quite stomach the thought of crossing the line and becoming a hijacker *just yet* . . . even if that airliner features only people willing to pay a very high price for exclusivity.

An airliner unlike any other . . .

And with a Jacuzzi in the back.

When I look to AA again, I see that he's poring over that barcode scanner device of his. Keeping himself busy with those all-important *coordinates*.

On the air, I can just about make out the scent of tea.

Freshly brewed.

And then something which I judge to be the scent of chicken pasta, with a smothering of mature cheddar cheese.

Once again, I feel a pang in my stomach.

I wonder if one of us—me or AA—should've brought along some provisions.

But the plan was always for one, or both of us, to get into the cabin.

And there'll be food *aplenty* there.

Still holding the torch tightly in my hand, gazing at AA's face in profile from the glare of the electrical light, I say, "What's your *thing* tell you?"

AA mumbles something to himself—something which may,

or *may not*, be a low blow at my ignorance. Really, to be honest, I couldn't care less.

In the end, though, he does make himself loud enough to be heard. "We're at cruising altitude," he says.

"Right," I say, "so, what's the plan?"

AA gives a slight sigh, apparently to himself, then he allows the device—the *altimeter*—to drop in his grip. "The plan," he says, "is for us to go and grab that memory stick. Nothing more, nothing less." He eyes me closely, the surface of his eyeballs looking glassy in the torch light. "Agreed?"

———

AA informs me that he believes it better for us to bide our time, to wait out a couple of hours so that we get to, what he terms, the Point of No Return.

What he really means by that is that if anything *is* to happen to the plane, then it's going to make more sense for it to continue flying along on its trajectory—make headway towards its planned destination—rather than double back.

Return to base.

And because I'm *all about* getting this mission over and done with, I flip the switch on the torch—no point running down the battery unnecessarily—shut my eyes and take a little nap. It's strange the mother-like effect trundling plane engines can have on my mind, almost like I'm back in the womb, listening to a maternal heartbeat, feeling it soothe me to sleep.

AA jabs me in the gut—with the barrel of his gun, no less—as he shines the torch in my eyes with his other hand. "Anna," he says, "Wake up—it's *time*."

I'm sure that I mumble something incomprehensible, and

vaguely offensive—I've never been the most relaxed of sleepers —then I rub at my eyes with my hands balled into tight fists, listening to that aged thirty-something *squeak* of protest they emit.

When I've finally got my eyes back in some sort of working order, I see that AA's working at the hatch, the torch now lying on the base of the duct, illuminating his hands for him. I feel just a touch put out that he doesn't seem to need me to be his torch-bearer any longer, and my only consolation is the knowledge that being a torchbearer isn't really anything to be proud about.

Still feeling the world drip back in around the edges of my brain, I reach down for my gun, down in its holster. I unbutton the holster and then slip the gun out, feeling its steady—should I say *comforting?*—weight in my hand.

I sharpen my gaze as AA fiddles with the last of the clasps keeping the hatch in place.

He looks back at me with narrowed eyes, lips pressed firmly together, his own gun snug firmly in his grip, and then he gives me a nod—one of those *interrogative* gestures; the ones which beg for a reply.

I give it to him, nodding in return.

With a quick flick of his fingers, AA manoeuvres the clasp that final fraction, brings it loose, and then, with a blast of too-white, bright fluorescent light from the passenger cabin, he kicks it through the hole.

I only just have a moment, as I go out after him, to glance at my watch.

To see how long we've got left.

4.52:43

WHEN I LAND on the floor of the passenger cabin, I almost lose my balance, despite bracing myself—despite bending my knees, as all of my well-intentioned PE teachers tried to engrave in my brain.

I catch myself by reaching out and grabbing hold of the headrest of one of the seats with my free hand, the one which doesn't lug along the gun.

I stand steady for a moment, breathing heavily, hearing my heart thumping away in my eardrums.

All those smells seem to become a thousand times stronger now:

Tea.

Pasta.

Cheese sauce.

Chicken.

And then, a little way to the back of that array of odours, I sniff—*clean, bitter and distinct*—whisky.

I guess somebody's as much of a nervous flyer as I am.

In the near distance, I hear somebody scream:

A woman, of course.

The scream itself is an odd sound, almost completely dampened by the plodding march of the aeroplane engines and the air conditioning system.

When I glance up, look over the passenger cabin, I realise why.

I take in the heads, all of them raised up out of their seats, staring towards the front of the passenger cabin. This cabin is nothing like any other cabin *I've* ever experienced.

For one, all the seats are slick leather—not one scuff mark *I* can see—and the ratio of seats to legroom is the stuff of dreams. I realise that each of these seats must be taking up the space normally assigned for two and a half—if not *three*—seats.

How the other half lives . . .

In all, from the alarmed heads staring towards the front, I count twenty passengers.

Most are male—I can tell from the bald spots, and the broad shoulders which, in the case of the taller gentlemen, just about peep out above the headrests.

There're a couple of females, though, too.

Including the woman screaming:

The one off near the front of the cabin.

I realise, with just a touch of pleasure, that nobody's looking in my direction yet, that they're all very much focussed on AA, standing at the front of the cabin.

Although AA isn't waving his gun around, or anything stupid like that—actually, he's holding it down by his side—the fact that he's got a gun at all is enough to get a reaction.

And why not?

I know, in these people's shoes, I would feel exactly the same.

Well, I might've shifted off my bottom, had a go at tackling the guy with the gun, but, that aside, we're not all that different . . .

I meet AA's eye for a quick moment, and his eyes quickly leave mine behind.

The passengers notice this swift exchanged glance, though, and several of them flash a look over their shoulders, to see me standing there, having emerged behind AA from the now-dispelled hatch in the duct above.

Deciding that it might be for the best, I shift my way along the aisle, headed for the back of the plane, away from AA.

In quick order, I locate the cabin crew.

Three of them:

Two female, one male.

They're all blissfully unaware of what's going on in the passenger cabin, located behind their red velvet—yes, *really*—curtain, making themselves busy with the dinner carts, and the coffee machines, and whatever else it is that they've got stowed away there.

The male member wears a dark-purple suit over a smartly pressed white shirt and a dark-purple tie. On the tie, I spot the logo of the airline emblazoned. It matches the one on the breast pocket of the jacket:

Pleasure Lines

It sounds vaguely pornographic, but, then again, I've never thought of myself as having any sort of nous when it comes to marketing.

The female members of the cabin crew have on a trouser suit, which is the same dark-purple colour as the male member's suit.

I catch a whiff of perfume and it nearly sends me into a foetal position.

The perfume *stinks* of sickly sweet petunias—ones which've been kept in a greenhouse for the entire duration of a record-temperature summer.

Even with my eyes streaming, I hold them at gunpoint, because anything else just doesn't seem appropriate. I beckon them out of their hiding place.

All three of them, apparently acting on instinct, raise their hands up above their heads, and move off along the aisle, towards where AA is already blabbing through some—apparently pre-prepared—speech.

Once I've eased the cabin crew down into the seats in the front row, I channel into what it is that AA's saying. That he's asking, straight-out, who has the memory stick here.

I can't help but roll my eyes at this, my back to the rest of the passengers, of course, and wonder why I allowed myself to slip off to sleep, and thus leave AA with executive control for implementing the plan.

But retrospect, as always, is an extremely fine thing.

I glance to AA, and then back to the passengers.

Not one of the twenty passengers comes forward, obviously, but I decide to lay my frustration to one side.

I look to AA, acknowledging that, at this moment in time, he has the Daddy Chair. "Where'd you want me?" I say.

AA breaks off his gaze across the rest of the passengers, looks over the cabin crew briefly. "You see any of them reaching for a phone back there?"

"No," I say, shaking my head, then glancing to the cabin crew.

All of them wear wide-eyed expressions, and are sitting on the edge of their seat.

Much like every other passenger on this plane.

AA looks them over. "Any of you speak to the pilot?"

The two women—one of them blond, the other brunette, I notice, a touch dizzily—say nothing at all. The male member of the cabin crew is bald-headed, tanned. When he replies, he has a surprisingly gruff voice and his English is accented. "No, she doesn't know anything."

A *female* pilot.

AA turns back to me.

His eyes are webbed with red veins. His complexion has turned a touch sallow. I wonder if he managed to get any shuteye up in the duct—although it wasn't the most comfortable place, I didn't have too much trouble.

His hair, too, sticks up in tufts.

I wonder if he devised this specific façade, offhandedly wanted to project a slightly unhinged appearance to the passengers—our *hostages*.

"Take a look in the first-class cabin," AA says, turning away from me as quickly as he speaks, turning his attention back on the passengers, still rooted to their seats, for obvious reasons.

Realising that I'm not going to get anything else out of him, I glance about me, spy another of those red velvet curtains, like the one towards the back of the plane, and I sashay through it, holding my gun out in my grip, ready to threaten anybody who needs threatening.

Almost right away, I run into another member of the cabin crew—another female.

I analyse pretty quickly, from the smooth, tanned skin, and the ample cleavage—not to mention the bright, sleek red hair and the decade or so of youth she has on the other two women—that this particular specimen has been picked out for those who can afford the privilege to travel in this first-class section of this *first-class* aeroplane.

She carries a silver tray bearing a bottle of champagne and glasses, which she promptly drops, throwing up her hands so I don't shoot her.

I figure out, soon enough, as I watch the bottle of champagne roll its way towards my feet, and the glasses all fall to the ground, that she was collecting up empties.

And why not?

Those in first-class areas of aeroplanes often also have first-class *tastes*.

From the backs of the heads, I can tell that there're only a half dozen passengers in first class.

I work quickly, keeping the stewardess in my sights first, guiding her back through the curtain I just emerged from, down onto the seats occupied by the three other members of the cabin crew.

AA will take care of *them* for now.

Then I turn my attention to the passengers in the first-class cabin, now all of them turned around in their seats, some of them staring at me out of disbelief.

One by one, I round them all up until only one remains.

As I approach the last passenger, seated by the window, and with a newspaper spread before him, clutching it with his chubby fingers, I take a deep breath.

I *really* don't want to pull the trigger on *anyone* for the duration of this flight.

Me and AA only came for the memory stick, after all.

But, as I call out for the man to put his hands up, to turn to face me, I get a nasty shock.

Dark-brown hair.

Slightly flushed cheeks.

And a well-knotted, silk tie about his throat.

Brian Mathewson.

I suppose I should've known from the tumbler of whisky which sits on his fold-out table.

Only a nectar-coloured dribble remaining in the base.

For just a second, my grip on the gun falters. I allow the gun to fall in my hands.

And then, right when I reach the pinnacle of my confusion, Brian slides out from his seat.

Inches his way past me.

On his way to the seats behind the curtain, with all the other passengers, he glances back over his shoulder.

Gives me a wink.

And I can't help wondering if I don't hear a *chuckle* too.

HIJACKING A PLANE was easier than I thought.
Here we are, me and AA.

All the passengers spread out before us, now to one side of the aisle, all in a neat row, all of them with their eyeballs focussed on ours.

Waiting for orders.

I have to admit that I feel a strength down deep in my stomach which only leaves me when I glance about the faces of the passengers, see Brian Mathewson there, grinning back at me, as if he hasn't a care in the world.

More than anything else, I want to rush up to Brian, stare him right in the face and demand that he tell us what the hell's going on here.

Just *what the hell* he's doing on this flight with us.

I glance back to AA, and I notice that he looks to have regained a little more of his colour. I wonder if he went and poured himself a coffee from the back of the plane. He has a slight shake as he holds his gun down at his side.

Nothing major.

But certainly something to keep an eye on.

God how I *hate* babysitting . . .

I can smell the salt from my sweat as I stand before these passengers, something like performance anxiety, knowing that all of these people are waiting to see what me and AA do next.

Sort of like having to do a class presentation.

At the back of my throat, I have this irrepressible dryness, and I know that I could really do with a drink of water—a drink of *anything*—and yet now, really, isn't the time.

As I stand up before the passengers, keeping an eye on them, I watch AA go—one by one—through the passengers, requesting that they each get up out of their seat and that he pats them down.

At first, somewhat *giddily*, I think that he's searching for a concealed weapon. It might be conceivable that on such an exclusive service, such as this flight, personal weapons are allowed.

But then I realise that, more likely, he's trying to see if any of the passengers have the memory stick.

A couple of times, between checking passengers, AA digs out his device, glances at the screen.

And I know that he's ensuring there hasn't been any sort of a course change—making sure that the cabin crew is holding to their promise, that nobody made the rash decision to notify the captain.

Since he doesn't react to any of these impromptu course checks, I assume that everything's ticking along just fine. And when he glances back at me, I can see that there's the faint outline of a smile on his lips.

He, too, noticed Brian when I brought him in here.

And he—like me—surely wants to get answers to just what Brian is up to.

I work crowd control, making sure that nobody shifts out of their seat, and I think back to Brian's briefing. I think about how, no longer than forty-eight hours ago, I was having dinner with my beau, Mark, in a pleasant Indian restaurant—one of those ones that has only space for four or five tables.

A candlelit dinner.

Romantic.

Even thinking back to it brings the scent of those spices to mind, and the sticky—*perfectly cooked*—rice.

I'd just been about to dip some of my Peshwari naan in my lamb jalfrezi when I felt my phone vibrating in my pocket. I thought long and hard—I really *did*—about taking a look.

In the end, though, I couldn't resist.

I never can.

And, with Mark tucking happily into his beef vindaloo, I had a quick glance at the screen.

A message from Brian.

One word:

Urgent.

I recall those ten seconds after receiving the message quite clearly.

I remember looking up, seeing the Indian waiter standing with his hands clutched to the white apron he wore over his charcoal suit; the matching shirt and tie underneath.

And although the two of us hadn't had anything beyond the

usual polite discourse during the dinner; nothing beyond me asking about the specials before going for just what I *always* order at an Indian restaurant; something crackled between us in the air.

When I turned my eyes back onto Mark, saw him chewing away—mouth closed, thank *God* for manners—he realised it too.

That I would have to go.

And though Mark didn't make a big deal of it, only reaching up, dabbing at his lips with his napkin, and then calling the waiter over to box up the two of our meals, I could tell that I had made a deep cut in the thread which ties the two of us together.

That flimsy, ever-so-delicate silk thread which threatens to break at any second.

As I went outside, got into the car which Brian had sent to my location—*disturbingly quickly*—I recall glancing up in the rear-view mirror, seeing Mark shuffling off in the direction of the Underground station on the corner of the street.

Before the car turned the corner, I observed Mark handing our cardboard-boxed dinners to a homeless man sitting on a set of concrete stairs to somebody's home.

And it was then that I felt my heart sink.

All the way down into my stomach.

Because I knew that I'd become one of those horrendous people for whom work will always—*without exception*—come first.

A workaholic.

"Anna?"

I glance away from the point I was staring at in mid-air.

The flickering fluorescent light of the cabin has an almost hypnotic quality on me.

I look to AA, who's apparently finished his search.

He nods in Brian's direction.

"Check him," AA says, and then stands sentry at the back of the cabin.

4.17:56

M Y BRAIN seems to return to me with a snap when my
    task is shifted to searching Brian.

Without comment, Brian rises up out of his seat.

I make no specific gesture or comment.

I don't want any of the other passengers on the plane to
know that we *know* each other—that *Brian's* the one who put me
and AA up to this job.

As far as *I* know this is all part of Brian's wider plan.

Or maybe, finally, he's cracked under the pressure.

Gone insane.

Although most of the passengers on board dress down—in
tracksuits, in jeans, some with baseball caps drawn down over
their faces—Brian remains in his standard-issue suit, looking, as
always, prim and unflustered.

And as I pad Brian in all the essential spots, he only gives a
sort of neutral smile.

If this is how he responds to a hijacking—albeit one he didn't only expect, but *planned*—then maybe it's a long-awaited explanation for how he manages to keep so many plates spinning in the world of publicity and politics.

The search done, Brian sinks back down into his seat.

He doesn't have the memory stick, although, from the shock he's clearly given me and AA, I was half expecting him to.

I cast a glance in AA's direction.

He gives me a slight nod, paces his way up to me, and then, in a low, guttural voice, says, "Anna, if you know *anything* about what's going on here then tell me, okay?"

When I look to AA, more specifically to his gun, which he holds pointed right at my stomach, I feel a chill run through my blood.

"Hmm?" AA says, as if prompting my memory.

I give a shake of my head. "No," I say, replying to him with a tone hopefully too quiet for any of the passengers to hear. "There's nothing," I add.

AA gives me a stiff nod, and he moves back to the other passengers.

I observe as his eyes go skittering over each and every one of them.

Picking through their appearances, no doubt building up some sort of a profile for each and every one.

I wonder if I should be doing the same.

I look over the cabin crew again; the male, the two older females, and then the younger redhead.

None of them wear easy smiles.

And every last one of them looks *scared*.

And why *shouldn't* they be?

"Anna?" AA says.

I look to him, see that he's reaching up for the overhead compartments.

"Someone here is lying," AA says, "somebody *has* the memory stick."

With a *click*, he brings open one of the compartments on its hydraulic hinge.

Then he waves his gun about the faces of the passengers.

One of the women gives something between a shriek and a gasp.

I see that AA's still shaking.

That he's gone pale again.

"And when we find them," AA continues, digging about in the overhead compartment, and then, with a violent action, tossing down a hard-shelled case about the size of a rucksack, "I'll stick a bullet in their forehead, how about that?"

When AA looks back at me, I see that there's a sharpness to his glare.

A *cruelty*.

"Give me a hand, huh?" AA says, a slight smile breaking out on his lips.

3.51:21

T HERE'S A CERTAIN POINT when mine and AA's search through the hand luggage seems to become a futile task. Actually, from the second that, between us, me and AA manage to get all the hand luggage spread out over the aisle, all of the pieces opened, some with the aid of their owners, and their keys, I realise that this's going to be in vain.

I think back to the cargo bay, to those suitcases all kept in place beneath those elasticated belts. I can't help wondering if me and AA have been a pair of idiots here—if, instead of cracking open that wooden container, taking a look at that Jacuzzi, we should've gone digging around in those suitcases.

But Brian told us that a passenger on board this plane would have the memory stick.

On their *person*.

Then again, Brian also failed to tell us that *he* would be on this flight.

And I try to stop myself thinking there, because it's making me increasingly angry to picture Brian's smug little face, his pudgy, rose-red cheeks as he plots and ploys, those hands of his clutched tightly together, one of his legs jigging with excitement.

Could this just be a game?

As AA—shaking his head—digs through clothes, makeup cases, and who knows what else, for the third or fourth time, I know that this whole search is futile.

That we're not going to get anywhere working like this.

The more I think about it, I wonder if Brian has brought me and AA here on a wild-goose chase.

Maybe it's some sort of a power game—one of those famed *ego* trips of Brian's which certain journalists tend to go on about in what, usually, turns out to be their final piece for whatever media outlet they write for.

Even journalists can't survive bad press; not the type which Brian cooks up.

This really *would* be an elaborate ploy, though.

A *seriously* crack-brained scheme to get me and AA in a heap of trouble.

Because, without having investigated the matter all that thoroughly, I can deduce that hijackers aren't generally treated with much in the way of leniency by any of the major countries of the world.

And neither are their co-conspirators.

Finally, AA straightens up from his work.

He continues to shake his head.

I can see that his eyes are completely bloodshot now, and something deep within me is saying that I should tread carefully. To make sure that I don't let him out of my sight . . . because it could well be the last thing that I do.

AA's breathing is profound and yet each lungful of air seems to be fleeting.

I have to admit that I can feel it myself—the air in the cabin, no doubt, having been recycled a good few times now, since the two of us got onto this plane, in those coffins of ours. I remember reading somewhere about the importance of not exerting yourself too much on a plane because of the poor air quality.

By all rights, I should just be reclined back in one of the chairs, stuck into a zombified doze.

But, no.

I'm in the midst of a hijacking.

When AA tosses away a canister of deodorant, barely missing a passenger, he lets out a sustained *roar* of rage. His complexion is paler than ever, and, without me saying anything, he sets off along the aisle, and disappears behind the red velvet curtain, into the cabin crew's quarters.

I allow myself to exhale, to breathe out all that nasty, already-breathed air from my lungs. I feel my gun still heavy in my hand, and I look about the frightened faces of the passengers.

All of them looking to me, wanting to see what's coming next.

Even as they eyeball me, I think back to the time in the hotel, to when me and AA met up, after, on Brian's orders, I was whisked away from my dinner with Mark.

Seven Hours Before The Job

THE AIR WAS FROSTY, and I pulled up the collar of my jacket, in some vague hope of keeping out the winter's breeze. But I had very little luck. It was the kind of wind which just cut through everything:

Cloth, skin, blood, *bone*.

And who was I to hold onto a hope of keeping it out?

I hugged my arms up to my chest, pressing the beige overcoat I was wearing down over the top of the neat, light-pink cocktail dress I had on beneath.

I knew that, in my tottering high heels, and showing off a good deal of my legs—kept apart from the night air only by the thin layer of my tights—I looked like one and only *one* thing standing here on the pavement outside the grey façade of a budget airport hotel.

There was nothing I could do, though, Brian's car dropped me off here. And I was given clear instructions to stay put.

I had to remain.

It was the agreed meeting point.

And since I was on the clock, who was *I* to disobey orders?

I couldn't shake the sense that some creep—*somewhere*—was getting his perve on. But, whenever I looked around, I saw nothing, of course. If there's anybody adept at keeping their nose out of the lime-light it's the *hotel* perve.

I could feel the chill nibbling at my toenails, exposed through the hole at the tip of my shoes. Now, thinking about it, having struggled with those decisions for seemingly hours before my date with Mark, it seemed imprudent to go with these particular shoes, almost purely on the basis that they complimented my dress.

But, then again, I never knew I was going to get dragged away.

Never knew I was going to *allow* myself to be dragged away.

When another of Brian's cars pulled up on the curb—one of those seemingly endless estate models in Brian's carpool, with tinted windows, and a sleek, well-polished, black finish—I moved slowly over to it.

Feeling my heart dip, I smelled a little of the spices from the curry I had been so looking forward to feasting on. As I brought my hands up to my mouth—to blow some long-awaited hot air across my palms—I could still smell the Peshwari naan bread.

Could taste its moist, coconut flavour on my tongue.

If it hadn't been for the smell—for the *taste*—then I might well have convinced myself that the date with Mark was all a dream.

And that now I'd returned to reality with an unpleasant *bump*.

This was who I am—who I *really* am.

And who was I to think any different?

The car door slammed shut, and AA slipped out of the back door.

He looked like he had been equally as involved in some Saturday night plan.

In fact, he was dressed up in a tuxedo, a pair of nicely polished shoes.

And he was wearing a dark, ankle-length suede jacket which swept about him.

Without a moment's hesitation, the car pulled away from the curb, and AA trod towards me.

And although he was wearing that easy—*familiar*—smile of his, all smeared across his lips, I could tell . . . I could just *tell*.

3.47:54

"**A**NNA, FOR *CHRIST'S SAKE!*"

I blink away my daze.

Turn my attention to my left.

And then my right.

Look at my watch.

When I bring my eyes away from the blurry vision I've created before me, I realise that AA stands at my side, that he's staring hard at me.

His eyes look worse than ever, that kind of appearance which suggests—to me, and I'm sure more of our audience—that AA has been up all night.

And I should know, too, because, last night, we shared a room at the hotel.

In his twin bed, he was tossing and turning until the small hours. Until I heard him, with a frustrated grunt, trudge off to the bathroom. Following the giveaway *rattle* of pills in a plastic bottle, he took a long few drinks of water.

I said nothing, lying in the darkness.

I only clamped my eyes shut.

And drifted off to sleep.

AA's up in my face now, his nostrils flaring, like some kind of wild animal. "What were you doing?" he says, his voice only just below a shout.

Just over AA's shoulder, I can make out the several sets of frightened eyes.

I scan them quickly, seeing if any of them have taken the opportunity, of me slipping away into a daze, to put some sort of plot into action.

Nothing that leaps out at me, but who knows?

Finally, my eyes rest on Brian's, and Brian, like before, remains cool as a cucumber.

Giving nothing away.

What a surprise.

AA's waving his gun about in my face, clearly distressed by my brief lapse into the not-too distant past. "I told you to keep an eye on things, and you're standing about here, daydreaming— just what the *hell* do you think this is?"

I give AA a shrug, not really knowing how to answer that question.

Deciding that it's probably better not to make an attempt.

AA takes a deep breath, and it seems to make his eyes bulge out of their sockets.

His shoulders rise and fall—*rise and fall*—then he appears to find some sort of inner calm.

As far as I know, AA's got a therapist.

Perhaps he's got all sorts of field techniques to keep his cool.

Now that AA's calmed himself down, he looks over the hand luggage:

The clothing, and the toiletries, and the reading material, all strewn about in the aisle.

It's almost as if he's seeing this sight for the very first time. He turns to me, almost with an accusatory glare, but that glare cools after a brief flicker. "We'd better get this cleaned up," he says. "Looks like a pigsty."

As AA makes that final remark, I observe the swift—*too swift* —glimmer of a smile which he flashes at me.

That easy-going nature of the AA I know, and—if not exactly *love*—that I at least have a strong preference for.

I nod, then look back at AA again.

My attention turns down to his hand, to the gun—*Hotflush*— he holds tight in his grip. "You think we should put them away?" I say.

AA's eyes widen, as if I'm some sort of predator, threatening to come down hard on him:

Kill him.

But that look, soon enough, vanishes.

He blinks it away, seems to return to his senses once more.

With several nods to himself, AA seems to hear me, and he slips his gun down into the holster, turns his attention to the mess we've left on the floor. "Come on, Anna," he says, "let's get to work."

3.36:38

ALTHOUGH THE SITUATION HERE is clear—that me and AA are holding these people hostage on this plane —I'm surprised at the passengers, our *hostages*, getting up out of their seats to come and help gather their possessions back together.

I half expect AA to fly into one of his rages, to yank out his gun and start waving it around again.

But he does nothing of the sort.

Apparently whatever he did behind that red velvet curtain has sorted him out for the time being.

Maybe it has something to do with those pills he offered me earlier.

I keep a cursory eye on the passengers, down on their hands and knees, reordering their things which, in our search for the memory stick, we threw about all over.

At the same time, I allow my brain to switch off just a little.

Allow myself to drift back to the night before.

Still trying to put together the pieces of the puzzle.

Desperately wanting to understand what we're involved with here.

Six Hours Before The Job

W E'D GOT THE ROOM at around half past ten at night.

To say that I was surprised about having to share a room with AA was an understatement. If there's one thing which Brian Mathewson *isn't*, it's poor.

And he's not *thrifty* either.

We checked into the hotel with fake documents given to AA by his driver—a pair of passports purporting that me and AA were husband and wife: the *Leiberwitzes*—and then, seeing as this *was* a budget deal, we lugged our own suitcases into the lift and headed for the fifth floor:

Our bedroom.

The bedroom itself was pleasant and clean—in that anonymous, budget-hotel sort of way—everything had that faint scent of disinfectant clinging to it, though that wasn't necessarily a bad thing. The heating was on a little high for my tastes, but since my roommate, AA, didn't see any reason to complain, I stayed quiet about that particular aspect of the deal.

Precisely five minutes after we'd got up to the hotel room, a folded slip of paper appeared through the crack beneath our door. Neither me or AA saw it sliding in so, for all *we* knew, it might've been there from the moment we checked in.

I decided that I'd be the one to read it, and was just a touch put out to find that it only had on a time, 'eleven p.m.' and a locale, 'hotel bar'.

When I passed it over to AA, I couldn't help smiling, seeing him squint at the swirly handwriting—the note written out in blue ink—as if he was long-sighted, or something.

When I said to AA, in a slightly jovial way, "What'd you make of it Sherlock?" I was taken aback by the stern glare he shot at me in return.

It was soon gone, though, in the blink of an eye, and he crunched the paper up into a ball and tossed it into the bin in the corner of the room.

With his back to me, looking out through the window of the hotel room, out across the apparently endless car park, he said. "It means we need to get ourselves dressed."

Before I could put in anything else, before I could interrogate him about *just what* we were to get ourselves dressed *with*, AA stomped on over to the wardrobe and brought the double doors open with a neat *snick* of hidden, unclasping magnets.

Within, I saw, sure enough, the light fleeces, the waterproof trousers.

The pair of trainers.

One pair for each of us.

Next, of course, there was the pair of guns.

.45s.

Our own weapons, snatched from our homes.

. . . Some days I have a *very* strong urge to throttle Brian Mathewson and his legion of thieves.

It was then that AA turned to me, a smirk on his lips. "Guess this is the assassins' equivalent of matching bath towels."

3.31:34

W E GET ALL the passengers' hand luggage cleared up, and replaced in the overhead compartments. It's at this point that, like the know-it-all kid at school, the male steward, shiny bald head and all, raises his hand.

I turn to look at him, feeling a twisting sensation down in the base of my stomach. "What?" I say, reminding myself that I need to maintain a certain *hijacker's* rapport with the hostages.

"I was just thinking," he replies, "that the passengers might require some refreshments—something to drink, some water"— he arches an eyebrow—"you look like you might be quite parched yourself."

I glance down at the male member of the cabin crew's name tag, pinned to the front of the breast pocket of his dark-purple suit jacket:

Enrique Suarez.

I look past Mr Suarez, and to AA, who's leaning up against

68

one of the seats near the back of the cabin, slotting the final piece of luggage into the overhead compartment.

When AA's through, and I see that he's stopped that quite scary, bubbling-away-just-beneath-the-surface look, I nod for him to come over.

Although AA combs his fingers through his hair, staring at Suarez in profile, he accepts the request, saying that two members of the cabin crew may accompany him to the back of the plane, while I stay here, monitoring the other two.

When Suarez makes to get up, AA gives a slight smile, reaches out his hand, and shakes his head. "No," he says, "you're staying *right* here."

Instead, AA selects the two older female members of the cabin crew—the blonde and the brunette—and they head off along the aisle.

I find myself standing before Suarez, who holds his lips pursed, his hands neatly clenched in his lap, staring at some point in mid-air as nonchalantly as if he's waiting for a bus.

As AA disappears behind the velvet curtain to the cabin crew's quarters, I see him slipping that device back out of his pocket—the altimeter, and whatever *else* that damn thing does.

I suppose that AA's paranoid about this being part of some protocol:

Some sort of a plan set aside for situations like this.

And yet, I'm fairly certain that not one member of the cabin crew has been able to get through to the captain. For all our other failings—that horrific mess we made of the passengers' hand luggage—we've kept a pretty close eye on the members of the cabin crew.

As I stand there, keeping a cursory eye over the passenger

cabin, I feel my brain shifting about again, and my mind being taken over by the memory of the night before.

Five Hours Before The Job

F IVE MINUTES BEFORE ELEVEN, the bar of the hotel was near enough deserted.

I don't know quite what I expected to see:

Men in business suits, suitcases tucked in neatly beneath their tables, tapping away at their phones, a half-finished bottle of beer on the table in front of them?

Single mothers shepherding children, a glass of orange juice for each, crumbs of cake scattered over the surface of the table?

An elderly couple, both of them wearing hats, with scarves wrapped about their throats, sitting on the edges of their seats, anxiously awaiting the shuttle bus to the airport?

But there was nobody.

Nobody aside from me and AA.

The bar wasn't much to write home about, either.

The sofas were all made of cheap, polyester fabric; several of them with tears exposing black stuffing within; and all of them with well-defined arse-grooves.

I speculated to myself that the hotel bar wouldn't have looked out of place in student accommodation.

Me and AA took a seat over by the window, looking out into the airport road passing by, and I promptly placed the elbow of my newly acquired fleece in something sticky and sweet-smelling.

The bar itself was winding down; the bar lady wiping down tumblers and stacking them on the walnut-textured plastic shelf behind. As she laid each one down, it was with a neat, practised *click* of the rim of the glass.

I breathed in deeply, and thought about ordering a glass of fizzy water and lime, then, thinking about the job ahead, and not wanting to give myself a full bladder before knowing what I was getting into, decided against it.

At exactly eleven on the dot—by the clock hanging over the bar—a blond-haired woman dressed in a long, flowing *black* trench coat, and wearing a wide-brimmed hat, clacked into the bar.

Already, I was feeling somewhat underdressed, and was silently cursing AA for having demanded that we 'change' into the clothing in the wardrobe before going down to the meeting in the bar.

That'll teach me to take a *man's* opinion on anything.

The woman wore heavy eye makeup, that smoky, brownish-black mixture bringing out the brilliance of her light-blue eyes. She could have been thirty—she could've been *fifty*. She still had her girlish figure and not many wrinkles around her eyes.

As she approached the table, I caught a whiff of blackberries and hazelnuts; odd that I should smell it so clearly, and that I should be able to recognise the odour so readily.

But that was how it was.

Instantaneous.

Without so much as making eye contact with either me or AA, the woman took the seat on the sofa opposite us, pausing ever so briefly to brush her leather-gloved hand across the cushion, then to hoik up the tail of her trench coat, before sitting down.

She removed the hat she'd been wearing—*black* to match her trench coat—and laid it down on the table before I had the chance to warn her of the innate stickiness of the surfaces here.

I saw that her hair was long, but that she'd coiled it up and plonked it down in the centre of her scalp:

A business-like bun.

She interlocked her fingers, looked between me and AA, and then tilted her head to one side. "I expect you're wondering where Brian is."

Although I slipped a sidelong glance to AA, I knew that it wasn't necessary that we so much as look one another in the eye to *know* that she had us sussed.

That *that* was exactly what me and AA were thinking.

The woman gave a slight smile, stretching her red-painted lips and making them *sheen* in the bright, orange lights of the bar. "Things are very simple," she said, "while"—she made a twizzling motion with her index finger in the air—"*this* all blows over, Brian's decided to go to ground, to stay out of the limelight."

"What's *this*?" AA put in, saving me the trouble.

The woman looked between the two of us, and then, in an almost seductive manner, she brought her hand up to cover her mouth from the bar lady—*obviously* not listening in and *most definitely* thinking long and hard about getting home.

"The memory stick," she said, her voice a harsh whisper.

I thought about the memory stick, the one which Brian had previously *handed* over to someone who'd become an arch nemesis, and for reasons that I—*myself*—found somewhat difficult to even *begin* to understand.

The one which had mine, and AA's—not to mention *tons* of others'—data.

I glanced to AA again, at last realising what this was all about.

She leaned back into the sofa, dipped her hand into the pocket of her trench coat, and then, from within, produced a pair of folded-up pieces of A4 paper.

She handed one over to me.

And the other to AA.

I took mine from her at once, unfolded it, saw that it was a print-out, with a variety of times and instructions for the next day.

I saw, with not a little horror, that the first event—'BE READY'—was timed at five o'clock the next morning. And there I'd been *hoping* I might be able to get some sleep before Brian subjected me and AA to his latest swivel-eyed whim.

"The way we're working this," the woman continued, "is that you've each got half of the plan."

I glanced to AA, seeing him already folding up his own piece of paper.

Just like *always*, he was trying to get ahead of the game.

"That way," the woman said, "if one of you gets into trouble then it'll be impossible to go through with the job."

I screwed up my eyes. "Why'd you want us to stop the job if one of us is incapacitated?"

The woman pressed her lips together, looked to AA, giving him an almost *knowing* glare. Getting up, she said only, "Dear, sometimes you need to know your place."

And with that catty remark lingering on her clacking heels, I watched that black trench coat disappear around the corner with a flourish.

When I glanced to AA, I saw he was looking somewhat green about the gills.

"You all right?" I said.

"Let's get some sleep," he replied, tucking his folded paper into the pocket of his waterproof trousers.

Before I folded up my own piece of paper, I glanced up at the header.

At the code name for this job:

HELL BIRD

3.27:40

I HAVE TO ADMIT that it's a somewhat surreal sight, observing the two stewardesses, a trolley between the two of them, dishing out cups of water and fizzy drink under AA's watchful eye.

I keep looking over the passengers sitting in their seats.

Some of them have returned to their reading material, to their technological devices, and I wonder if me and AA should *really* be allowing that.

I wonder if—way out here, in the middle of the Atlantic Ocean—anybody will be able to get any sort of mobile phone signal.

I hope not.

As I'm scanning the passengers' faces, I can't help but catch Brian's eye.

He's looking at me, over the top of a newspaper.

When he catches me looking, he feeds me another of those sly smiles of his, and then returns to his reading.

I suppose it must be a fine thing—a very fine thing *indeed*—to feel one-hundred-per-cent, totally and completely in control of any given situation or context.

Because I have no doubt at all that he's in control now.

If only there was something I could do to shake him up a bit.

When the stewardesses get through with their drinks trolley, and AA deigns to escort them through the velvet curtain at the back of the plane, I take it upon myself to wander over to where Brian's sitting.

He sits beside a woman of about forty, or fifty. When she observes me approaching, she recoils, gripping the armrests tightly, her nails sinking into the deluxe leather and all the blood draining from her knuckles.

I can't say I blame her.

As I approach them, I catch a slight smell of musk—*body odour*—mingled in with whisky:

Brian Mathewson's smells.

He sits tight, in his seat, continuing to look over his newspaper.

When he finally can't ignore me any longer, as I stand there, in the aisle, staring down on him, he gives a slight smile to the woman sitting next to him, brings his newspaper closed with a slight *rustle* of loose pages and neatly tucks it into the pocket in front of him.

He turns side on, and heads out of his seat.

Towards me.

I can feel the eyes of every passenger—and the two seated cabin crew members—on me as Brian lightly reaches out and touches my wrist. He leans into me, still with a slight smile, and says, "This way, dear, let's not keep them waiting."

Without any further input from me, Brian leads me to the

front of the passenger cabin, where I stand before the other passengers. He bows his head slightly, apparently waiting for me to do—or *say*—something.

Only problem being that I have no idea what that is.

AA emerges from behind the velvet curtain towards the back of the cabin, and, his eyes never leaving mine, he escorts the two stewardesses back into their seats; back alongside the younger woman, and Suarez.

AA nods to Brian, his eyes skittering all over the place, and he says, "What's this about?"

Brian looks out over the passengers, watching us, as if we're on a stage and they're all merely the audience. He takes a deep breath and then, speaking low in a voice only me and AA can hear, he says, "Kill me."

3.24:32

I T TAKES ME several moments for my brain to process exactly the words that've tumbled out through Brian Mathewson's lips. And when the words finally do clunk through the mechanism—like a penny churning through an aged, rusted-up coin slot—I screw up my eyes, regard Brian as if he's crazy.

I'm on the cusp of spitting out something, of asking Brian, please, for an explanation of what he's just said—that we're to *kill* him—when AA beats me to the punch.

Before I can react at all, AA grabs hold of the back of Brian's suit jacket, gives him a quick shake.

When I look over the rest of the passengers' faces, I'm not surprised to see the shock and awe there, all spread out among them. Then AA slips his gun out from its holster, holds the barrel to Brian's cheek. I feel my heart beating hard in my throat, and it's only then that I *do* react.

I whip my gun out, feel its nice, steady weight, and I point it, momentarily, at AA.

It's right then, as I peer over the sight, that I catch Brian's eye, out of the corner of my vision. And it must be a skill which Brian has developed for years and years, because he manages to communicate a message directly into my brain:

Leave AA to his work.

I haven't even processed the thought consciously before I turn my gun, which was previously pointed at AA's chest, onto Brian himself.

I stare along the sight, feeling a strange and—*quite alluring*—power from pointing a gun at my boss.

Brian remains calm, though his head is tilted to one side from how AA holds the back of his suit. Brian's lips are slightly parted, and I can see that they're just a touch moist, from the whisky he was drinking back in first class.

I can only watch on as AA drags Brian away from the watching eyes of the passengers, through the velvet curtain which leads to first class, and out of our sight.

The passengers all fix their gazes on the velvet curtain; their reading material, their electronic devices, all forgotten for the time being.

They've even forgotten about me, because, when a man dressed in a grey tracksuit, with a baseball cap drawn down over his face, a pair of large, wrap-around sun glasses attached to his face, gets up from his seat, cranes his neck towards the curtain of the first-class area of the plane to get a better look, I shout out; stop him right there.

Point my gun at him.

Like an obedient hostage, he holds up his hands, returns to his seat.

All of us concentrate on hearing anything at all coming from the first-class cabin.

We're waiting . . . waiting . . . for what we *think's* going to happen . . . and then, from out of nowhere, and nothing like as loud as I might've imagined, there's a gunshot.

Everybody flinches at the sound.

One Hour Before The Job

A S I LAY IN BED, on my side, feeling my ribs aching— throbbing with dull pain—I listened for the longest time to AA getting himself ready in the bathroom.

I heard the *tinkle* of him replacing his toothbrush in the glass provided by the sink, and then the slender *schlick-schlick* sound of him going about shaving.

The curtains were still drawn, not that there would've been daylight anyway.

At this time of the year, it won't get light till around eight or nine in the morning.

Drawn-out, bitter winter nights.

Although it felt as if my heart was pounding within my skull, I managed to fork myself out from beneath my duvet, to tread on over to the window, to the curtain.

Despite knowing what I'd find there, I still peeled the curtain back.

Peered across the sad, apparently endless, asphalt car park all lit up by the even, orange streetlights that seem to be perpetually on at this time of year.

The sky was overcast, so I couldn't see the moon at all.

When I turned back into the room, seeing that the bathroom door was still mostly closed, and still hearing that *schlick-schlick* sound of AA shaving, I moved my attention down to AA's bedside table.

To the drawer, left partially open.

The folded-up A4 piece of paper just visible.

I took a deep breath, gave a quick thought to my professional morals—and then to my *personal* ethics—and decided that taking a peep, really, wouldn't do any harm.

I just about managed to get one hand on the drawer handle when I heard AA's voice, even, and slightly playful. "Uh-uh-uh, Anna," AA said. "Remember what the important lady *said*."

Feeling the colour rise in my cheeks, I backed away from the bedside table.

I shifted a glance over my shoulder to AA. He was wearing only the over-washed, grey-white hotel towel, his face still half covered with shaving foam. He held his razor down at his thigh, as if it might make a useful weapon.

Not the way they're made *these* days.

He brought his razor up, waggled it a little, at the tip of my nose.

And then, with a parting, familiar smile—and one which seemed to vanish the moment he turned back to the bathroom— he said, "Playtime will come later."

With a final glance back at the drawer, the note still temptingly visible through the crack, I turned to the wardrobe.

Busied myself with the task of getting ready for the pickup.

3.21:21

I N THOSE LONG MOMENTS, as the gunshot—not much more than an overhead compartment being slammed shut—enters the group consciousness of the plane, I lose myself in the night before, in the hotel, attempting to—*somehow*—keep myself rooted to the spot.

Because I know that it'd only take *one person* to spark an outright revolt.

I turn my attention back to the passengers, bring my gun up to my chest just to make sure that everybody knows who's the *mummy* here.

I get a few looks, and then, as if this whole routine has been meticulously pre-planned—*I wish*—AA ducks his head through the curtain of the first-class cabin.

AA briefly glances about the passengers, the ones we're holding hostage, and I feel a group gasp pass about the room.

I have to admit that I feel just as frightened as they do,

because this isn't the AA I know, quite cleanly—*succinctly*—put, he seems unhinged . . . more unhinged than normal, that is.

"Anna," AA says, and then jerks his head back, into the first-class cabin.

I look about the faces of our hostages, and then shift back to AA.

I'm not about to leave the passengers alone.

Not even if AA decides to shoot me down himself.

Instead, I go for a compromise.

I inch away from the stare of the passengers, and go over to the velvet curtain—over to AA.

When I stand near him, I catch a slight whiff of sweat, and of something rotten. I glance down, to his side, notice that there's a damp patch on his shirt, where I suppose that bullet wound of his has been weeping.

What *is* it with men and doctors?

They never seem to want to go . . .

Already, I can see that the stubble has begun to grow back on AA's cheeks—that's the thing with dark-haired men, like AA, they never seem to ever get quite shot of those beards of theirs. "Look in here, Anna, quickly," he says.

I feel my heart beat against my ribs.

Although I'm not one who usually has much trouble with seeing dead bodies, I have to admit that seeing the body of my boss holds a certain sway over me.

Perhaps I am human after all . . .

I peer in through the curtain, to the first-class cabin, and there—*I just knew it!*—I see Brian Mathewson, leaning casually up against one of the seats, giving me a coy wave and a raised eyebrow.

I also notice that one of the seats now has a freshly shot-in hole.

I turn back to AA, and I can't help but feel all the eyes of the passengers upon me, looking to feed off my reaction to the —*apparently horrific*—sight there in the first-class cabin.

There's not much acting required on my part, though. I'm sure that my look of surprise, although it is with a slight sense of dreadful inevitability, is enough to convince the passengers that Something Not Very Pleasant resides just beyond the curtain.

AA eyeballs me, keeps his voice low. "Just keep an eye on them, all right?"

And although I feel a sigh rising up my throat as I turn back to my supervision duties in the passenger cabin, I can't say with any great conviction—or *honesty*—that I expected anything else.

When I turn back to the passengers, I notice that the bald steward—*Suarez*—has raised his hand once more.

Realising that I'm still holding my gun, I slip it back into its holster, not seeing any great reason to be brandishing it.

I stand before Suarez, concentrate on keeping my expression stern, neutral—*professional* . . . something which AA might take on board as a meaty piece of advice.

Suarez meets my eye, his lips are pert, and he still clutches his hands in his lap as if he's unperturbed by all that's happened so far.

Yeah, right, like I buy *that*.

"We demand to know what's going on," Suarez says.

I breathe in deeply, feeling that recycled air move about my chest.

The drone of the plane engines throb through my eardrums, almost as natural as the sound of my own heartbeat now; it's almost difficult to imagine a time in my past when I didn't hear them.

I cock my head to one side and, despite everything, despite the situation, I manage to jabber out, "My associate just *shot* that man."

This seems to quieten Suarez a touch. His tanned skin goes a little pale. But his eyes remain locked on mine. "Do you think you'll get away with this?" he says.

I give a shrug. "We just want the memory stick—the sooner somebody hands it over to us, the sooner this will all be over."

Suarez—the three stewardesses all serving to create a backdrop of concerned expressions—replies, "Nobody has this memory stick, can't you see?"

His almost flawless English cracks a little, and I can tell that he's under strain.

That his mother tongue is threatening to break through.

But, then again, why *wouldn't* it be?

When I turn back to the passengers, I see that AA is sticking his head through the velvet curtain, that he's beckoning me over again.

And I go to him.

AA holds the device in his hand, checking up on our coordinates once more—*apparently*.

He speaks quickly, and I can see that his face is slick with sweat. I can smell the salty odour all over him. "I'll keep an eye out," AA says, "you go and speak to Brian."

I think long and hard about rejecting this request.

But, in the end, the curiosity in me makes itself heard.

And I slip past AA, through the curtain, and into the first-class cabin.

3.17:12

B RIAN AWAITS ME, of course, that same *smug* grin spread all over his cheeks.

But I console myself with the knowledge that—*at last*—I'm going to get some answers.

Some *kind* of answers, anyway.

Whether they're truth or a lie remains to be seen . . .

"Great work, Anna," Brian says, grinning all over.

I suppose that, if I allow myself to get close enough, he'll clap me on the shoulder.

I'm vaguely aware of AA barking out something beyond the curtain, to the passengers. It appears that he's taken exception to passengers using electronic devices, and that he's setting about gathering them up.

I look to Brian. "AA," I say, "he's a total mess."

Brian flashes his eyebrows at me. "I know, isn't he?"

A little taken aback that Brian doesn't so much as attempt to parry *that* blow, I put in, "Just what're you up to with all this—why didn't you *tell* us that you'd be on the plane?"

Brian pouts, tilts his head to one side. "Can't a man have his secrets?"

I breathe in then sigh out.

The plane bounces a couple of times.

I grab hold of a nearby headrest.

Tighten my grip on it in a way that looks *far* too nervy to be anything other than instinct.

When I look back to Brian, that self-satisfied smirk of his seems to have grown by factors of ten. "Don't like flying, Anna?"

"Not a big fan," I reply.

"I never knew," he says.

And I can't help feeling that it's a *big* mistake to allow Brian to know of *any* sort of weakness that I may have, let alone letting him know *right now*, when he can extract maximum advantage from the situation.

He doesn't even need to *sense* my ill ease.

He knows it for a fact.

Thankfully, the turbulence is just a couple of bumps, nothing more—because I can't quite face strapping myself into a chair, and having to conduct this impromptu chat sitting beside Brian.

It's *always* preferable to be standing when dealing with him.

Reasonably convinced that the plane's not going to drop out of the sky in the next couple of minutes, I meet Brian's playful gaze again. "I suppose that Jacuzzi tub in the cargo bay is yours?"

Brian beams back at me. "Yes, yes," he replies, with a shake of his head, "you know me *so* well, Anna, a man of luxuries, that's me." Brian rubs his thumb and forefinger together, as if he's making a subtle allusion to money, but then he says, "AA's got that neat little *computer* of his, hasn't he?"

"Yes," I say, thinking about the device with the coordinates.

Brian gives a shake of his head. "There's never any beating that man—one of the most resourceful employees I've ever had the fortune of encountering."

"Right," I say, "if you ever wanted somebody to bring a plane down, then it's AA."

Brian closes one eye, jabs his tongue out of the corner of his mouth. "I don't think you realise the stress AA's been under these past few days"—Brian throws up a loose hand as casually as another man might flourish a handkerchief—"*personal* issues, I believe."

"Really?" I say, not really all that concerned, and then, deciding the time's right to change the subject for good, "Where's the memory stick?"

Brian brings a finger up to me, points it right at the tip of my nose. "That's the question, isn't it? That's what's brought us all here—on this flight."

"Uh-huh," I reply, and wait.

Hopefully, like all good arch villains, Brian will spill his masterplan before too long, so that I—his humble henchwoman—might be able to put it into place.

But he seems content to keep me in suspense.

"Tell me, Anna," Brian says, "where do you think we're headed?"

I give a shrug. "Somewhere in the Caribbean?"

Brian squashes his lips together, gives a nod. "Yes, a good enough guess."

Feeling my patience waning a little, I shift my weight from

one foot to the other, tilt my head to one side and say, "Well, are we or *aren't* we?"

It's always important to pin down publicists to yes-and-no answers.

Of course there's never any confidence that you'll get the truth out of them.

But at least in the future, you'll have evidence that they lied.

Even if it's only the evidence of memory.

Evidence you can only use yourself.

"You know what I think, Anna?" Brian says, sticking his hand into the pocket of his suit jacket.

For a long, drawn-out second, I'm sure he's going to produce a gun . . . but, in the end, he comes up with a sort of plastic key.

"I think it's time you went to see the pilot."

"What?" I say, taking the plastic key off him.

Without another word, Brian dips his hand into the other pocket of his jacket, and produces a slip of paper.

I have to say, after this job, I'm going to be *well and truly through* with slips of paper.

I take it from him.

When I unfold it, I see there's a list of coordinates all written out there.

Coordinates which mean *nothing at all* to me.

"Well, come on, Anna," Brian says, stifling a yawn with the back of his hand as he descends into a seat. "Time's a wasting."

3.06:57

I T'S NEVER A GOOD SIGN when an assassin's hands start shaking.

Perhaps it would be acceptable if my normal method of taking care of people was anything other than a gun. A rope, a knife, all those means which don't demand such precise, exacting control over the weapon. But now, as I eye up the keyhole in the door to the cockpit, I feel as if I'm almost treading on holy ground.

As if I'm *desecrating* holy ground.

Perhaps it's just the weight of all the movies, all the stuff I've seen or read, about how pilots now somehow seem to occupy the same sort of space once preserved for politicians or monarchs, or *Yetis*.

But, as Brian Mathewson has often taught me, those people are only kidding themselves if they think that their position can protect them.

And, from what I've heard, Brian Mathewson is working hard on getting the yetis to come out of the closet . . .

As I slip the plastic key into the hole, I speculate about how Brian's really worked out a very nice way to have the first-class cabin all to himself. I suppose, to Brian, faking his own death is all part and parcel of a good day's work.

I feel for my gun, down in its holster, at my side, and I bring it into my hand.

Then I turn it towards the door, ready to act if needed.

As I feel the locking mechanism *twitch* against the key, I know that there's no turning back.

That I've *officially* become an aeroplane hijacker.

I breathe in deeply then push the door open.

At first the bright light takes me aback.

It's only then that I realise, back in the passenger cabin, all the blinds on the windows had been drawn down. That the only light present had been the fluorescent, flickering glow from above.

I hold up my forearm, shield my eyes from the glare of daylight.

All I can make out are the pair of forms.

In their seats.

Both of them staring back at me.

I blink several times, clear my mind of the simmering daze brought on from the bright light, and, just like that, I can make out the pilots fine.

First, my eyes linger over the pilot to my right, sitting behind the—*to me*—incomprehensible and extensive buttons and levers . . . and who knows what else.

I look to his white, short-sleeved shirt, the pair of golden stripes stitched onto the shoulders. And I see his face, much younger than I might've expected, and with a smattering of fine, blond stubble. I guess that he must be somewhere in his twenties. And then I twig that, most likely, he's the co-pilot.

The air smells lightly of grease, that vague odour of a garage.

I almost expect to see a mechanic, dressed up in oil-smattered overalls, appear before me; wiping his dirtied hands with an equally filthy rag.

The co-pilot's strong, blue eyes stare long and hard at me, in a way which reflects the searing, endless blue skies which stretch out beyond the nose of the plane.

His eyes stare at my gun.

I shift my attention to my left, to the pilot—*a woman, like Enrique Suarez said.*

She looks me over, her features narrowed, a fair few wrinkles in her brow. I guess her age to be in the fifties, and, by the look of her well-tanned, leathered skin, she's spent a good portion of her life doing what she's doing now.

Globetrotting.

She has sleek white hair, drawn up into a ponytail which remains still as she, like the co-pilot, stares at the gun I hold in my hand.

Neither of the pilots speak, and I suppose, the way things are playing out, it makes more sense for me to be the one to break the silence.

"Here," I say, remembering the scrap of paper, and holding it out to the pilot.

The pilot remains frozen where she is for several moments.

And then, with a rapid glance to the co-pilot, she reaches out for the piece of paper.

Unfolds it.

Glances over the numbers written there.

The coordinates.

She looks up at me, her eyelids drooping a little, her mouth taking on a pout. "What's this?" she says, and I realise that she has a thick Welsh accent.

I eye the pilot back. "It's where we're going," I say.

She glances back down at the slip of paper, hands it over to the co-pilot, then, with a shake of her head, looks around at me again. "Nothing there," she says. "Just *sea*."

I feel my stomach dip as the weight of the pilot's gaze rests on me.

As I come to realise just what this means.

Forty-Five Minutes Before The Job

ALL DRESSED UP in my light fleece and waterproof trousers—*all black*—I stood alongside AA on the curb outside the hotel.

Like AA, I kept my gun and holster in the front pockets of my fleece, not exactly wanting to excite whatever security systems surely keep an eye on the surrounding area of an airport.

I could still smell the slight fragrance of soap clinging to him from that extremely long shower he took, and which meant my own shower was curtailed to only a few drips.

Not that I begrudge it at all.

Although I could tell AA was jumpy, that every time I happened to cast a look over him, I'd see him blinking rapidly, or scratching at the back of his neck, I did my best not to look at him.

To be fair, I'm not the greatest in the morning either.

When the van pulled up at the curb of the hotel: a white van with no other markings—and I couldn't help thinking to myself: *subtle Brian*—I could feel my heart beating hard against my ribcage. My blood running a little cold. I couldn't help wondering if Brian could've sorted me and AA out with something a little more substantial than only the fleeces and waterproof trousers.

We were instructed to leave the clothes we arrived to the hotel in the night before in the wardrobe of the hotel room, and given strict assurances that they would be duly dry-cleaned and returned to us once the job was finished with.

In my mouth, I could still taste the bitter flavour of the instant coffee I hurled down my throat, the granules still stuck between my teeth because I wasn't given sufficient time with my toothbrush.

If there's anything I hate more than getting up early, it's being *rushed*.

Without a word to me, AA rounded the van, stepped up to the back doors and then popped them open. He at least saw fit to adhere to the Rules of Chivalry:

Ladies first.

I clambered aboard, into the darkened interior of the van.

AA stepped in behind me and brought the doors shut with a pair of percussive *thuds*.

Before I really managed to get my bearings, the van's engine rumbled to life and a light blinked on from somewhere. It did a decent job of illuminating our humble surroundings, which was to say that they consisted of a pair of wooden boxes . . . *coffins*, for want of a better word . . . laid out in the back of the van.

I glanced back at AA, seeing that he, too, seemed just a little phased by the sight confronting us. As I headed over to one of the wooden boxes, the van lurched to life, gently accelerating away from the hotel.

As we trundled along in the van, I could feel the soles of my feet becoming itchy.

I knew that feeling well.

A feeling of *unease*.

Something at the back of my brain trying to tell me that I was about to ensnare myself in some Very Deep Trouble Indeed.

But, like an idiot—as seems more and more the case these days—I ignored the feeling.

With a final look to AA, I got down on my haunches, taking care with the continuous motion of the van, trying not to face plant, and gently knelt down in the wooden box.

I couldn't help but think back to my cat, Lizzie, and how she might've reacted to such a box. She would've been having a *whale* of a time because, if there's something all cat owners know only too well, cats are the greatest fans of boxes on planet Earth.

But I'm not a cat.

A slight smile snuck onto my lips as I slipped AA a sidelong glance, and saw that he was lowering himself down into the wooden box beside mine as if he was getting into a well-filled, steaming-hot bath.

The van jerked hard to one side of the road, and I almost lost my balance, almost ended up with my head smacking *hard* into the metal interior wall.

As the van trundled on, apparently back to its normal, *predictable* driving patterns, I turned myself around. Lay myself down in the box, in the fashion which AA had already done.

I looked to him, said, "Did it tell you to lie down in the coffin on that note?"

Apparently not realising that I was speaking to him, AA retained his thunderous expression.

Not amused at all.

Finally, though, when he did see me looking, he gave a vague smirk. His features a little darkened from the insufficient light. "It's instinct, Anna," he said, "we've all got to learn to die sometime, haven't we?"

2.58:11

W HEN I RETURN to the first-class cabin, I find Brian right where he was.

Cool as you like, newspaper clasped in his hands, a pair of spectacles resting on the tip of his nose as he peruses the day's— *yesterday's?*—stories.

As I approach him, I can't help thinking that the pose he strikes, that one of gentle amusement, is one which has been shared all down the ages by bankers, merchants and, most of all, manipulating royal advisors.

He senses me standing over him and he reaches up, hoiks his glasses off his nose then lays them on the folded-down plastic tray before him. He folds his newspaper smartly in half and then clutches it to his stomach. He gives me a gentle smile. "How did you get on, Anna?"

"Fine," I say, not feeling all that eloquent at present.

Brian cocks his head to one side, smiles wider. "So, they're going to fly us off to those coordinates I provided?"

"That's how we left it," I reply, thinking about how the pilot turned her attention back to the controls, that scrap of paper in her lap, and then tapped away at some instrument or other.

I wonder, once all this is through, whether I should take some flying lessons.

Assuming I'm still alive, that is.

"Good, good," Brian says with another smile as he unfolds his newspaper, replaces his glasses on his nose, and, apparently, continues where he left off.

How can he be so calm?

How can he be so *cool*?

"Brian?" I say, unable to restrain myself.

"Hmm?" he replies, without taking his eyes off the newspaper.

"What if the pilot's contacting somebody on the ground— what if they scramble fighter jets to intercept us, something like that?"

Brian carefully turns the page of his newspaper. "No, they wouldn't."

"Why not?" I say, feeling as if I'm stepping out-of-bounds, and yet, given the circumstances, it doesn't seem too much of a big ask.

Still focussed on his newspaper, Brian reaches up and taps the side of his nose.

He gives a slight smile and scans down the page.

"Look," I say, determined to get more out of him, "if you'd told me that we'd be responsible for hijacking an airliner I'm not sure I'd have accepted the job. You didn't give me a chance to back out."

Brian breathes in a breath that can only be the precursor to a sigh. He turns the page of the newspaper again. "Anna, really, we've been over this already—you've had *plenty* of opportunities to back out before now." Now he does look up over the top of his newspaper—eyes me very closely over the rim of his glasses. "We both *knew* that it would come to this."

"Mutual destruction?" I say, unable to keep myself from blurting it out.

Brian smiles, returns to his newspaper. "Something like that."

2.43:53

BACK IN THE PASSENGER CABIN with AA, I feel myself getting feisty, feeling at a loose end.

There's a bout of turbulence during which me and AA cling on tight to the overhead compartment. Suarez does his best to admonish us—to tell us to sit our arses down in a seat and buckle up.

Neither of us pays any attention.

I cling on for dear life. Each time the plane bounces over an air pocket—or whatever the hell it is—I feel that sensation of weightlessness, and feel as if I'm simply going to plummet, right down to the surface of the ocean.

That the entire plane will simply *explode*.

It's while I'm standing up that I notice the younger, redheaded stewardess staring at me in profile. When it begins to bother me—when I get that odd, *uncomfortable* itching sensation just below the surface of my skin—I turn to look at her.

Meet her brilliant, green eyes.

And she quickly looks away.

I tell myself that I've still got it.

The *killer's* look.

I spend as much time looking over AA as I do looking over our passengers-slash-hostages, and I can't help noticing all those little exaggerated gestures of his. How, every half a minute or so, almost without fail, he reaches up to smooth back a non-existent loose strand of hair. Tucks it back behind his ear. And then, a couple of moments after, he glances down at his gun, fiddles with something near the safety, before gripping it tighter.

To finish off his odd-ball routine, he rolls his shoulders, as if he's trying to loosen tension out of them.

I can't help but look down to his side—trying to work out whether or not that wound of his has stopped weeping. It looks dry to me, but it's difficult to tell because the shirt itself is black.

I think about Brian, in the first-class cabin, and shake my head.

Think about him casually leafing through his newspaper— not a care in the world.

And I think about how Brian should've been the one to go into the cockpit, the one to go and pay the pilots a visit.

Because now I know that whatever I said in there will be on the Black Box, some sort of recording device. Just like always, Brian has managed to find a way to get off scot-free.

A demonic puppeteer.

After another bout of turbulence, I find myself crossing eyes with the redheaded stewardess again, and perhaps for no other reason than boredom, I venture over to her.

Go and see what she *wants* from me.

When I stand over her, I'm conscious of the gun in my hand.

I slip it down into its holster, not wanting to scare this girl crazy without cause.

I lean up against the side of the plane, against the plastic wall which, somehow, doesn't quite feel substantial. Then I say, "Are you all right?"

She sits in her seat, seatbelt fastened, with her hands clasped tight in her lap, over the top of her dark-purple *Pleasure Lines* trouser suit. "Yes," she replies, with a slight smile.

I can tell, though, that the smile is an act.

Her complexion is pale and her pupils are dilated.

No doubt she's experiencing extreme stress.

I look to the seat beside her, where Enrique Suarez reclines back in his chair, arms drawn up to his eyes, covering them, apparently asleep.

Behind these two, the other two stewardesses also doze.

In fact, when I glance about the passenger cabin, I see that, for the most part, all the other passengers are in some state of sleep.

I suppose that—even in a hijacking—a person can't remain tense the whole time.

I look back down to the redhead stewardess.

"My name's Tabitha," she says, and then, with a slight, schoolgirl giddiness, "you can call me Tabby."

Her accent is something of the English schoolmarm. It brings to mind a privileged childhood, expensive schools, and I wonder just what her parents might think of her career choice; about her having become a stewardess.

But, more than that, there's something about that name which brings to mind the antiquity of the nineteenth century.

I think about making some comment on it, then decide not to.

There's a distinct difference between being a hijacker and being a bully.

And I've no intention of crossing over into being the latter.

"Anna," I say, not seeing any reason *not* to give her my real name.

Tabby inclines her head slightly towards me, her eyes narrowed just a fraction in a playful manner which, I suppose, is eminently popular with the more *exclusive* passengers:

The ones who reside in first-class.

"You're afraid of flying, aren't you?" Tabby says.

That comment takes me aback, mostly because it's true.

I feel my chest tighten a touch, a chill run through my blood.

I slip a quick glance back to AA, who, I see, is leaning up against the wall of the cabin, his eyes drooping low now, his mouth slightly latched open.

Great, just about the last thing I need . . .

I wonder what exactly he might've taken when he slipped off to go and use the toilet.

If he's going to be *any* use to me at all for the remainder of this job.

"Hey?" I say, calling out to AA.

AA comes around quickly.

He blinks away his daze.

Squares his shoulders.

Gives me a business-like nod, suddenly looking alert.

I turn my attention back to Tabby. "I've never trusted planes," I say.

Tabby nods back at me. "It's okay, it's just that I can tell the type, the *nervous* types." She gives a bright, wide smile, showing off all her pearly white teeth. "After all the air miles we clock up, you get good at reading people. Not really anything much else to do aside from look at faces."

I reach down, feel for the grip of my gun.

For the longest time, I keep on reaching downwards, but, try for the life of me, I can't get a hold of it. Finally, when I feel my fingertips make contact with the holster, I realise that it's not there.

I jerk my head down, to Tabby—the innocuous redhead.

She has my gun.

And she's pointing it at me.

My heart feels like it might explode as I call out to AA.

Fifteen Minutes Before The Job

THE WHITE VAN took a hard left, and then a hard right, and I couldn't help feeling that the driver—for whatever reason—was attempting to throw off a tail . . . somebody attempting to follow.

I propped my arms up onto the rim of the coffin, looked over to AA.

Just glancing over his face, seeing how he had his eyes clenched tightly shut, his arms crossed over his chest, sent chills right down to my bones.

It was almost like I'd stumbled across a corpse.

A *dead* body.

In those moments, I found my mind ravished by fleeting, *bizarre* speculations. That, perhaps, Brian was trying to set me up. That he had slipped AA something—given him some kind of poison—so that he might frame me for the crime.

Maybe this job—Hell Bird—was nothing more than a ruse to turn me over to the authorities. Perhaps the game was up . . .

But, after another brief bout of swerving—brutal accelera-tion followed by even *more* brutal braking—the van began to move much more steadily.

Overhead, I heard the enormous *roar* of a plane taking off.

As the sound faded, the van drew to a stop, and I heard, from the cab of the van, the driver speaking with somebody through the window.

Footsteps sounded all around, and I heard the *clunk-clunk-clunk* of something hard, and probably wooden, against the metal back doors.

Moving quickly, realising that neither me or AA had twigged the reason for the lids to the wooden boxes, I got to work.

Seeing AA was still on his back, apparently dead to the world, I called out to him in the huskiest whisper I could manage. "Lid! Get the *lid* on!"

As if summoned by a slap to his cheeks, AA wriggled himself upwards a touch, reached out for the lid to his own wooden box and drew it down—entombing himself within.

And I did the same.

Inside the wooden box—the *coffin*—it was very quiet.

And very dark.

Somewhere in the distance, I heard coughing, some mutter-ing, and then, with an ear-wrenching *creak* of hinges the doors opened wide.

I listened in to an *official-sounding* voice.

Somebody in a uniform.

Somebody with the power to dispense approval or disap-proval at his whim.

"What's in them?" the voice said.

"Jus' designer food stuff," the driver of the van—I supposed —said.

A V IAIN

"Such as?" the voice replied.

The driver took a sharp intake of breath as if he was thoroughly fed up, but not with the official, more with his own boss. "You know, pickled squid, pitted olives, caviar, all that usual shit they can't get in paradise."

Lying in the coffin, I felt the suspension of the van retreat downwards—the official setting one foot inside of the van, I guessed.

I reached for my gun.

During the journey, I'd strapped on my holster, and slipped the gun inside.

I knew I might need to be brought into action.

This driver, after all, was *only* a driver.

At least as far as I knew . . .

I slipped the gun out from my holster, pointed it upwards, at the lid of the coffin.

Rested my finger on the trigger.

Right at the moment when I felt all the muscles seize tight in my hand—when the tension reached its most fraught moment—there was a percussive, short series of taps on the lid.

Tap. Tap. Tap.

I was ready—ready for the lid to slip back at any second.

And then I would shoot.

In the near distance, I heard the driver mumble something.

It drew the official away from my coffin.

And I felt the suspension of the van heave downwards and then back up, to its previous position, like it had been when we'd been driving along.

I drew my gun back from the lid.

Shut my eyes.

And waited for the van to drive on.

2.37:15

I T'S FUNNY how quickly things can turn around just by the simple fact of a gun changing hands.

I find myself staring long and hard at the diminutive redhead stewardess—*Tabby*—and wonder just how I managed to let her fool me.

Then again, I guess I've never been the intellectual type.

And, in my defence, it has been a solid six or so hours of being on this plane.

Enough to sap anyone's strength—let alone when you're supposed to be hijacking said plane too.

"Put it down!" Tabby says to AA as she stares along the sight of my gun.

I can just make out, in the periphery of my vision, AA hovering about the scene.

He's just as confused as the rest of the passengers, blinking away their dazes, cottoning on to the latest development.

Behind Tabby, I can make out the other members of the cabin crew.

They all wear anxious expressions.

Enrique Suarez is the first to get up from his seat.

"Sit down!" AA screams out, pointing his gun at Suarez.

For a long second, Suarez seems trapped in no-man's land.

He glances to me.

Then to Tabby.

Back to AA.

It's no longer clear who's in charge.

I think about the distance between me and Tabby.

Like any sensible person, when she snatched my gun off me, she immediately rushed up to her feet and took several steps away.

I know that if I'd been thinking straight—if my instincts hadn't been muffled, *dampened*, by the simple fact of being ten thousand kilometres up in the air—then I might've had a chance of snatching back my gun almost as soon as Tabby stole it.

But, no . . .

I feel the eyeballs of the passengers, all of them glued onto us.

It feels almost as if I'm standing in the middle of a stage.

As if this isn't really happening at all.

The plane hits turbulence.

The floor bounces out from beneath my feet.

And I take a tumble.

I land *hard* on my back, not having either time or coordination to break the fall with my hands.

As I hit, I feel a sharp pain in my ribs.

It flashes right through me.

I bite down hard on my tongue.

Taste blood.

When I glance up, I see Tabby standing over me.

And the other members of the cabin crew all backing her up.

I look over to where AA was standing.

There's no sign of him now.

As Tabby steps closer to me, the gun still pointed at my head, in a way which seems *far* too casual for an amateur, I just about get out, "Where'd he go?"

2.14:31

I T TAKES A COMBINATION of seatbelts—ones which're sourced from the overhead compartments, and clearly ordinarily used for pre-flight security demonstrations—to get me tethered up to Tabby's satisfaction.

Between them, the cabin crew, the two older ladies—the blonde and the brunette—shovel me into a window seat, before having Enrique Suarez plunk himself down in the aisle seat beside me.

He wears the *biggest* shit-eating grin I've ever seen in my life.

And why not?

After all, they've managed to turn the tables on this pair of fearsome—if slightly *green*—hijackers.

I can't help but feel that *I'm* the baddie here.

As I sit tight, by the window, my mind runs through funny little fantasies.

Me lunging hard, my arm swinging through the air, planting a karate chop right on Suarez's Adam's apple. And, with him gurgling away for air, me sliding past him, dodging Tabby's expertly aimed gunshots, before knocking her flat on her back.

Taking my gun away from her.

But, in reality, I know that's not going to happen.

I've never been one all that keen on brute force.

With a gun in my hand, it never really seemed necessary.

Tabby is in frantic conversation with the other two stewardesses and, as a result of her command, she sends one of them scarpering towards the back of the plane.

The other towards the front:

Into first-class.

I can't help but slip Suarez a glance in profile and say, "Aren't they afraid that my"—I pause for a fraction of a second, thinking about how to put it—"*partner* might apprehend them?"

Suarez doesn't look around at me, he continues to stare along the aisle, as if transfixed by something. He mutters a reply out of the corner of his mouth, "I wouldn't worry about *them*," he says, and only now looks to me, "I'd worry about yourself."

"Why?" I say.

Suarez gives a wider grin, nods to Tabby, now holding my gun down at her side, apparently unperturbed by *anything* going on.

She strides over to us.

Without a word, Suarez gets up from his seat.

He looks back over his shoulder at me.

I get the message.

Even though I'm all tied up with the seatbelts, I can still move my legs.

I meet Tabby's green eyes, and give myself up to being her prisoner.

She takes a firm hold of the back of my fleece as we go.

"Where're we going?" I say, as she leads me towards the front of the plane.

"To visit the pilot," she says.

Five Minutes Before The Job

ALL I COULD SMELL was the thick, earthy scent of wood.

A slightly damp feel to it.

Getting caught at the back of my throat.

I felt the van trundle to a stop.

The driver's door slammed.

Footsteps sounded around the van.

Mumbling voices.

And then, without warning, the doors creaked open.

I overheard the conversation.

". . . Bloody toffs, always get up my nose, we should do something to rile them, huh?"

"Yeah, like what?"

"Oh, I dunno"—I felt the speaker grip the wooden box I lay within, attempting to raise it—"Uff, I tell you, this's a heavy one, all right, whatcha reckon they got in here?"

The other voice became quieter, as if afraid that they might be overheard.

I suppose they were worried about the driver listening in. "Why don't we take a look?"

"Let's get 'em up the ramp first, eh?"

The feet end of my wooden box rose.

My head pressed hard against the other end.

It sent pain throbbing through my scalp.

Dancing down my spine.

A few dozen heart beats later and the head end of the wooden box rose up too.

I listened to the manly grunts coming from the pair of baggage handlers, and I couldn't help but feel just a *tad* offended.

If there's one assured way to bruise a lady's dignity, it's to make a quip—no matter how subtle, or how unintentional—about her weight.

As I listened to *yet more* grunts from the baggage handlers, I felt the box hit an angle and then level out. Then there was only the gentle trudge of the baggage handlers' boots over asphalt.

The thick stench of kerosene piled through the air.

Its sharp scent making me quiver slightly.

A little daylight leaked into the box.

When I glanced up, I realised that, on the underside of the lid, there was a pair of plastic handles.

Apparently it was so I could manipulate the lid at will.

Brian Mathewson—he really *does* think of everything.

About half a minute later, I was greeted with the metallic, echoey sound of footsteps on, what I imagined to be, a walkway. And then the little daylight which'd entered my wooden box dissipated completely.

I felt the men drop me a good metre or so.

When I landed, I felt the agony dance through my chest.

My ribs burning *hard* with pain.

"Come on, then," one of the baggage handlers said, "let's have a look-see."

Still clutching my chest, trying to foster some warmth to ward away the constant, gnawing pain, I broke out of my daze.

Turned my attention upwards.

To the handles there.

I grabbed on tight—*clung* to them.

Felt the plastic bite into my skin.

And I could feel the force working against me.

The strength of the two baggage handlers, obviously accustomed to lugging around heavy items all day long, working against me.

But I had the advantage of my deadweight.

And—from the sounds of their grunts earlier—my *sizeable* weight.

I put everything I had into driving myself downwards, into the base of the wooden box. Preventing them from getting so much as an inch of give.

Finally, the upward force gave way, and one of the baggage handlers, with a harsh puff of air said, "Nah, it's nailed shut tight —shall we go get the other one?"

"Yeah, the driver'll be wondering."

As the two of them trod out of the cargo bay of the plane, I allowed myself to breathe easily again. And I wondered just what the driver told the two baggage handlers.

Surely they knew already that this was a very *exclusive* flight, with *exclusive* cargo, and that the fewer questions asked, the more the clients would appreciate it.

But, then again, how often does a passenger run into a baggage handler?

I lay back in my coffin, listening to the men making all sorts of noise lugging AA in.

I heard them drop him with an even louder *thump* off over on the other side of the bay.

I gripped tight to the handles on the lid—ready for the men to return and launch some sort of a sneak-attack.

But neither of them did.

As I lay there, I listened to the pair of baggage handlers—chatting among themselves now—slip on out of the cargo bay, leaving me and AA very much alone.

In the distance, I heard the van's engine starting up, the driver leaving us.

His job—his part in *Hell Bird*—was through.

The chatter of the baggage handlers, too, drifted away outside.

Off to go and rummage through other passengers' property, no doubt.

It was only as I reached up for the handles, ready to push the lid off to get a little fresh air, that I heard the sobs coming from the other coffin.

From AA's coffin.

My chest tightened.

My ribs tingled.

And my breathing shallowed.

But I stayed put.

Waited for take-off.

2.08:33

T ABBY LEADS ME ALONG, through the first-class cabin where, I can't help but notice, Brian is no longer located. I wonder if I'm maybe suffering from one of those delusions that people in horror films—psychological thrillers—so often experience on planes.

Seeing people who aren't there.

But I remember, all too clearly, AA, and Brian.

No, I'm certain that it's all true.

And that, for better or worse, we're going to be landing in just over two hours.

By then I need to have my hands on the memory stick.

Or else.

The door to the cockpit has been left open, and I can't help but run the quick day-time fantasy through my brain that—*just perhaps*—AA has played a blinder, got himself into the cockpit and is now holding a gun to the pilot's head.

But, when Tabby urges me in through the door, I see that things are much as they were earlier.

The lady pilot sits in the left seat. The co-pilot in the right.

Tabby nudges me in the back and I look around, see that she indicates a retractable seat—*currently retracted*—up on the wall.

It is located at a right angle to the windows of the cockpit so that I have to turn my head side on to look through them, or to glance back at the pilots.

If they *deign* to speak to me, of course.

Without any further prompting, I deduce, by some sort of horse sense, that I'm supposed to yank the seat down. To feel the hard springs against my grip.

And although having my hands tied up by the seatbelts makes the task slightly more difficult, I manage okay. I bring the seat down.

Then I sit.

I'm all too aware of Tabby pointing the gun at me the whole time and actually find myself wishing that she would just be a *tiny bit* less professional.

Give me at least a *hope* of escaping this situation.

But why would she?

She has me *right* where she wants me.

The pilots seem busy pointing out something on some little screen in front of them. I wonder, from the floaty shapes, whether it might be weather patterns. I hope, for my sake, that the representation on the screen means lots—*and lots*—of turbulence-free air.

However, when the pilot turns to look at me, she speaks again in that Welsh accent of hers. "Flying into a spot of bother," she says with a slight smile, "those coordinates you've got us flying along, they don't seem to be accounting much for regional weather patterns."

Although I know I should show a better poker face, I can't help but reply, "Why *are* you following the coordinates? Why're you doing what *he* says?"

"Because," the pilot says, with a slight smile, "he's Brian Mathewson."

2.04:46

W HEN I LOOK UP to Tabby, to see if she's registered *anything* about what the pilot's just said, I notice nothing at all. But I can tell, from the way she keeps the gun on me at all times, how she has a way of making it *seem* like she's not watching me—*when she really is*—that she knows exactly what she's doing.

And I wouldn't put it past her that she knows *exactly* what's going on here.

I turn my attention back to the captain, deciding that I should try a different tact.

"I'm Anna," I say.

The pilot busies herself with some switch hanging above her head—flicks it into place.

A red light sparks up.

Ahead, through the windows of the plane, I make out fluffy white clouds, and soaring blue skies.

But only as far as the eye can see.

A little further on I can see extremely ominous-looking black clouds.

And rapid *flashes*.

"I'm Captain Hughes," the pilot finally replies, without looking around. "But if you'd been paying attention to the pre-flight briefing you'd already know that."

"Unfortunately the PA doesn't seem to carry to the cargo bay."

Captain Hughes gives a shake of her head as she works away at another switch, on the endless board of switches in front of her. "So that was where you were stowed away." She glances back, to Tabby, nods at the gun. "That's how you got that aboard."

"Come on," I say, "you know as well as I do that the normal rules don't apply to this flight."

Captain Hughes gives a slight pout, a shrug, and then exchanges glances with her co-pilot. She casually jerks a thumb at him. "This's First Officer Milton."

First Officer Milton doesn't bother to turn to look at me.

And I can't help thinking—even with my relative lack of martial arts—that I could quite easily snap that fragile, bird-like neck of his.

If only I had a second . . . if only I had the *need*.

I turn my attention away from murder and back to Captain Hughes. "You said that those coordinates I handed you earlier would end up in the middle of the sea."

Captain Hughes doesn't reply, apparently busy again with that gadget which may, or may not be, a weather forecaster.

I look back to Tabby, who—*annoyingly*—is still completely focussing my gun right at my head.

I wonder whether I should mix things up, if I should take my chances.

If I should just *make* Tabby take the shot.

Surely the cockpit of an aeroplane isn't the *greatest* of places to fire a gun?

As the plane warbles on through the air, the conversation between myself and Captain Hughes seemingly over for the time being, I think about the pickup, about how the plane made that stoppage to collect Brian from whichever of his mansions he'd been hiding away in.

And *of course* the pilot would've had to know about *that* stop.

I was only kidding myself when I imagined Brian wouldn't have this *entire* flight all stitched up.

Right then is when it strikes me. Everything comes together at once.

I feel a sharp, painful sensation right between a few of my ribs, and I can't help wondering just how *ominous* the name of this job, Hell Bird, really is.

Will Brian be dragging us all to the sea?

To our *doom*?

Is that his masterstroke?

. . . Right now I'm seeing, for the first time, that the idea of recovering the memory stick was all just a ruse to get me and AA aboard . . . or, considering that AA's gone AWOL, a ruse to get *me* aboard.

But that still leaves question marks over the passengers, and, if Brian really *does* intend to bring this plane down, then why's he involving all those innocent passengers back in the cabin?

1.41:32

WHEN I LOOK at my watch, to the countdown timer, I'm somewhat surprised to note that about half an hour's gone by—that I've been in the cockpit for half an hour with Tabby pointing my gun at me.

As I tilt my head up, look back out through the windows of the plane, I can't help but notice the sight stretching out before us.

The deep, black clouds.

And night already sweeping towards us like some sort of irrepressible *evil*.

By now the air smells stale, and the heating system seems locked in a constant battle with the air con. There're only small victories:

One system or the other taking precedence for only a few minutes before the other bites back hard.

One of the stewardesses brings in cups of water—the brunette.

When I spy those plastic glasses all standing up proud on her tray, I can't help but hope that I'll be let free.

That the pilot and Tabby will allow me to free at least one of my hands so I can take a drink.

But, no.

Without a word, the brunette stewardess presses the rim of the plastic cup to my lips—surprisingly tenderly given that I'm a *hijacker*.

As I drink for a long while, I almost forget the whole situation.

I realise that I must be parched, that my body has been *crying out* for something to drink for so long. Even my ribs seem to throb a little less by the time the stewardess has tilted the contents of the cup down my throat.

Right as the stewardess pulls back from me, her tray filled with those plastic cups, the whole plane jerks harshly to the right.

Since my seat sits at right angles to the windows out of the cockpit, I feel myself falling forwards.

Thankfully, though, the seatbelt keeps me pinned in place.

However, the stewardess wobbles for a long moment, balancing the tray with the emptied plastic cups for seemingly hours, before losing her balance.

She bangs her head *hard* against the wall of the cockpit.

I'm still struggling to regain my own balance, sat in my retractable seat, when I observe Tabby crouching down, seeing to the brunette stewardess, attempting not to lose balance herself.

My eyes fix onto the gun—*my gun*—which dangles from her fingertips.

If I can just get a little more wiggle room.

If I can *just* get myself free . . .

While this goes on, the pilot—Captain Hughes—perches

forwards on her seat, grappling with the headset which she had previously hung up on a hook.

As she sits with her back to me, her silhouette is a picture of concentration.

The co-pilot, too—First Officer Milton—drags his own headset down over his blond hair.

Through the window, the bulky, *black* clouds dominate everything.

Night has fallen.

There's no light any longer.

Not even from the moon.

I sense controlled panic on the part of Hughes as she jabbers away instructions into the mouthpiece of her headset. Apparently communicating with Milton.

Milton reacts, flipping switches, turning the odd dial or two.

I hope that what the pilots are doing isn't as random as it seems.

When I glance back to the brunette stewardess, I see that she's gradually getting back to her feet, with Tabby's aid. The task is made more difficult, of course, because Tabby has my gun in her other hand.

I think—*a little dizzily*—about offering to hold it for her.

But I see enough sense to realise *that* particular trick has approximately *zero* chance of working.

Once the brunette stewardess is back up and on her feet, she clutches at a spot on her temple.

Through her leathery, tanned hands, I make out the glimmer of blood:

Thick and crimson and gleaming in the fluorescent lighting of the cockpit.

I know blood well.

The stewardess still seems somewhat stunned by the whole experience as Tabby carefully leads her away from the cockpit; the plane bouncing from side to side, up and down, trying to find that most delicate of equilibriums:

The one between flying and falling.

My stomach long ago left me, and I'm making peace with my new physical state.

It helps a little to be able to gaze out through the windows of the cockpit—kind of like how seeing out through the windscreen of a car helps with travel sickness.

But this isn't quite the same thing.

For one, there's no nausea at all.

It's just a profound, almost *intimately held* knowledge that tells me I'm going to die.

That we're *all* going to die.

Now that I'm alone with Hughes and Milton—now that I don't have a *gun* pointed at me—I feel that it's easier to focus.

Both pilots, sitting with their backs to me.

Headsets clasped tightly over their ears.

Lost to the real world.

I look down at the seatbelts tying my hands together. I try to decipher just how I can extricate myself from this mess.

After Experiment One, I find that *tugging* at the knots doesn't work. I wonder if the cabin crew's competence in binding my hands using such *makeshift* means is evidence of the oft-rumoured highly charged *sexual* antics which supposedly abound within the trade.

I don't have to try too hard to picture the male cabin crew member, Suarez, tying up some boyfriend, that's for sure . . .

The plane continues to bounce around.

Both pilots have on full seatbelts.

There's still no sign of Tabby.

I know—*soon*—I'm going to have to take my chance.

Most likely, I won't get another one.

I give up for the time being on trying to get the seatbelts binding me undone, and I turn my attention to the seatbelt which holds me down to the seat itself.

I can see the eject button—bright red and impossible to miss —and I reach around to my side, sure that somebody's going to shout out, tell me to stop, at any second.

As I feel the spring-loaded mechanism push back against my fingertips, the plane seems to drop *hundreds* of metres. The blood rushes up to my head, and, when I turn to look out through the windows of the cockpit, I see that rain streams down the glass, obscuring everything except for the never-ending darkness.

Both pilots continue to concentrate.

They give nothing away.

But I can tell—from how they clench their teeth—how they *grip* the controls, that they're fighting to keep this plane in the air.

Just *where* is Brian taking us?

Finally, I press down on the eject button.

I either hear or feel a light *click* and—just like that—I realise that I'm free.

Somehow, the arrival of my freedom overrides any fear I might have for flying, and I stand up on my two feet. Neither of the two pilots notice me as I turn towards the door of the cabin.

And it's then that I catch sight of Tabby.

Just emerging back into the first-class cabin having—*apparently* —delivered the brunette stewardess back to her seat, so that another member of the cabin crew: the blonde or Suarez; can see to her.

Acting faster than I can think, I press my back up against the wall of the cockpit.

Feel my heart tickling my throat.

Right then, the cabin lights flicker.

Go out for a second.

When they come back on, I find myself standing right beside Tabby, at her shoulder, as she peers back into the cockpit. She holds my gun, expertly held in a two-hand grip, pointed to the floor.

I watch her gaze pass over the retractable seat.

See that it's vacated.

And that's when I pick my moment to strike.

As the plane bucks hard to the left, I launch myself out of the darkness and right into Tabby's shoulder with all the force I can muster.

1.24:22

W E TANGLE on the floor of the cabin, outside the cockpit, for a long time.

I lie on top of Tabby, having the upper-hand.

At any second, I expect to hear the gunshot.

To feel the burning-hot sensation of a bullet ripping through my flesh.

But it never comes.

I eventually manage to get my knees down on her chest, pinning her shoulders to the ground.

She peers up at me through her narrowly slitted green eyes.

I look about Tabby, trying frantically to find the gun.

But it's nowhere in sight.

I glance up, peer down the aisle, back into the passenger cabin beyond first-class. I see some of the passengers leaning out of their seats, trying to get a better look at the melee taking place. I know that there's no time, that if I don't get my hands back on my gun then there's going to be a mutiny on my hands. That I'll have no chance if a few of those male passengers—no doubt herded by Suarez—get it into their heads to bring me down with brute force.

My heart beats harder still. My blood runs cold and all the way up to my throbbing temples. I can feel the aching pain in my chest take hold again as I exert all the pressure that I dare to keep Tabby where I can control her.

On the floor.

I bring my face close to hers, find that my words come out with a seething menace. "Where *is* it?" I say.

Tabby glares back at me.

She says nothing.

Acting on impulse, I reach out, take her head in my hands.

I bash the back of her head against the floor a couple of times.

When she opens her eyes again, it seems to have had no effect.

Nevertheless, I try asking again.

"Where is it?!"

Again, nothing.

I peer along the aisle another time—see that a couple of passengers *are* out of their seats now, and that Suarez is also up and about, despite the 'FASTEN SEATBELTS' sign being lit.

There's no time.

Not now.

Seeing that several of the passengers are inching their way into the first-class cabin, I know that it's now or never.

And I pick *now*.

With a single movement, the plane feeling as if it rises hundreds and hundreds of metres in the space of a few seconds,

I lunge off towards the side of the plane, and away from the cockpit.

Aware that every second counts, I eye the hatch in the duct—still left open—where me and AA first entered the passenger cabin.

Sensing that I'm being boxed in, I take a wild run.

Somebody shouts something out.

The plane descends sharply.

I feel nothing but air beneath me.

But—*somehow*—I urge my feet onwards.

To the duct just ahead.

And as the most severe turbulence yet takes hold of the plane, I leap up, dig one foot down on a headrest and launch myself upwards.

Grabbing onto the rim of the hatch.

Dragging myself up.

And inside.

1.17:48

C rawl. Crawl. *CRAWL!*

I tell myself that over and over again, having no patience for my cumbersome, exaggerated movement. My kneecaps and palms ache from where I scrabble along. Pain prangs through my ribs as I put all the force into lugging myself forwards.

The air smells strongly of disinfectant.

A slight scent of burning electrics too.

My mouth tastes so dry that the glass of water the stewardess served me seems almost as if it was some kind of feverish dream.

Unreal.

As I shuffle my way along the inside of the duct, I can't help but think of all those times I've thought long and hard about joining the gym and never seen the point.

Since I've never been a big eater—not even when pregnant with my two children—it's never been much of a challenge for me to keep the weight off.

Being skinny, though, means you don't have much strength.

Certainly nothing which might challenge the male passengers back in the cabin.

When I reach a turn in the duct, I allow myself to relax a little.

The plane continues to swoop about as it navigates the storm:

Up and down.

All over the place.

I breathe in deeply, feeling my shoulders arching back as I do so, then I breathe out again, trying—*desperately*—to bring my thoughts clear.

To keep myself from panicking.

Against all odds, I manage to get my heartbeat ticking along at a more reasonable rate.

The sweat ceases to seep out of every pore of my body.

When I'm certain that none of my pursuers are coming after me into the duct, I clamp my eyes shut and press the heels of my hands into the backs of my eyelids.

That's good.

It feels *relaxing*.

All that breaks me out of my pleasant-minded state is the sudden jerk of the plane to the right, followed by another of those unearthly sensations of falling through thin air.

Some deep sense of self at the back of my brain tells me to expect impact at any second.

For the plane to smash against the hard surface of the sea.

Ending all this madness.

For good.

. . . But the end doesn't come.

When I open my eyes again, blink about me into the darkness of the duct, I can see that the world is still very much here.

In fact, I can just about make out a sallow light emanating from a hatch.

A little way along the duct.

I think about what to do.

Whether I should return to the cargo bay.

Or if I should just stay put.

Go back?

Time's running out.

Sooner or later, when we eventually *do* land, I'm going to be captured.

And it'll be the end for me.

At last.

It takes another few moments before I get my head around moving from my spot.

Before I can convince myself that shifting from where I'm slumped—up against the wall in the duct—might well be a good idea.

My eyes trace the sallow light leaking into the duct, and then lock onto it.

Well, the only other option is the cargo bay, so I might as well . . .

The plane shudders hard as I crawl my way through the duct.

I can smell the gentle, salty odour of my own sweat making its way up my nostrils.

More than anything, I just want to get back home, slip in underneath my duvet, pull my cat Lizzie onto my lap and sleep away the afternoon.

But I'm a long—*long*—way away from home now.

And there're no guarantees that I'll ever get back.

When I reach the hatch, I twist the clasp holding it into place. There's something about the change of smell in the air, something which sticks to the back of my throat, and which sends a chill down my spine.

But I push *those* thoughts away.

Lock my mind back onto the task before me.

Getting this hatch open.

My fingers shake a little as I twist the clasp free from its housing.

Then I feel the hatch itself come loose in my hands.

With another quick motion, I pull it from its place and the sallow light becomes bright.

It sets me in its glare.

I shield my eyes from the brightness with my forearm for several moments.

Then I stick my head in through the hatch.

I'm up fairly high—near the ceiling of the plane, of course—and I find myself looking down on a toilet. This must be the toilet at the back of the passenger cabin.

As if in confirmation of this fact, I find my nose picking out all those smells of disinfectant, and of soap, and that scent of paper mixed in with urine and faeces.

I hold myself still, considering my next move.

And then I see no other option.

This might be my one chance to regain the upper-hand.

My eyes move over the toilet itself—*shining steel.*

To the plastic basin.

The rubber button which is pushed to start water flowing.

Moving quickly now—feeling the adrenalin flush through my veins—I hang my legs down through the hatch, and then, with a single, swift movement, I drop down onto the floor.

It's hard to tell whether the impact of my landing comes from the soles of my trainers making contact with the floor, or if it's all just in my mind.

If the shock passing up through my legs sends some kind of a signal up to my brain.

Making me hear things.

I reach out, slide the lock to the toilet shut, not wanting to think about whatever *ping* sound or green-light-turning-to-red might be taking place outside in the passenger cabin.

It'll become apparent, soon enough, if Tabby and co. have rumbled me.

If they realise that I've ended up here—at the back of the passenger cabin—in the toilet.

I allow myself several seconds, just so that I can breathe in some deep breaths, right down to the pits of my lungs, trying to urge some strength back into my body.

When I'm feeling slightly stronger, I reach out for the roll of toilet paper, tear off a sheet or two and then blow my nose. It's when I push down on the silver lid of the bin, thinking only to drop my sneezed-in tissue within that I notice something in there —among the paper.

My heart hangs in my throat.

But not with disgust—*repulsion.*

Instead, I pick out the details slowly.

The long and *curved* handwriting on the piece of paper.

From the elegant 'A' all the way through to the stylised 'S'.

A name.

My name.

I overcome my temporary repulsion at sticking my hand down past the silver lid of the bin and digging about within the contents.

I feel my exposed flesh brush up against the bits of discarded paper; the ones which've served various purposes—purposes which I *really* don't want to get into thinking about.

Finally, I fish the crunched-up ball of paper out from the bin.

Lay it down on the counter.

Smooth out its wrinkles.

As I look over the letters, I can hardly believe my eyes.

And yet I know that there can be no other explanation.

Because here it is, right before me:

KILL ANNA HARRIS

This paper must've come from the blond woman, the one who met me and AA at the budget hotel the night before.

I think about seeing this very paper in the drawer of AA's bedside table.

How he prevented me from seeing what was written on it.

Now I know the reason why.

Now I know the reason why the blond woman gave us clear instructions *not* to share our information with one another. It hadn't anything to do with completing—or not completing—the job. It had to do with setting me and AA against one another.

Making us *fight*.

Just as that revelation clocks through my brain at frightening speed, I hear something in the duct above my head. I turn my attention upwards.

And wish I still had my gun.

1.02:41

FOR THE LONGEST TIME, I can't harness onto the face staring down at me from the gap in the duct I just came through.

Not because I'm having difficulty making out the features, but because I simply *can't* place those features *here*.

On *this* plane.

But, although it's inexplicable, there's no other explanation:

Amy Douglas.

She wears her blond hair up in a ponytail. Her face is gaunt, and her cheekbones sunken. She looks as if she could do with a week or so of good meals.

The familiar scent of her perfume—strawberries—wafts through the stale air of the toilet.

I've only just managed to square what my eyes are seeing when I hear a loud, irrepressible knock at the toilet door.

"Who's in there?"

Tabby.

On the other side.

I wonder if she's managed to regain my gun.

But I don't plan on finding out.

Without a word, Amy hangs her hand down to me, her frail fingers seeming insignificant. But before I have time to fully think through whether or not Amy's actually going to have the strength to lift me back up to the hatch, I grab hold.

Her dainty fingers close in—vice-tight—over my hand.

And, with a strength I never thought she possessed, she lifts me up.

When I get level with the hatch, I can do the rest for myself.

I grip on tight, lug myself in through the space, back up to the duct.

There're no more knocks at the door and I know, on instinct, that Tabby's not going to call or knock again. I know that she's working on getting the toilet door open.

As me and Amy crouch down at the hole in the duct, the two of us frantically working to bring the hatch back into place, I can hear the *clickety-click* of a mechanism being manipulated by some tool.

Or by a key.

It wouldn't be a giant leap of logic to believe that members of the cabin crew have keys to any given part of the plane.

Including the toilet.

I feel my chest rising and falling—my ribs feeling tight, and near pain the whole time—I shift a glance over Amy, see that she's wearing a tracksuit top over a pair of jeans.

Right as me and Amy manage to bring the hatch into place, I hear the toilet door give and—with a *squeak* of its hinges— brighter light from the cabin spills into the area.

Up in the duct, me and Amy press our backs up against the

wall, looking away from the cracks in the hatch and both of us —*I believe*—hoping that Tabby will just go away.

"Anna?"

I hear Tabby's voice from down below.

"I know you're up there," she says.

I hold my breath tightly in my chest, and I sneak a sidelong glance at Amy.

Amy looks just as confused as I do.

"I don't expect you to come down," Tabby continues, "that would be extremely *naïve* of me—all I thought I should say is that we'll be landing in an hour and, when we do, an entire team of well-armed, extremely well-trained militants will continue the chase."

Tabby stands there, in the toilet below us, hidden from sight by the hatch.

And then, as if a coin drops somewhere at the back of my mind, I realise *why* . . . the note . . . the one which I retrieved from the bin, the one which I smoothed out . . . the one which the blonde in the trench coat gave to AA.

I feel the rapid beat of my heart against the underside of my tongue.

Then, without another sound, no words from Tabby, I hear the toilet door slam shut.

Almost without thinking about it, I bring my hands up to my face, close my eyes, and I press my palms *hard* against the backs of my eyelids.

A Week Before The Hit

I COULD HEAR KNOCKING coming from my front door. When I reached out for my mobile phone, sitting on my bedside table, when I tapped the screen to bring it around from its own sleep, I could see that it had just gone three in the morning.

As I rubbed my scalp hard, trying to force consciousness on myself, my tortoiseshell cat, Lizzie, lying curled up on my duvet, enjoying the warmth of my legs, gave a pained, half-asleep *yowl* of protest.

The knocking at my front door stopped.

I lay on my side, waiting, prone for any other sound.

But there was nothing at all.

Nothing which I could sense.

Glad that the knocking had stopped, I hauled my duvet back up so that it covered my ears.

I turned over.

Already feeling that sleep was getting the better of me once again.

Then my phone started buzzing.

With a sharp intake of air, feeling it bustle through the gaps in my teeth, I reached out, grabbed my phone and looked at the screen:

Unidentified Caller.

Quelle surprise.

I thought long and hard about answering.

The thing is, if you make a habit of answering phone calls long before sunup—or long *after* sundown—then whoever calls you will deduce that you're *quite happy* to be contacted at any time:

Twenty-four hours a day.

And that's certainly *not* a habit I want to encourage.

Outside, I heard a breeze stir the leaves in the trees.

I felt an ice-cool draught drift about my room.

My cat Lizzie made a noise between a *purr* and a *miaow*, had a *big* stretch and then laid her head down again to return to sleep.

As for me, though, I was wide awake.

I fooled myself with the hope that the person knocking at my door might be a group of kids paying a rather tame night-time prank. And that might've been a great story, except for the fact that—down the street where I live—you don't go knocking on strangers' doors . . . unless you want to get your head kicked in . . .

But I knew, at the same time, that people didn't just *happen* to pick out my door to knock on in the middle of the night.

Because, let's face it, this wasn't the first night-time visitor I'd ever had.

With a slight sigh, I barely had the energy to hoik myself out from beneath my duvet. I just about managed to perch on the edge of my mattress, and get my feet into my ridiculously comfortable, woolly slippers.

A long yawn later, and wondering just how I might look to the stranger at my door in a pair of tracksuit bottoms and an over-washed t-shirt from a concert for a band called *Mothers Hate Knives*. I didn't recall the band, or buying the t-shirt. And only then did I realise that the lettering on the front of the t-shirt, in addition to being half-peeled off, was also glow-in-the-dark.

Classy.

I managed to just about get myself up to my feet, when I noticed the figure standing in the doorway to my bedroom.

In those quick, fleeting seconds, I calculated how long it'd take me to rush for my wardrobe, extract the gun which I keep nestled within.

Too long.

With a burbling *purr*, Lizzie rose up from my bed, leaped down to the floor, and promptly coiled herself about the intruder's legs.

In the near darkness, I noticed that the intruder was wearing a balaclava, and that they had on a loose jacket, coming down to just below the hip in length.

A slight smell of strawberries floated through the air.

And I thought—*then*—that I knew.

Knew *exactly* who it was . . . and yet the actual, *conscious* thought didn't cross my mind until I heard the intruder speak.

Until I heard *her* speak.

"Sorry for breaking in, Anna."

147

Amy.

Amy Douglas.

Even as the revelation of who this person was who'd just invaded my home sunk in, I couldn't quite square it with my brain.

I was expecting anything—for Amy to try and shoot me, to kill me where I stood:

In my rock-concert t-shirt, and nothing else.

Because, just like me, Amy Douglas was an assassin.

Although it was a long—*complicated*—story.

Just like all of our stories are, I guess . . .

The last I saw of Amy was when her father—a former Chief Constable—and his goons, kidnapped me and AA, took us off to this bunker by the sea.

Amy, though, saw sense in the end, and aided mine and AA's escape.

I supposed I should be thankful for that, but I really found it difficult to get past the detail of her wandering into my house in the middle of the night.

But, hey, at least she knocked . . .

Back when she was playing the assassin game—or letting on that she was—Amy managed to sneak her way inside Brian's operation and get hold of a memory stick with a whole ton of sensitive data held within.

And Brian just allowed her to take it.

He was playing her for a fool.

Trying to ease her into a false sense of security.

To make her believe that she was in control.

And that her father might have a chance at taking down Brian.

For the most part, it seems to me, Brian succeeded.

But that didn't make any difference about the sensitive data being out in the Big Bad World, ready for taking by anybody who wished to.

It was still pitch-black out, and the clock in my kitchen was nudging towards half past three in the morning. I really wanted to get back to sleep—I was meeting my boyfriend Mark at ten in the morning, and we were going to go spend the day somewhere 'romantic' . . . I've learned from experience of being with Mark that it's better just to trust his sense of 'romantic'.

His sense is far superior to mine.

As we sat at the kitchen table, both of us with a cup of tea I'd prepared, I observed Lizzie coiling her way about Amy's legs, clearly wanting to be hoisted up to Amy's lap.

During that whole complicated business of Amy working as a spy for her father within Brian's operation, Amy came to live with me. And though I might've tried to explain the nuances of just where Amy stood in terms of good and evil to Lizzie, I had never quite got around to it.

Anyway, Lizzie has always been something of a flirt:

Never too bothered about anything as deep as ulterior motives.

Tonight—*this morning*—Amy was wearing a denim jacket over a pair of black jeans.

Thankfully, she'd seen enough sense to whip off her balaclava, so that I didn't need to contend with *feeling* like I was sat opposite a breaking-and-entering merchant.

The balaclava now hung off the back of her chair.

"So," I said, blowing across the surface of my tea, "what's this all about?"

Amy's blond hair stuck up in tufts all over from wearing the balaclava. Her quick, laser-like blue eyes fastened onto mine, and, like they always seemed to do, suggested they had no intention of letting go.

She broke off our gaze, turning her attention back to her cup of tea, to the swirling mulchy brown contents. "I came to tell you that I'm not working for my father anymore."

"And which father's that?" I say, a touch playfully.

Amy well knew, from our last outing together, that she attempted to buy more time to investigate Brian by having him believe that she was his daughter.

She went so far as to knock together a diary:

A *forgery*.

Not bad for a former cop.

Amy side stepped my quip. "I want some more protection," she said, "I want to build a group of people around me who I can depend on."

"And you've come to me *why*?" I replied.

"Because, Anna," Amy said, glancing back up at me—something of a scolded puppy in her look, "I saved your life."

"Only after you put it in danger."

Amy gave a shrug, as if this was a minor detail and returned to staring into her cup of tea.

"Look," I said, "if this is something about you being on the run from your father—and needing somewhere to stay for a while—perhaps I need to remind you that we tried that already."

I paused to take a sip of tea, and, I suppose, in retrospect, for dramatic effect too.

"If you're looking for somewhere to hide out for a while then I can put you in touch with my neighbour, Mrs Pietersen."

I thought back to my experience at Winged Women; a centre for women escaping from abusive domestic situations; an organisation which I took shameless advantage of when I was running away from the goons which Amy's father sent after me.

When it was all over I *did* hand over a sizeable donation, though, for their inconvenience.

Amy stared into her mug of tea, and I had the urge to tell her that it wasn't poison, or that it wouldn't taste of rotten eggs, something like that. I'd be the first to admit that I'm not the greatest tea lady in the world, but my brews are certainly nothing to turn your nose up at.

"Anna?" she said.

"Yes?"

"I'll leave you in peace if you'll please just tell me that you'll be one of those people."

For the longest time, I just sat there, at the kitchen table, unable to quite keep my brain from drifting off on some tangent. Thinking about the gun I had stashed out in the hallway, near the front door. Or wondering if I might be able to surreptitiously clamber up the stairs and fish out my gun from the wardrobe.

When Amy looked back up, though, I could see tears spilling from her eyes, glistening on the surface. "Please," she said, her voice not much more than a *rasp*.

I grabbed up her teacup, laid it in the sink, ready for washing later.

Sighed.

"All right," I said. "You can count on me."

0.54:11

"WHAT'S THAT TIMER, Anna?"

For a second there, I forgot Amy was here at all.

Slowly, I turn to face her.

I realise, in the glow of the light which comes in around the hatch to the toilet, it's possible to just make out the display on my watch.

"Is it how long is left of the flight?" Amy says.

"Yes," I reply, "got it in one," and then shift myself away from the wall of the duct, thinking about what we're going to do next.

I know there's no time. I believe Tabby's threat about the armed team.

But I also believe the other thing she said.

That she won't come looking for us before the plane lands.

From my experience of flying long-haul, I'm fairly confident that the plane won't start its landing procedure for another twenty-five minutes, at the earliest.

There *is* this weather knocking about too.

Just as that thought crosses my mind, there's a large bout of turbulence.

I feel as if the plane was an enormous salt shaker and some giant baby's clenching it tight in its fist, throwing it all about.

Once the worst of the turbulence is over and done with— once I've managed to withdraw my teeth from my lower lip and put the taste of blood in my mouth to the back of my mind—I turn to look at Amy, and I say, in an off-the-cuff sort of way, "You haven't seen AA or Brian around here, have you?"

She shakes her head.

"No," I say. "Didn't think you would have."

We remain there, in the duct, for another few minutes.

It's then that I give a shake of my head, look in Amy's direction. "Well," I say, "you think we'd better get moving along here? Get ourselves into some better position?"

"A better position like how?" Amy replies.

I shrug. "Not near the toilet for a start."

Amy glances back at the hatch to the toilet, and I have no idea at all what she might be thinking.

She's probably thinking that I have no idea what to do next . . . and she'd be right:

One-hundred-per-cent.

Since there seems to be nothing else going on and—for better or worse—me and Amy are going to be trapped up here in the duct until landing, I blurt out, "How'd you get on the plane?"

"I followed you."

I roll my eyes. "Of course you were." I pause. "But that doesn't answer my question."

Amy goes quiet for a long while and I wonder if she's going

to butt in with something that'll take my breath away, that'll turn this whole situation on its head.

And what do I know, she does . . .

"Your neighbour," Amy says, "that day, when I came around yours . . . asked you that question. I took your advice. I knocked on my neighbour's door—on Mrs Pietersen's door."

Another bout of turbulence hits the plane.

I grab hold of a plastic strut in the duct and cling on for dear life.

When I breathe in now, the air seems thick. I draw in all those fragments of skin and hair, and whatever other nastiness floats about pressurised cabins. No matter how hard I force air through my nostrils, they remain blocked. I wish I could still taste something—that I could *taste* the dried blood sticking to my lower lip.

But, no.

"You don't like flying, do you, Anna?" Amy says, in that intensely annoying, bright and sparky way that people who aren't scared of anything use . . .

"No," I reply, still clinging to the plastic strut. "Not really."

"Silly, though," Amy says. "I mean, it's safer than crossing the road—safer than driving by far."

"Yeah, but how many cars have you ever seen out in the middle of the Atlantic?"

Right then, there's one *long* dip followed by—what feels like—the plane lifting up a thousand metres on a torrent of hot air.

The plane tilts to one side.

I breathe in deeply.

Feel the force of the trapped air push at my cheeks.

Without further prompting, I feel Amy's hand brush my white, blood-free knuckles.

I flinch and look back into her blue eyes.

She's smiling. "It's okay, Anna," she says. "It'll all be over soon."

Yeah, I think to myself. *The being over part is what I'm afraid of . . .*

Still gripping tightly to the plastic strut, I clamp my eyes shut. "Tell me about what you've been doing, why you showed up at my house—why you wanted someone to *rely* on."

"I wanted someone to *depend* on because, like I said, I've been going it alone."

"Yeah," I say. "I've heard that one before."

"No, Anna," Amy replies, in a *far too* carefree voice, as if we're not straddling a razor's edge defying the laws of physics and coming close to paying a *large* price. "This time I'm serious—but I can understand why you wouldn't believe me. I let you down."

I tell myself that if she brings up saving my life again—or AA's for that matter—then I'm going to have to throttle her to death.

If there's one thing I *cannot* handle it's being in other people's debt.

"I was following you," Amy replies, "because I wanted to protect you."

This causes me to open my eyes, and to look back into hers. "Protect me *why?*"

Amy smirks a touch, and I see that she's now propped up on her knees, as if this was some sort of a girls' own camping trip and the two of us are sitting around a blazing fire.

"Because there're people trying to kill you."

0.45:45

THE PLANE rocks *hard* to the left.

This time it feels like something strikes the side.

One of the engines lets out a high-pitched *groan* of what sounds nothing like satisfaction.

In the panic, more from the sound than the movement of the aircraft, I release the plastic strut.

Thankfully, though, Amy reaches out, grabs hold of my wrist.

Holds me with that—*surprisingly strong*—grip of hers.

When I grab back onto the plastic strut, Amy releases me, as if she knows, by instinct, that I need to have my space.

Maybe she was serious about wanting to keep me safe.

Without further prompting, Amy goes into it.

"I turned up on Mrs Pietersen's doorstep and she wanted to ship me off to some . . . *institution* . . . this place out in the countryside where she said I'd be safe."

"Winged Women," I put in.

"Yeah," Amy replies, "that sounds like it."

Despite the plane constantly shifting about beneath us, Amy finds the nerve to peel her fingers free from the plastic strut. She presses her index finger into the pit of her chin.

A gesture which—I suppose—might look normal on a model posing for a photoshoot.

Or a toddler doing an imitation of some Very Deep Thinking.

"Anyway," Amy continues, "I managed to convince her to take me in—told her that I'd be all right in a couple of days, that I wasn't being pursued by anybody, and that I just needed somewhere to lay my head for some thinking time."

"And she took you in?" I say, surprised at myself for managing to get out *that* many cohesive words.

Amy nods. "At first I thought she might have somebody by to pick me up, not allow me to stay with her for more than a couple of nights. But, after a while, she seemed happy enough to take me in, for me to have the run of the attic bedroom."

I think back to the attic bedroom of Mrs Pietersen's house, and how the window looks right into my spare bedroom.

It also gives a passable view of the street outside.

Not only the front of my home, but the side passage to the back garden too.

Yes, if I was pressed to think of one place where I might put up a night-vision, twenty-four-hour camera, then the window frame of Mrs Pietersen's house would be just the place.

Here Amy smiles. "A couple of times your cat, *Lizzie*, she came wandering into Mrs Pietersen's kitchen—Mrs Pietersen has a plate all set out for her on the kitchen floor, and, a couple of times, she came all the way up into my attic bedroom, snuggled with me for a while."

As I grip the plastic strut tighter still, sink my teeth deeper into my lower lip, I make a mental note to schedule a serious cha[t] with my cat.

Not that it'll do any good.

Cats are a law unto themselves.

Amy continues, "I was watching your back, Anna, for anybody who might be lurking in the shadows, ready to strike."

"And was there anybody?" I say, unable to keep myself from blurting it out.

I don't imagine that I'd ever make even a passable poker player.

Amy shakes her head, then looks away from me, as if ashamed.

And perhaps, what with all this spying business, she *should* be. Just a tad . . .

"That night, though," Amy continues, her eyes brightening a spark, "when you went out on that date with your boyfriend."

"With Mark," I say, promptly scolding myself for having given her information she can likely use against me later.

"Uh-huh," Amy goes on, "well, I got myself a table in the restaurant opposite the Indian where you two were eating."

I scour my mind, trying to dig up some sort of recollection of the street outside the restaurant, but—try as I might—I can't bring up anything.

"You know," Amy continues, "the fish-and-chips place?"

I *don't* particularly know, but I do know, as something of a fact, that the majority of fish-and-chip shops—if not *all* of them —have steamed-up windows. The perfect hide-out for any would-be sleuth . . . which, apparently, is what Amy aspires to be.

"Anyway," Amy says, "when I saw that car pulling up, I recognised it, right away, as being one of Brian's, so"—here she clicks her fingers—"just like that, I got up, paid and nabbed myself a taxi." Here she gives me a wide grin. "I've always wanted to tell a taxi driver to 'Follow that car!' and I got my chance that night."

The plane lurches hard to the right.

I sink my teeth deeper into my lower lip.

Taste yet more blood.

But I still manage to witter, through my almost-sealed lips.

"Good for you."

Amy either doesn't hear my quip or she side steps it . . . quite *neatly* in my opinion. "When the car dropped you off at the airport hotel, I held back, saw you there on the street, looking for AA."

I feel my chest tighten, recalling how I'd felt like somebody was watching—a 'perve' if I rightly remember . . . now, though, I know the truth.

It was Amy.

"I waited for you to check into the hotel and then I went and got my own room."

Here Amy wraps up, as if she's looking for some input from me to keep her sustained—almost like the needy kid in class desperately seeking Teacher's approval.

I breathe in deeply, again a mistake seeing as the air is clogged with all sorts of unpleasantness. "Go on," I say, "how'd you manage to get on the plane?"

Amy gives a smug grin. "Actually, getting on the plane was the easy part—the difficult part was in working out which plane you were going to get on."

"And how did you do that?" I say, unable to keep the sarcasm from giving my words a venomous bite.

Amy grins wider still—*if possible*. "Well," she says, "I managed to get talking with the security man."

"The security man?"

"Uh-huh," Amy replies, "and he allowed me into his place, to look at the security cameras. When I asked him if we could take a look at the footage from that evening, in the bar—I'd seen you and AA down there earlier," she adds as an aside, "the security man was only too happy to do so."

I can't help but mentally draft a Letter of Complaint in my mind hearing this.

What has privacy come to?

Then again, I suppose that blond hair and blue eyes can get you a very long way in life indeed.

Amy goes on, "When I saw you and AA, it was just a matter of taking a glance at the piece of paper you were holding—it had the flight info and everything on it. First thing I did was log onto my computer and grab a ticket."

Even with the plane bucking hard—*up and down*—seemingly trying very hard to find an uneasy compromise with gravity, I manage a vague grin. "Yeah right," I say, "and I almost bought all that—right up to that point."

I jerk my head to indicate the passenger cabin some way below us.

"This isn't the sort of plane where you can just stroll up and buy a ticket—let alone buy one online."

Amy just smiles back at me, and she gets a somewhat *sneaky* twinkle caught in her eye. "Cyber Crimes, Anna," she says, "I did learn a few tricks back when I was a copper."

And there was me thinking that I'd got the upper-hand for the first time in this conversation . . .

"All right," I reply with a shake of the head, "so you managed to get on the plane—*brilliant* work."

I halt for a moment, grip tighter to the plastic strut as the plane heaves to one side.

When it returns to something like stability, I say, "That doesn't answer what you're doing up here, in the duct, why you aren't sitting your bottom down in the seat you paid good money for."

Amy gives me a squinting smile, then says, "Let's just say that I had a good inkling of what you and AA were going to be up to." She looks away from me. "When I heard some fumbling about in the ducts above my seat, I knew that it wasn't the normal, mechanical aeroplane noises—I'd already given the plane a butcher's, and been unable to locate you and AA travelling in the traditional fashion." She nods to the toilet hatch behind me. "It's not the first time I've had one of those open on this flight."

"No," I reply, "I suppose not."

"So, Anna," Amy replies, "Any questions?"

As the plane feels as if it will drop out of the air at a moment of its choosing, I find my brain narrowing, some sort of a background processor forcing me to focus.

"Just one."

"Shoot," Amy replies, her word choice somewhat inappropriate.

"Why did you assume I'd be safe with AA—that he wouldn't kill me?"

At this Amy tilts her head at me, gives me a squinty, slightly squiffy-eyed look. "Because I know AA," she says. "He'd never do anything like that." She stops for a moment, almost catching herself, and then adds, "Not to you."

My eyes meet Amy's for a second, and then they drift away into the gloom of the aeroplane duct.

And I can't help wondering just what the hell I've done to deserve this.

Actually, I can think of plenty of reasons . . .

0.32:03

F OR THE TIME BEING, I decide to say nothing to Amy about the note . . . the one I found in the toilet bin.

The one which read:

KILL ANNA HARRIS.

I don't want to shatter her illusions about AA.

As the two of us continue our sit-in, both in the duct, I turn my mind to wondering about where AA and Brian have got themselves to—they just *disappeared*.

There's a whole host of things I want to ask Amy. I want to ask whether her surveillance encompassed AA too. *She* might have some explanation for his strange behaviour.

But I can't get any words out.

All my energy is expended in clinging tightly to the plastic strut of the duct.

Without me saying anything at all, Amy decides to take this opportunity to wander away from me, to shirk off into the shadows, apparently off on her own mission.

I still don't quite buy that—out of some kind of *goodness*—she's decided to appoint herself my Official Protector.

I'm inordinately grateful when she returns to me, comes back out of the gloom.

But that mostly has to do with my fear of dying alone.

Because is there anything worse than the combination of 'passing on' whilst being drowned in a plane?

If there is I don't even want to think about it.

Amy comes close, and I'm a little struck to take in the fragile bone structure of her face, her sweet looks, and to know that, beneath that exterior, beats the heart of a fully paid-up maniac.

Just like me.

"Listen," Amy says, like I've got any other option . . . if I'd wanted to cover my ears then I'd need to unpeel my fingers from the plastic strut. "I think the best thing to do now is for me to go back to my seat."

"What?" I blurt out, unable to get a hold on my inexplicable, knee-jerk panic.

Amy glances back over her shoulder in a way which tells me, in no uncertain terms, that we're not alone. Still acting somewhat distractedly, she turns back to me and says, "Anna, you're going to have to trust me, okay? You're going to have to trust that I'm on your side—that I'm looking out for you. Do you think you can do that?"

Although every bone—every last *nerve*—in my body screams out, *No!* I manage to get out a Big Girl nod.

"Great," Amy says, flashing me a brief smile. "Now, the good part about this—about me venturing down there, returning to my seat—is that they'll have no clue of my association with you."

The plane shakes about, giving a sensation as if it's passing over a few dozen invisible, hundred-metre-tall speedbumps.

I'm sure my expression reflects my panic.

"I can do more for you down there," Amy says.

It's then that it hits me—out of nowhere. "The gun."

"Hmm?" Amy says.

And then I realise that Amy—*apparently*—wasn't present for the duration of mine and AA's hijacking. That she doesn't realise we were armed at all.

Or perhaps it's just that she doesn't know where the gun is right now.

"I lost it," I say, already feeling somewhat stupid to speak the words aloud. "Tabby—the redhead stewardess, the young one, from first-class . . . she managed to snatch it off me. And then—"

The plane hits a long piece of turbulence and I feel my whole body shake.

After a few seconds, I can't tell whether it's the plane shaking or just me.

Finally, I return to my senses.

Amy stares at me.

"Red hair," Amy says, making a gesture to indicate Tabby's flowing, scarlet locks. "About my age?"

"Uh-huh," I say, hoping that the plane will stop shaking.

Or *I'll* stop shaking.

Either would be nice.

Amy turns her gaze downwards, her thoughts clearly working on something which is well beyond the remit of my brain right now.

Finally, she comes up for air. "Now that I think of it, I've seen her around before . . . around Mathewson Media—around Brian's offices."

I feel as if a dead weight has settled down on my shoulders.

And that I have no hope of lugging it off.

"Why doesn't that surprise me?" I finally get out.

0.27:55

As the plane shudders on along its trajectory—one which I hope is *mostly* upwards—I sit alone in the duct, Amy having left me here.

Alone.

If there's one thing that frightens me above even flying, it's having to depend on other people.

And, right now, I find myself having to depend on Amy.

And there was me thinking that the whole deal—our whole *run-in*—was about Amy being able to depend on me.

Why didn't I see *that* reversal coming?

As I press my back up against the wall of the duct, I wonder if Brian accounted for all this *drama* when he wrote down the exact timing of the flight on that sheet of paper.

The sheet of paper which *Amy* saw through the hotel security camera.

Although it's become apparent that the pilot knew all about

Brian, and his wishes, I can't help but think that there's surely going to be *some* delay.

If nothing else, because of the weather.

Even with the plane bouncing all over the place, I decide that *something* needs to be done.

That I need to suck up my fear and just *get on with it.*

After all, I'm *supposed* to be looking for that ever-elusive memory stick.

That's what I'm getting paid for.

Assuming this *isn't* a trap, of course.

And that seems like a *large* assumption right now.

It takes just about every last shred of energy for me to release the plastic strut, to allow my fingers free—one by one—and to reach out, onto the surface before me, steady myself, and attempt to gather my bearings.

No sooner have I done that than I feel the whole plane shift around me.

There's a loud *whine* from one—or more—of the engines.

As I crawl my way along through the duct, I close my eyes.

Try to forget I'm on a plane at all.

Yeah, and that's *far* easier said than done given the constant shift of air pressure. How the world, all around me, never stops moving. How I feel as if every last mechanical jerk which vibrates up through my palms might well be the last sensory detail that floats through my head.

Think positive, Anna. Think happy thoughts.

I crawl my way through the duct, feeling the hard surface bite into my kneecaps, and my joints stiffen up as I shuffle my way along.

When I glance up, peering into the darkness, I half expect to see AA staring back at me.

To see a gentle smirk on his lips as he holds a gun.

Squeezes the trigger.

Because that's *his* role.

But I make my way through to the end of the duct.

I know because my scalp bumps into the hard surface.

I glance to my left, back in the direction of the passenger cabin—and then I look to my right, in the direction of the cargo bay.

To my mind, there's only one place I can go now.

Only one place where I'll have even a *hope* of escaping the plane alive.

And without being discovered.

For now, I really couldn't care less about the memory stick.

That's all extra stuff.

Real-world stuff.

Right now I'm battling for my life.

At least it *feels* that way.

As I scrabble along . . . through the duct, and back towards the cargo bay, it's with a nasal *hiss* that the plane shifts to one side.

And my head makes contact with the wall.

That's the last I know as the blackness seeps in.

0.0:01

A BLEEP-BLEEP, *bleep-bleep* sound brings me awake.
I stare at my watch.

See that four zeros blink back at me.

I tune into my surroundings.

Pad the ground around me.

The duct.

In the plane.

I recall it now.

Hitting my head.

Something's different, though.

I reach out, push my body weight up against the side of the plane, gently easing myself up onto my knees. My knees throb from all the crawling I've done. As I move a little way, I'm surprised at how easily I can crawl. It's not like before where I struggled to so much as lift a finger.

Now I notice the engine noise.

The throbbing, never-ending *rumble* has been replaced by a much lower pitch.

There's no more turbulence.

But I can still feel the plane shifting around.

Taxiing.

I guess this isn't the sea . . . that the pilot somehow managed to find land among those coordinates I brought her . . .

I look about me, into the darkness, recalling which direction leads back to the passenger cabin. And which direction leads to the cargo bay.

I remember that I'd got it into my brain to move towards the cargo bay.

And that was when my head struck the wall.

When I knocked myself out.

I think quickly.

Remember Amy shifting off into the gloom.

Returning to her seat for landing.

And then I recall the threat Tabby made.

About there being militiamen showing up.

I decide that now—*now*—is the time for me to get moving.

But which way?

In the end, I decide on the cargo bay.

Little, old conservative me believing that delayed death is preferable to the *immediate* option.

At least if they find me in the cargo bay, it won't be Tabby doing the shooting . . . and with my own gun.

I'd be spared that embarrassment.

If only for a few dying seconds.

I return to the familiar hatch.

When I roll myself onto my back and kick my legs down

through the gap me and AA made, I feel how swollen up my ankles are.

I've never been a big fan of long-haul flights and I don't think this job—*Hell Bird*—is going to shift my thinking an inch.

Without really thinking it through, and feeling the gentle, smooth motion of the taxiing plane, I drop down into the cargo bay.

Thankfully, I remember to bend my knees as I land.

I absorb the shock through my rubbery calf muscles.

The cargo bay—like the ducts above—is completely pitch black.

As I walk about, I stumble over the edge of—what I recall to be—part of the wooden crate lugging the Jacuzzi along.

Brian's Jacuzzi.

Despite the situation, I manage the hint of a smile.

I have to admit—with all that's been going on—I find it hard to believe that Brian thought this an apt time to bring a Jacuzzi along for the ride.

As I stalk around, I can't help wondering to myself if Brian might already have got hold of the memory stick. Has he somehow concealed it somewhere about the Jacuzzi?

From all my experience with Brian, I might have got down on my hands and knees to check the Jacuzzi out . . . to see if my wild hunch was right.

But then I hear the sobbing.

I turn my head to look into the darkness.

"Who's there?" I say, but I'm pretty sure I already know the answer.

The plane is turning now—perhaps headed towards the terminal, and closer to those militiamen.

I take a step in the direction of the sobbing. "AA?" I get out.

Silence from the shadows.

Neither confirmation or a denial.

Another step.

I know AA's still armed.

That he still has his gun in his hand.

That—if he wished—he could go through with his portion of the job.

KILL ANNA HARRIS

Get paid.

Another heaving sob.

Almost muted by a sharp intake of air from the engines.

I get the feeling that the plane will come to a standstill before too long.

And I need to be ready.

"Come on," I say. "If you're going to do it then *do it*. I'd rather it be you than a bunch of drugged-up macho men."

Nothing from AA.

As I get closer to the shadows, to where I sense AA standing, I feel the plane grind to a stop.

It rolls back a few centimetres and then finds the chocks—or whatever they're called.

I stumble slightly.

But stay on my feet.

Right then, from above, a shimmering, white fluorescent light flickers to life.

I can make out the cargo bay now.

Can make out AA.

And I see that Brian holds him tight.

With a gun stuck up the underside of his chin.

Ten Minutes After Landing

MY EYES CROSS BRIAN'S.

I take him in, standing behind AA, wearing the same suit as before, the silk tie still about his throat. His pudgy cheeks rosy in the light from the cargo bay.

I catch that strangely sour, woody scent of whisky on the stilted air.

Although I know that it'll spell my immediate doom, I can't help but look forward to the cargo bay door opening up. Letting in some fresh—*Caribbean?*—air.

More than anything else, I wish I had a gun.

Brian presses the gun he holds harder into AA's chin.

I see that it's AA's gun.

I can see that from the lettering '*Hotflush*' embossed on the grip.

As I stand there—stock still—almost unable to breathe, I observe a bead of sweat roll down the side of Brian Mathewson's face.

All around us, the sounds of the plane drop away to nothing.

The engines power down.

Only then do I realise that the world was throbbing before—senselessly vibrating.

Finally something inside me switches.

I manage to catch my breath.

Get enough puff into my lungs to *speak*, in any case.

"What is this?" I say. "What the hell's going on?"

Brian continues to press the gun up into AA's chin.

His expression is cold, calculating.

All his conscious strength is being pumped into making out that he's thoroughly neutral about the whole affair.

And what do I know?

Perhaps he is.

My eyes skim over to AA—to his wide-open eyes; far more afraid than I ever might've been able to imagine them being. I suppose that he believes he'll be dead soon—that it'll only take a quick bullet to the brain and then it'll all go away.

Suffering—*life*—whatever you want to call it.

"What happened to your gun, Anna?" Brian says, his voice totally flat, his face expressionless.

I say nothing in reply.

A smile tweaks onto Brian's lips. "You didn't drop it some-where, did you?"

Again, I say nothing at all.

I turn my attention to AA—it's difficult not to when he's staring at me with blood-soaked eyes, as if he was a stuck pig. "What's going on, Brian?" I say, my voice as flat as his.

Brian considers the question—or seems to—he tilts his head to one side, and then he examines AA in profile. "Did you manage to find the memory stick, Anna?"

I shake my head.

"Have you figured out yet that it's not here?"

Once more, I shake my head.

Brian sniffs a laugh . . . then he exhales long and hard.

He glances off towards the door of the cargo bay, and then, without another word, brings his gun down to his thigh. "Well," he says, "I'd better not sully *my* hands with any more of this unpleasantness. From what you just said, you seem well aware of the *men* on their way—men who are *far* more adept at handling a delicate situation such as this one."

"An execution?" I say, hoping to—at the very least—get a flinch out of him before he leaves me behind forever.

But, Brian Mathewson, as ever, just gives a slight chuckle.

"You always did have a flare for the dramatic, Anna."

With that parting quip, he grips tight to AA and then thrusts him towards me—all at once causing AA's deadweight to knock me back.

The two of us sprawl about on the floor.

Unable to find any purchase.

I feel AA's elbow dig *hard* into my ribcage. The pain is so extreme for a few moments that I can hardly manage to draw breath.

AA, too, gives several groans before rolling off me, and onto his side.

Finally, when I manage to get a grip back on myself, I shift my attention back towards Brian.

Brian steps over to the door of the cargo bay, AA's gun still fixed on the two of us. "It was a shame that AA couldn't take care of you on the flight over . . . if he'd been *really* spirited then he might've got it done back in the hotel room."

Brian reaches out for a lever, brings it down hard.

From somewhere within the plane, there's the creaking of a mechanism whirring into place.

Behind him, the cargo bay door shifts downwards.

It takes an inordinately long time to open completely.

A waft of *warm* air flows in.

I feel it brighten my spirits.

As if there was any hope remaining.

"Brian?" I say, as he stands, silhouetted in the door to the cargo bay.

"Hmm?" he replies, allowing AA's gun to slip down to his thigh now.

Apparently the *threat* of me and AA has been thoroughly vanquished.

"Why'd you go to all this trouble?" I say. "Why did you bring me and AA all the way along on this plane?"

Another smirk arrives on Brian's lips. "Well, that would give the game away—wouldn't it?" He steps out onto the gangplank which has formed from the doorway of the cargo bay.

He looks to his left, and then to his right, then he takes a step down.

"Brian!" I call out after him.

He glances back over his shoulder, a slightly amused expression on his face.

I manage to choke the words from my throat. "Don't you . . . don't you *need* us anymore?"

The tropical sun now shines on Brian's face, and he has to squint slightly to look back into the cargo bay. Into the darkness.

He smiles even wider now.

"Oh, Anna," he says, "what you must learn is that as one era falls, another rises."

And—just like that—he disappears from sight.

Leaving us for dead.

Twenty Minutes After Landing

FOR A LONG FEW SECONDS, there're no words.

What would be the point?

My employer—my *boss*—all that I've really ever known in the professional world of assassins, has disappeared without a trace.

Left me—left *us*—to be slaughtered by a bunch of men carrying weapons.

I look to AA, but see that he's lying on his side, and—most likely—not going to be any sort of help.

I glance about me, to the Jacuzzi, the unpacked object.

And then I turn my attention upwards, to the duct, to the hatch me and AA worked so hard on, so many hours ago, to get open.

All for nothing.

All of it a game.

Just a minor amusement for Brian Mathewson.

In those sad, distant moments as I acknowledge the fact of

my approaching death, I bring into mind my children: Ben and Josie.

And I think that, forever more, they'll be frozen for me, in their children's bodies.

I don't feel much.

I have no urge to cry.

I only feel the emptiness opening up within my chest—this sense that there was still so much to be done, so much to *live* for . . . . but now it's all gone, slipped between my fingers, escaped my grasp . . .

Outside, I can hear the *crunch* of boots marching towards the cargo area.

I glance back to AA once more.

He stares back at me.

His cheeks appear hollowed out—his eyes more so.

When I realise that he's speaking—that he's trying to summon the *strength* to speak—I notice how dry and cracked his lips are.

On the point of dying and I can't help thinking about how AA looks like shit.

Wow, I always thought I was shallow, but I've even surprised myself with that one . . .

Finally, inching closer to him, hearing the marching boots coming still nearer, I manage to make out what AA's trying to say.

". . . Amy . . ."

"No," I say—the sound of boots louder still—"I'm *Anna*."

"Amy," AA repeats.

I can only roll my eyes.

I know that AA's strung out on whatever drugs he was knocking back in the hotel bathroom, in the plane toilets. Nothing save the ramblings of a madman.

And yet I indulge him.

The way I see it, one of us should have a dying wish granted.

"She *told* me," AA continues, "about this . . . about *all* of this . . ."

And it's right then that the first militia man steps up into the cargo bay, a rifle slung across his chest. With a seemingly *endless* strand of companions at his heels.

One Hour After Landing

I'VE VISITED all sorts of prison cells.

But this one is *by far* the worst.

I can hear the constant calling of seagulls.

I can smell the stale, fishy stink of the sea. All mixed up with the exhaust fumes of a nearby port, the existence of which I only know of because of the constant *parp-parp* of ship horns.

The odd strike of a ship's bell.

Above all else, I feel absolutely parched, the back of my throat like a dried-out sponge. When I draw my feet up onto the retractable wooden bed, the chains which hold it in place at right-angles to the concrete wall all creak out ominously . . . as if it's ready to drop.

The floor is slightly damp, as are *all* floors which're located close to the sea. But it's the dark, yellow-brown colour of the puddle which most concerns me.

And which prompts me to keep my feet *well* above the waterline.

A rusty steel door, puckered with pivots about the edge of the metalwork, keeps us from coming and going as we please. The door has a tiny window, smudged with a browned tint which makes it impossible to look through.

At least our impromptu gaolers saw fit to leave me and AA in the same clothes with which we hijacked—or should that be *attempted* to hijack?—the plane.

The light-weight black fleeces. The waterproof trousers.

No guns, though.

That's an issue.

I glance up, to the small—*barred*—letterbox-sized window.

I can make out the searing blue sky above.

I wonder what time of day it is.

Decide that it doesn't matter.

At least they didn't kill me and AA back in the cargo bay.

I have that to be thankful for.

Though for them to only bring us here—to this cell—seems a mite cruel.

Why not cut out the waiting?

I glance over to AA, lying on his own bunk. He lies on his back, one arm flailed down towards the ground, his fingertips almost brushing the concrete floor. His tongue lolls out of the corner of his mouth and his closed eyelids flicker as he—*apparently*—dreams about somewhere faraway.

AA passed out soon after the men marched us off the plane, and onto a windowless armoured vehicle. When we arrived here, none of the armed men managed to bring him round from his dreams. They had to drag him along the winding corridors of this concrete—*apparently sea-front*—holding area.

The past forty minutes having been a total blur, only now do

I have a chance to think back on what he said. That little titbit about Amy. About her *knowing* what was going on.

Just thinking about it sparks anger in the pit of my gut.

Because if she *did* know about this.

If she knew *anything* about this . . . well, let's just leave it that if Amy wanted me to trust her at all then this is just about the *very worst* start she might've made.

Just as I thought, she was bluffing me.

Setting me up for another fall.

And—*wow*—did she hit it right on the nose.

AA turns in his sleep. He's grinding his teeth now. He no longer has the at-peace expression he once wore, when he first passed out. That makes me feel slightly better, because if *I'm* not having a good time here then why should he?

Finally, and with a slight jolt, he wakes up.

He rolls a little, and I think about leaping up, coming to his rescue.

Stopping him from rolling right off the edge.

In the end, though, I decide against intervention.

I could really do with a touch of slapstick comedy right now.

AA lands on his side, half breaking his fall by outstretching an arm.

He gives a loud, percussive, "*Oof!*" and then eases himself back upwards with his elbow.

He squeezes his eyes shut several times and reaches up to his temple as if he feels a headache coming on.

Poor baby . . .

Finally, with lots of heavy breathing—all that *macho crap* men do to express hardship—AA manages, with the aid of the retractable bunk behind him, to arrive back in a sitting position.

He blinks at me, clearly having trouble in seeing straight, and then, with a large gulp of air, rocking his shoulders back, he says, "How long was I out?"

"Three days," I reply.

"Fuck off," he answers, not missing a beat, and then, "How long?"

"About an hour."

AA nods at this, apparently accepting the answer. Then— perhaps ill-advisedly—he attempts to reach back behind himself, grasp hold of the retractable bunk and lift himself up onto it.

He fails after a couple of tries and decides—*apparently*—that the floor's a better bet.

He rubs his scalp, displacing his hair which'd been slicked flat from his sleeping.

He screws up his eyes and looks at me. "We locked up again?"

"No," I say, "this is Brian's seafront room—he thought he'd give us a room with a view, really impress us."

AA gives me a scowl in return, tries to stumble back up to his feet.

Fails again.

Once more he decides to play it where it lies.

He squints at me. "Why're you being catty?"

" 'Catty'?" I say. "Catty *how*?"

"Just"—AA twizzles his fingers as if it explains some great intangible—"the whole *thing*."

"We *are* Mister Articulate this morning."

"Is it morning?"

"I dunno."

And I decide to leave *that* conversation where it is, and to move onto the *far* more important matter.

I direct my best glare at AA.

"Why didn't you tell me Brian ordered you to kill me?"

AA meets my eye for precisely one second—I know because the digital second timer of my watch sits just in the corner of my vision—then he looks away.

Up to the letterbox-sized window as if he might be able to contemplate the 'view'.

Whatever the result, he turns his attention swiftly back onto me. "When did you find out?" he says, not with any sort of apologetic tone . . . just flatly—like Brian spoke to us.

"On the plane," I say, "from the toilet bin."

AA screws up his eyes, shakes his head, stares long and hard at the concrete ground.

"Shit," he says, "I'm sorry."

"That's more like it," I say.

"No," he says, looking back up at me, "I knew this was coming all along."

"Knew *what* was coming?"

"That Brian was going to have you, uh, taken *care* of."

This just hits me *completely* the wrong way.

I feel a tingle through my ribcage.

My chest tightens.

And I feel an almost unbearably hot sensation flow through my blood.

Right up to my temples.

It pounds there—*hard*—for several moments. When I finally have the strength to look back at AA, I am *PISSED OFF* in block capitals.

And yet, I can't make the words come.

Still, it appears that my glare does all the work words might've done, because AA looks back at me like a scolded puppy —a puppy that's just relieved itself in my favourite shoes . . . well, it couldn't have been my *favourite* pair since Lizzie decided to urinate in those a few weeks ago.

AA's eyes skitter about in their sockets and then he looks back up to the window above us, as if that's going to provide him with the answers.

Finally, he looks back at me.

What *is* it with men and admitting their mistakes?

Or trying to make them be *honest* for that matter?

"Amy," AA continues, staring at the concrete floor rather than me. "She told me the plan—what was happening."

Just thinking about *that* bitch really sets off my alarm.

The one in my chest which sends pain skittering all about my nervous system.

But I try not to make it show.

And probably fail.

"Anna," AA goes on, *finally* looking at me, "you've got to understand that it was for the best—that if you knew the ins and outs of the thing then you would understand."

"Why not try me now?" I say, surely sounding extremely 'catty'.

AA swallows hard, and I actually see his Adam's apple bobbing in his throat.

That was something I imagined only happened in cartoons.

"Have you got any water?" he says.

"Nope. They didn't think to leave any."

AA looks around the cell. "And what about"—he pauses for a long moment as if I'm going to have no trouble filling in the gaps.

Thankfully my mind *is* that scatologically calibrated, because I reply, "No, doesn't seem to be any sort of bucket either."

He looks back at me. "Do you mind if I . . ."

"Number one or two?" I say.

He seems to consider this for a long time.

"It doesn't matter," I butt in, "you're not doing *anything* in here with me."

AA looks like he's going to protest, but, in the end, he sees the light.

Decides not to contest me.

He gives a dejected, but understanding, nod.

"Fine," I say, "then tell me everything." I make sure to meet his eyes, just as you might look an untrustworthy, unfamiliar *dog* in the eye. "Now."

One Hour And A Half After Landing

A DOESN'T HOLD BACK from then on.

He does the *honest* thing.

At last.

He tells me about how Amy came to see him several weeks before she came to see me. And how she informed him of her father's plans—how Brian and her father, ex-Chief Constable, Charlie Branwick, had something of a reconciliation . . . and *that* after her father had decided to make it his mission to bring Brian Mathewson down.

Then again, I've learned never to take whatever anybody says at face value.

Not just in my business, but life in general.

AA informs me that Brian and Charlie Branwick have—together—been working out how to cut the ties of the more 'unsavoury' aspects of Brian's business.

All those on board the plane were, in some way, involved with Brian Mathewson.

All of them illicit members of his company.

It does make me wonder why they weren't more terrified to hear of his 'execution' on the plane.

Then again, I suppose—from my personal experiences with Brian Mathewson, especially the more recent ones—his death would be somewhat bitter-sweet.

Perhaps those people on board had the same sinking feeling as *I'd* had.

Just as I knew before, AA explains to me again—perhaps he thinks I'm *slow* . . . probably onto something there, actually—that Charlie Branwick lost his job as Chief Constable because of his ties to Brian Mathewson; because he was having to sweep so much beneath the carpet.

Somebody had to fall for what Brian was up to . . . and no *way* was it going to be the politicians at the higher end of the chain.

It turns out that the other members of Brian's elicit payrol have all been given decent accommodation—they've all been handed a nice place, on the beach, and, of course, a fine monthly allowance so that they 'disappear' on this tropical island paradise which, somehow, doesn't exist on any map.

From the sound of things, as AA tells me, his assassins haven't been extended the same privilege . . . apart from *Tabby* that is . . . and there I was thinking that *I* was Brian's favourite girl.

It seems that Brian believes assassins to entail a much larger risk.

And one patently not worth taking.

He set me and AA up so that we would have some hefty charges placed against us—hijacking.

Any sort of a plea bargain would be a last-ditch fantasy:

Who *ever* heard of a publicist tugging on everyone's string?

Really having the influence to change things for good . . . or evil?

When AA gets to the part where Amy heard all about her father and Brian working together, and the most important bit— from my perspective—about how they'd planned on having AA *kill* me, he gives me a deeply apologetic pout, and he almost succeeds in making me melt.

Not quite, though.

Knowing that someone has been told to kill you—knowing that a *friend*, no less, has been appointed to kill you . . . well, that does take a little forgiving.

Maybe I should try some empathy for my many—*many*— victims down the years.

He tries to explain it away, saying that if he had refused, kicked up a stink of any sort, then Brian would've set somebody else on my case.

Once AA's got through with most of the details, I have to admit that I'm not feeling *quite* as angry as I was from the outset.

He reasons away how he couldn't *possibly* have told me—that we couldn't *possibly* have ducked out somehow—because Brian would've known that *we* knew.

It would've led to them knowing there was a spy in their midst.

Tipping people off.

And that would've led to Amy being discovered.

Then, most likely, an assassin coming after me and AA.

Wherever in the world we decided to up sticks to.

It all sounds quite *reasonable*.

Until I feel one sticking point leaping out in my mind.

"About Amy," I say.

"Uh-huh," AA says, now having managed to haul himself

back up onto the retractable bunk, and sitting on the edge of the suspended wooden bed.

He's switched back to being somewhat blasé, and I can't help feeling that *he* believes he's winning here. That he's managed to get himself back into some sort of Good Book with me . . . yeah, like such a book even exists . . .

"She told me that she bought a ticket to get on the plane."

AA glances back at me.

His expression serious now.

"What'd you mean?"

I relay, word-for-word, as far as I can remember from my aviation-fear affected brain, what Amy told me while we were there together in the duct.

AA looks away, turns to some serious thinking of his own.

He tucks his hands beneath his chin in such a way that makes me wonder if he's had some sort of training as a male model.

I could just about imagine AA on a fifty-foot-high billboard flogging perfume, or a designer tuxedo . . . or some smarmy marketing course for professionals.

Finally, he looks back up at me, then says, "She probably just wanted to stick to the story."

"Yeah," I say, and then, looking AA in the eye. "Or one of you is *lying*."

Two And A Half Hours After Landing

THAT COMMENT of mine leads to a pretty long and uncomfortable silence.

And one which *I* have no intention of breaking.

I can't help but think back to Amy coming to my house. How she *broke in*.

How she sat at my kitchen table, with my cat Lizzie winding herself about her legs.

How she spoke so sincerely.

So from the *heart*.

I can't shift the idea that the one lying here is AA.

As I hear boots approaching down the corridor outside the cell, I decide that I should lose the Frosty Girl act for just a few seconds. I have no idea if the guards-slash-soldiers-slash-macho men are going to separate me and AA.

I turn to AA, now lying flat on his back, dozing and—*apparently*—unlike me, not having heard the approaching footsteps just yet.

"Is that the reason?" I say, trying to get it out as quickly as possible.

I hear a key slipping into the sturdy, rusted-up lock of the cell door.

I speak more quickly. "You know, why you've been so worried —so *stressed*—because you knew you'd have to kill me?"

The door creaks open on its hinges, one of those *movie-style* effects. I wonder, a little dizzily for a moment, if somebody's actually had the job of picking out the spookiest, most *unpleasant* door they can manage for the prisoners.

Then I snap back onto AA as I see a pair of men rounding the door.

AA gives me a smirk in return. "Yeah," he says, and then, lifting his shirt to show off the bullet wound in his side . . . the one that's gone ever so slightly *green* . . . he adds, "And this too."

I look to the soldiers.

One man. One woman.

They're dark-skinned—*locals*, obviously.

They wear grey-blue camos.

Bulletproof vests.

Seems that they might be expecting crossfire . . .

I breathe in deeply and wait for them to look us over.

Both guards, of course, are armed.

The two of them with rifles.

They hang down over their chests.

Because I can't help it, my eyes drift down to their waists, to their sidearms.

Snug in their holsters.

For now.

"Time to go," the male soldier says.

His voice has that Caribbean *twang* to it . . . an accent which I might describe as Jamaican, but which is probably widespread throughout the area.

I glance to AA, as if we've got some sort of top-secret plan nailed down.

He nods back to me.

The two of us get to our feet.

If there's one thing I've learned in a lifetime of messing about with guns—the same way that Rat in *The Wind in the Willows* messes about in boats—it's that you never argue with someone who has one . . . especially when you don't have one yourself.

You've got to make them believe that *they're* in control.

And that's when you can leverage power.

The female soldier looks to me. "You," she says. "Come with me."

Since the male soldier stands still, continuing to stare suspiciously at AA, I suppose that AA's not coming along for the ride with me.

It appears that my initial suspicion, that me and AA are to be separated, is coming true.

I turn my attention to the open door, the corridor outside.

And, taking care not to excite my female escort, I step through it.

Unlike our cell, there're no windows out in the corridor, only a few dim, fluorescent lights—the ones that're generally used as backup lights when there's an earthquake, some sort of a natural disaster. I suppose, here, in this jail, the idea is more about saving money than seeing out the apocalypse.

I glance back over my shoulder, then, meeting the female soldier's stern expression, I don't deign to repeat the action.

When we reach the end of the corridor, there's a dead-end.

Or, at least, what *seems* like a dead-end at first. In actual fact there're two ways to go:

Left or right.

The female soldier soon clears up any confusion I might be having in short order.

"Right," she says.

I take the right turning, still feeling the female soldier on my heels, and—more notably—the sharp, burning sensation just between my shoulder blades knowing that she has a gun which could quite easily be pointed at *me*.

If she's taking me down some dead-end corridor to execute me then this'd be the place.

A sad ending, but—*still*—an ending nonetheless . . .

However, I'm given a stay of execution because the female soldier barks out, "Stop!" to me in a way which, without even processing the word through my brain causes me to do just that.

In the gloom of the corridor, I can just about make out the door in the wall.

The female soldier barges me out of the way, throwing her shoulder into my upper arm. As I recoil away from her, I feel the tingle of pain through my ribcage and I have a strong urge to give her a bunch of fives.

In the end, though, sense *does* prevail.

I hang back as she—first—raps her knuckles against the door and—second—waits for the response from within. She slips me another suspicious glance before giving me a firm nod.

I take this as an invitation to reach for the doorknob for myself.

And I do so.

Just like everything else in this jail—or whatever this place is —the doorknob is damp.

And a little cold.

When I turn the doorknob, step into the room, I'm almost blinded by the bright light flooding into the space.

I bring my forearm up to shield my eyes.

Then, when my eyes finally adjust, I take in the room.

A battered old desk which looks like it's seen more beatings than paperwork. Then there's the withered, dying—*dead?*—pot plant in the corner; its leaves turned brown and crinkled.

Finally, behind the desk, I eye the black woman sat there.

In uniform.

A beret perched on her cropped, frizzy black hair.

She has rich, chocolate-brown eyes.

Eyes which remind me, for a dizzy second, of my boyfriend Mark.

She sits perched forward in her chair, with her elbows propped on the table. She unclasps her hands and indicates the chair in front of the desk. "Please, Mrs Harris," she says, in the same Jamaican-slash-Caribbean accent of the female soldier. "Sit down."

Even though I know this isn't the time or place for me to mount any sort of high horse, I just can't help myself. "*Ms* Harris," I say, supposing that 'Miss' might be a stretch.

The black woman makes no response.

She continues to indicate the chair standing before her desk.

With a quick look back to the soldier—who rests her hands over her rifle as if it's some sort of teddy bear—I lower myself down onto the chair.

When I breathe in, I catch that same stale scent of the sea.

But it's also enhanced with a strong smell of body odour.

And of a lemon-smelling perfume.

I glance out the window, for the first time being able to properly admire the view without being rendered half blind by the daylight.

A glimmering seascape—no *boats*, or any other sign of a port that I can make out—only bare nature beyond.

A bay.

I suppose that the sounds of boats—the sound of a port— must've come from the other side of the jail.

And I don't feel that this is the time to ask this stern-looking black woman to confirm or deny my assumptions.

I turn back to her.

See that she's smiling lightly now.

Like the two soldiers, she wears the blue-grey camos.

Though, I can tell, she benefits much more from the uniform's bagginess, hiding her—no doubt—doughy figure.

Sometimes I wonder if I said half the things I think out loud I'd end up being called some kind of Skinny Bitch . . . most likely I would . . .

"*Ms* Harris," the black woman continues, "my name is Grendelin."

"Nice to meet you," I say, glancing back to the female soldier now lurking over by the window looking out over the bay. "You can call me Anna if you like."

When I turn back to Grendelin, I see that she's smiling wide and proud, her teeth clean and white and *extremely* straight. Although I feel strongly that she might be luring me into some false sense of security, I find her smile somewhat infectious.

Against all odds, I find myself smiling back.

"Now," Grendelin says, "Brian Mathewson, he would like us to kill you and . . ."

Grendelin twirls her hand in the air as if this might prompt me to spill AA's name.

It does.

"Adam Alderknot," I put in, my guts feeling frozen at the mention of my prospective execution.

Grendelin jabs her tongue hard at the inside of her bottom lip, making it bulge outwards. "However," she says, "we believe that you might well be something of an asset."

I feel my chest tighten.

The pain jangle through my ribcage once more.

" 'An asset' how?" I reply.

Grendelin breathes in deeply, moves her tongue along to her cheek, which she pushes out in the same fashion. "Your skills would be useful for us—for keeping order here."

Grendelin shifts her attention out through the window, to the scene across the bay.

As she loses herself in thought, the room drifts into a profound silence.

I decide that I need to pick up my end of the conversation. "Hasn't he . . ." I begin, wondering at how wise I am being to continue, ". . . *paid* you to take care of us?"

"Mm," Grendelin says, still staring out through the window.

She turns back, looks at me with those chocolate eyes of hers.

"But he doesn't *have* to know—and, anyway, we *would* be killing one of you."

My heart skips a beat.

Three And A Half Hours After Landing

S OON AFTER, I'm shipped back to my jail cell.

On the way there, though, I'm given something of a looser rein.

I suppose that's just one of the benefits—one of the *rewards* on offer—for giving someone what they want.

I tramp along the corridor, working out the relative merits and disadvantages to what I've agreed—in parlaying AA's life for my own.

In the end, I sell it to myself as a strategy.

That it's just like Amy and AA worked out between themselves.

It's *better* that I keep the truth from him lest he blow up, or cause a ruckus. I need time to think—to think about how I can get the upper-hand over Grendelin.

As I tread back towards AA, I find myself glancing in through one of the small windows in the doors to the other cells.

I come to a halt.

I expect the female soldier who, despite having allowed me a little freedom, still has a rifle close to hand, to bark out for me to keep going.

To continue on to the cell I share with AA.

But she says nothing.

Apparently *allowing* me to look in through the window.

There, in a cell very much like the one myself and AA are sharing, sits Tabby, perched on the edge of the retractable bed, staring at the floor between her flat-soled stewardess shoes.

She wears the same stewardess's uniform from before, too:

That dark-purple trouser suit with the *Pleasure Lines* logo emblazoned on the breast pocket.

She seems terribly out of place, of course.

But, then again, where else does a stewardess look at home other than on a plane?

I look to the female soldier, and find myself asking, "Can I speak with her?"

The female soldier spends a long while considering. She glances beyond me, up the corridor, and then back over her shoulder. If I had any cash on me—if the soldier *thought* I had any cash on me—then I would take this as a not-so-subtle hint for a bribe.

As it stands, though, it doesn't seem on the cards.

Then, apparently decided, and without another word, she reaches down into her pocket.

Digs about there, causing an unseen set of keys to jangle.

Finally, she brings a key up, sticks it into the lock, and gives it a sharp twist.

When she pushes the door open, I find myself—*inexplicably*, and not a little hypnotically—drawn to the female guard's sidearm.

As I come up for air, the female soldier notices this.
She gives a wry grin, knowing that she still holds the power.
That she's very much the one in charge.
Of course she is.
She has not one but *two* guns.
I step past her.
Into the cell.
Into *Tabby's* cell.

Three Hours And Three Quarters After Landing

TABBY'S CELL has all the dressings of mine and AA's.

The retractable bed.

The off-colour puddle on the floor.

And the barred letterbox-sized window high up on the wall.

That same scrap of bright blue sky shines through the glass.

Tabby's hair seems flame red in the dour, tight cell—almost *inflammatory* in the greyness of the room. I'm all too aware of the female soldier standing in the doorway, watching every one of our moves with great interest.

Tabby lifts her head up to me, and I take in her bright green eyes.

Suddenly full of hope. And surprise.

She gets to her feet.

Stands before me.

Her eyes lock onto mine.

"Anna," she says.

I hold out a hand as if I'm some sort of Roman empress.

But Tabby obeys me.

She comes no closer.

I look to the female soldier, standing in the doorway, her eyes glued on the two of us. Her hand just hovering over the rifle which hangs down over her chest.

Then I turn back to Tabby.

"What happened?" I say.

"Oh," Tabby says, "nothing much—only this man carrying a rifle got on the plane a little after landing, made me get down on my knees. They put me in handcuffs." She holds up her wrists to show me the swollen red welts.

My heart bleeds for her.

It's a personal issue of mine, but I find it very difficult to feel any sort of sympathy for somebody who's disarmed me.

Someone who's made me feel *weak*.

I decide to move on from the pity party. "What did Brian promise you?"

Tabby stares at me.

"Come on," I say, "don't hold out—just tell me what he said, what mission he had you running along on."

Tabby gives a shake of her head, and then a slight shrug. "I did jobs mostly out of town," she says. "*International* jobs."

I look to the female soldier—still in the doorway, but glancing down the corridor now.

That sidearm of hers looks mighty attractive.

Sticking out of its holster.

All ready for *grabbing*.

I turn back to Tabby, who continues with her story.

"I always pose—*posed*, I guess, in the past—as a stewardess, a sort of undercover bodyguard for whatever purpose Brian required. I flew all over the world, ready to head off on whatever flight Brian needed me on."

I think back over all the flights Brian's sent me on down the years.

Try as I might, I can't seem to bring any sort of recollection of having seen Tabby before. And, despite her distinctive looks—her blazing red hair, those eyes of hers direct from the Emerald Isle—I can't recall.

But it could quite easily be the case that, all those flights, all those members of the cabin crew, have blurred into one congealed mass in my memory.

I've never really been one for remembering faces without some extreme drama to tag them with. The funny thing is that when you're the last person somebody ever sees, their face becomes etched on your mind forever.

It comes back to you in dreams.

Or—*sometimes*—in the middle of the daytime.

But I haven't killed Tabby.

Yet.

"You didn't fly armed?" I say.

Tabby shakes her head. A smile tweaks her lips. "But as you saw on the plane, I'm fairly adept at getting my hands on a gun when I need one."

I don't smile back. "And losing it just as quick."

Tabby arches an eyebrow, her smile transforming into a smirk. "Sneak attacks have always been something of a weakness of mine."

"All right," the female soldier says, taking a step into the room. "Time to go."

I look to Tabby, who treads towards me, that same smirk on her lips.

For the longest moment, I'm certain she's going to stab me with some shank. But, right at the last moment, she wraps her arms around me. Squeezes me tight to her chest.

I feel her warmth, in the humid air, and I breathe in the salty scent of sweat.

I wonder, for a long moment, if she's going to whisper something in my ear.

But she doesn't.

I eye the female soldier stepping towards us, and I try to wriggle free from Tabby's grasp . . . more than anything else not wanting to get *her* into trouble.

But she holds on tight.

The girl doesn't appear to have any sense whatsoever.

"Come on!" the female soldier says, reaching out, grabbing hold of Tabby's shoulder, peeling her away from me finally.

When I catch Tabby's eye again, I expect to see some desperation there.

Perhaps a tear glistening in the corner of her eye.

But that same smirk remains.

Set in stone on her lips.

I look to the female soldier, who continues to hold tight to Tabby. I give her a nod, and then step through the doorway, and out into the corridor.

A couple of heartbeats later and the female soldier follows.

It's only a matter of seconds after leaving the cell behind that my eyes slink downwards, to the female soldier's waist. To her sidearm.

Gone.

For some reason, my first instinct is to call out.

To *warn* her.

But it's too late.

I hear the gunshot rip through the air.

The female soldier turns to me as she drops.

Her eyeballs roll back in their sockets.

Showing me white with blood-streaked veins.

Through the doorway, I eye Tabby, standing prone, pointing the sidearm—nothing more than a 9mm. But it did the trick. And, from the result, the female soldier lying dead, face-down on the floor before me, Tabby sure knows how to handle herself.

Then again, Brian always does hire the best.

Tabby lowers the gun in her hold, both hands squeezing the grip tight. Her eyes are wide and her lips slightly parted. Her red hair, once perfectly smooth, back when she was on air hostess duty, is now more like split and frayed rope.

Coming apart.

Her eyes—slowly—work their way upwards to meet mine.

I think back to the touching little moment, in her cell, only seconds ago.

The embrace.

That was just a ruse to bring the female soldier close to us. Before Tabby could reach out.

Snatch the sidearm off her.

I hardly have time to appreciate this morsel, though, because Tabby brings the gun back up.

Getting *me* in her sights.

I just about have the presence of mind to leap to my left as she pulls the trigger.

Four Hours After Landing

W HEN I LAND, I lie for too long on my side.
      Feeling that sharp prickle of pain in my ribs.
I tell myself to get up.

Anna, get up!

For a second, I stare at the face of my watch, seeing that four
hours have already passed since me and AA were carted off the
plane. Working quickly, my ears still recovering from the near-
deafening sound of the gunshot, I lever myself back upright.

Back onto my feet.

And I run—*flat out*—until I reach mine and AA's cell.

The door is open.

And the male soldier stands inside, his rifle raised, pointed
at me.

AA is slumped on the bed. His head turned in my direction.
The surprise sketched all over his face.

Thinking quickly, I raise my hands, but it's too late.

The male soldier fires.

The shot blasts just past my ear.

A puff of cement dusts the back of my neck.

A distant ringing fills my skull.

When I turn my head, I see Tabby sidestepping along the corridor—bounding towards me—the purloined sidearm pointed right at me.

I try to warn the male soldier within the cell, but I can see his eyes are wide with fright, and he's readying another shot.

I only have time to jump out of the way—to keep on going along the corridor.

Tabby's gunshot fizzes past my other ear.

This time I hardly hear it.

The ringing from the first shot goes on.

Even despite the situation, I think about how stupid I must look, ducking and diving as I fly along the corridor, attempting to outfox Tabby . . . trying *not* to get myself wiped out.

When the bullet finally does bite me—down in my right calf muscle—it hardly registers at first.

I turn the corner.

Bound along an upward slope leading out of the jail.

The pain comes soon after.

Throbbing.

Burning.

Impossible to bear.

I bite down so hard that I feel my teeth sink into my tongue.

Bring out blood.

This time in my mouth.

I bound onwards, loping along, one hand gripping tight to my right thigh, urging that leg on.

Desperate to drag myself up and out.

To safety.

Whatever that means.

However temporary it might be.

All that matters now.

Over my shoulder, I'm dimly aware—through the persistent ringing in my head—of the gunfire being exchanged. Cracking back and forth.

It's bought me time.

I just have to keep going.

Head for the light at the end of the tunnel.

See if there's an ending at all.

Four Hours And Five Minutes After Landing

O UTSIDE, the fresh air should be an elixir.

But it's more like salt in the wound.

I grimace in pain as I leave the doorway behind.

I don't turn around to look back along the corridor.

To see if anybody's pursuing me.

I don't care anymore.

About anybody or anything.

Everybody—*it seems*—has betrayed me.

So maybe it's time for me to betray *them*.

I take in my surroundings, a dirt track leading up to this cement structure. The sea begins just a matter of metres away. No wonder, even back in the cell, I could smell the salty breeze.

As I limp on along the dirt ground, hearing the soles of my trainers scuff against the rough surface, I can see a hill growing up from behind the concrete construction.

Not having any other reference point to head for, I decide to crest the hill.

'Agony' is the only way to describe walking with my shot-through calf muscle.

Every couple of steps, I have to shut my eyes tight, as if I can just will the pain away.

But, of course, that doesn't work.

I make for the bent and bashed-in crash barrier which skirts the barely tarmacked road. I'm glad to have something to hold onto—a sort of outdoor banister, leading me up the hill. Away from the concrete structure, and the cells.

Perhaps the pain takes my mind off anything else, but I manage to reach the crest of the hill in what seems like no time at all. And when I turn back to look over my shoulder, the pleasantly cool breeze caressing my cheeks, I can't see anybody following me.

I hope sincerely—*in my darkest of hearts*—that they've all killed one another.

Mutually assured destruction.

Hopefully that was the result.

Surely that was the result.

I turn back to the road ahead, and I grip the crash barrier tightly, easing myself along the road. Each step feels like a victory. As if I'm not only getting away from the apocalyptic firefight, but away from Brian too.

It's only when the concrete structure has left my range of sight completely that I begin to feel at all at ease—and, even then, I'm expecting a bullet to whizz past my head, if not right into it, at any given second.

But I stagger on.

Now I can see ships bobbing about the sea, and, closer in the foreground, an active port. Lots of warehouses; corrugated steel shacks. Blurry forms moving between them. Several workers carting around sacks of varying colours.

My mission, now, becomes clear.

I need to get aboard one of those boats.

Get away from this island.

Escape this *mess*.

Then everything'll be okay.

Then I'll *truly* have a fresh start.

Who knows, perhaps I'll never go home?

Maybe I'll sample what it means to go AWOL.

See how I like it.

Whatever it is, it must be better than the life I've lived up until now.

A trained killer—morally bankrupt, and worse . . .

Right as I eye the future opening up before me, I hear a familiar voice from behind.

"Anna?"

AA.

I knew it was too good to be true.

I turn and look to AA, and, though I say it to myself, I can't help but think that he looks in just about as poor shape as I've seen him.

His complexion pale.

Green almost.

Black hair slicked with sweat.

All over the place.

I look beyond AA, back down to the concrete compound. "What about Tabby?" I say.

AA pouts, then gives a shake of his head. "Nah, when my soldier decided to up sticks, go off and have a shootout with Tabby, I took my chance. Snuck on out of there."

I turn back to the coast, enjoying the calming effect the twinkle of sunlight has across the surface. The air is pleasantly warm out here, with the cool breeze taking the dampness out of it. "Think she's dead?" I say.

"Dunno," AA replies. "Does it matter?"

I feel a lump form in my throat. Although I tell myself that I'm being a weak little girl— *afraid* for her life—I can't help but speak aloud. "When you and Amy were sneaking around, plotting . . . whatever it was that you were plotting . . . did you hear or see anything about Tabby—anything that she might've had to do with Brian's 'masterplan'."

There's a long pause and then AA replies, "No, why?"

I breathe in deeply, right to the pit of my lungs.

And then I exhale.

"Because, when Tabby snatched the sidearm off the female soldier, she took aim at me. Fired off a bullet in my direction."

AA screws up his features—his forehead wrinkling. "Anna," he says, and then digs down into his pocket. He produces a piece of paper—folded up.

It takes me a couple of heartbeats before I realise what's going on here.

What that piece of paper *means*.

As AA unfolds it, I look to him, rather than the paper. "That piece of paper," I say, "the one that I found in the aeroplane toilets—it wasn't yours, was it?"

AA looks me long and hard in the eye.

Then he gives a shake of his head.

I stare back off out to sea, to the faint bluish glow on the horizon.

I get the feeling that, in a couple of hours, this whole scene will be steeped in twilight.

And I'd like to be *far* away when that happens.

"Brian," I say, half to myself, "he must've palmed that note off to Tabby—made it clear that he wanted *her* to rub me out if for whatever reason you didn't manage it."

I turn to AA, look him right in the eye.

"Is there anything I need to know, Adam, you can tell me— you know that."

AA holds my gaze.

A thin, almost transparent film forms over his eyes.

Once more, he shakes his head.

I turn away from him.

Head along the road.

Down towards the docks below.

Four Hours And A Half After Landing

EVERY SINGLE STEP I take, the pain is sharper. It digs into my right calf.

Sending me a clear, *easy-to-understand* message that I should stop.

Perhaps get some medical attention.

Considering that, it doesn't seem so bad that it takes me—and AA, apparently—twenty minutes or so to get down to the bustling streets. To the dockworkers dressed in t-shirts, cargo shorts and flip-flops. All of them are glistening with sweat. Their expressions are dogged—*determined*.

As we walk among them, I breathe in the sweet odour of sewage all around, and I only realise that I'm walking in rivulets of thick, brown water when I sink my foot down into a puddle.

When I bring my foot back up, I see that my trainer is sodden. Its fabric covered in gunk. I grimace slightly but know—*at present*—that there're far more pressing things to consider than the state of my footwear.

When I tell AA my plan about wanting to get the hell off the island, he seems to be on the same wavelength. And although I still haven't cleared up who, out of Amy and AA is telling the truth, the whole truth and nothing *but* the truth, all that matters at the moment is that I have a companion.

Someone who shares my driving passion to leave this island behind.

We can sort out all those subtle intangibles later.

When the dust's settled.

When we're back in England.

After a long haul through several side alleys—on either side of us the warehouses made of rusted-up corrugated steel towering above—and some extreme agony for my right calf, we manage to reach the pier.

Where all the boats are.

Even for me, someone who knows as much about sailing as flying, I can tell that the boats on offer here are made for local travel.

Not a transatlantic liner among them.

Still, without mumbling so much as a word to AA, I limp along the promenade, dodging coiled-up, frayed ropes. Each time I need to avoid one of the snaking ropes, it necessitates me hoiking my right leg upwards.

Sending pain jangling up my spine.

On the air, I catch the strong scent of rust. To me, it smells just like blood. Over and over again, I glance down at my right calf. See that the blood sticks to the back of my waterproof trousers.

I bite down hard on my tongue, the pain in my mouth relatively *more* bearable than the pain in my calf muscle.

Up ahead, I eye a captain—a black man in about his fifties,

maybe early sixties, with a silver, diminishing afro clinging to his scalp. He leans up against one of those bollards for wrapping a ship's rope around.

When I get closer, I see that he wears only a white string vest —well, I suppose, once upon a time, it was white—and he folds his arms across his chest before smiling widely at me and AA.

His teeth are yellowed and crooked.

He has several sores on his lips.

But I'm glad to be welcomed.

He nods down at my leg. He speaks with the same Caribbean accent. "Whatcha gone done there, hmm?"

I give a shake of my head. "Just a fall."

He scratches his scalp with his knobbly, horned fingernails. "Whatcha been doin' that for?"

I shrug, look to AA and, for my troubles, feel *another* flash of pain up my right calf. "Climbing—without ropes. You know how it goes," I say, and hope that he'll gobble up this *idiot-tourist* line.

"Dontcha want to call out an air ambulance?"

"Is there one around here?"

The captain chuckles, then shakes his head. When he looks back over me and AA, he says, "Nah, ain't nothin' like that." He jerks his thumb over his shoulder, in the vague direction of the coast. "You gotta go to the town if you're needin' some medical attention."

I glance to AA, as if he's the one in charge here, and then I turn back to the man. "We'd like to get off the island," I say.

The captain sticks out his lower lip as if considering the plausibility of such a request. Then he gives a shake of his head. "Not in my boat, you won't."

I feel my hopes dwindle.

Another flash of pain up my calf keeps me honest.

"Is there," I begin, wincing through the pain, "is there a boat around here that can get us off the island?"

The captain shakes his head, long and slow. "Nah," he says, "this's just a little port—if you're fixin' to get off the island then you'll need to head into town. Or fetch a plane outta the airport."

"Either," I say, feeling the pain cut right to the bone. "Either is *fine*."

The captain gives a nod. "Then back to the town port?"

"Yes," I say, becoming almost exasperated now.

The captain unfolds his arms, brings a pair of fingers up to his lips and then whistles long and shrill and *hard*.

All of a sudden, I feel a thrill jangle through my chest.

I look around us.

Expecting to see a fresh wave of soldiers bearing down on me and AA.

Ready to shoot us here and now.

All I see, though, is a boy of about thirteen, or fourteen. He has his hair buzz-cut short and he skips toward us, expertly navigating the various brown puddles and scraps of rope lying about on the floor. He finally jerks to a halt before me and AA, and the captain.

He clasps his hands behind his back and stands to attention —*straight-backed*—in a manner which I can't help thinking must've been taught him by some elder, or his mother.

"Gramp?" the boy says.

The captain snorts hard, sucks back the mucus and then gobs it out over the sea wall, into the calm harbour waters behind. He nods to the boy, but addresses me and AA. "This's my grandson, Redge—he's a good help these days, doesn't mind helping out his Gramp with the boat now and again." The captain narrows his eyes. "Once he's got his school work done, that is."

I look to the boy—Redge—and see him flip a gaze off in mine and AA's direction.

Curious.

Looking for adventure.

He looks away as soon as I meet his eye.

The captain combs his fingers through his withered and retreating hairline. "Ready to ship out?"

Five Hours And A Half After Landing

WHEN I HAVE THE SEA BREEZE rushing through my hair, blowing it back over my shoulder, I can hardly believe that—just over an hour ago—me and AA were caught up in crossfire.

The boat is about the same size as a large car:

One of those four-by-four monstrosities which Brian Mathewson finds so preferable.

It makes just about as much *noise* as one of those four-by-fours, the engine making my teeth rattle if I don't make a point of leaving my jaw latched some way open. Soon enough, though, I become accustomed to its intensity and it takes on more the quality of a purring cat.

Just thinking about Lizzie makes me a little homesick.

And I haven't even been gone twenty-four hours . . .

When the choppier waters wash against the side of the boat, I can't help but feel glad that the captain advised *against* us shipping out into deeper waters.

I look to AA, and see that he's resting on the stern; the bright, late-afternoon sunlight pinning him down to the wooden bench. He seems almost in another world, sucking up those rays as if they were some kind of drug . . . like those painkillers, or whatever they were, he was knocking back on the plane . . . in the hotel room.

I stand in the shade, leaning up against the side of the boat, feeling the sun's warmth on the fibreglass coating. Although my calf feels as if it's caught fire—and is *still* burning—the warmth of the sun up against my skin seems to keep my spirits up.

Now's not the time to let the situation overwhelm me.

Not if I want to survive.

As has already been made quite plain, Brian Mathewson appears to have this island firmly beneath his thumb.

While the captain, wearing a pair of scratched-up, wrap-around sunglasses, casually stands at the wheel, making minor adjustments to our course, I eye the man's grandson, clambering all over the boat. He works at bits and pieces, nailing something with a hammer, or else screwing something down.

A *most* industrious boy.

It's only then that it strikes me.

I look around and then limp back to AA.

I slump down on the wooden bench, sit beside him, feeling the fiery pain throbbing through my right calf muscle. I suppose that the only minor benefit of getting shot in my calf is that my ribs now, by comparison, feel a hell of a lot better.

AA turns his head to me, smiling. "Well this is nice, isn't it?" he says.

"Yeah," I reply, "*great*." Then I look to the captain, his back to us, and the captain's grandson currently occupied tying up a well-rusted steel rope which has, apparently, come loose. I lean into AA so I won't be overheard. "Adam?" I say.

"Mm?"

"Have you got any cash?"

AA gives a profound sigh, then he winces, reaches down to his side and gives it a rub.

I guess *both* of us have been in the wars now.

He shakes his head.

After another fifteen minutes or so of sailing, I notice the giant concrete barriers of what must be the main port of the island. I can see the cruisers, and the ocean liners, all docked up.

When I catch the captain's eye, he gives me another one of his familiar smiles.

I feel nausea penetrate my stomach.

Then I turn back to AA. "What're we going to do?" I say.

AA shrugs. "Do a runner?"

I give him a hard punch in the upper arm for that quip.

He gives a mock slap of his forehead. "Oh, that's right," he says, "your *leg*."

When I turn back to the captain, and his grandson, I catch the captain looking us over. That smile of his gone now. The captain turns back to his work, making adjustments to the wheel, before I get any sort of solid read on his expression.

But I can't shake the feeling that he *overheard* us.

Or, at least, appreciates the issue.

Without another word between me and AA, the captain carefully guides the boat in through the port. I feel humbled by the ocean liners and cruisers towering above us, like *skyscrapers*. As if this is some sort of a floating city.

I wonder if people ever get lost on such enormous ships.

If there's a smattering of skeletons—those who were never found—in the distant nooks and crannies of the vessels.

As we approach a more humble section of the dock, complete with rotting wooden planks on the jetty, the captain's grandson coils a rope about his wrist and then dives off the side, landing with his feet a neat shoulders-width apart on dry land.

Or whatever a jetty counts as.

He makes himself busy, tying the rope up to a wooden bollard, and then he gives his grandfather—the *captain*—a salute before dashing off along the dock.

Away from the boat.

The captain brings the purring engine to a stop. Everything, all of a sudden, becomes so much quieter. I become more aware of the odour of fuel in the air.

It sends a quiver right along every one of my nostril hairs.

It gives me a fresh new throb of intense pain in my right calf muscle.

The captain lunges forward, resting one of his legs up on the side of the boat. Next, he digs down into the pocket of his jeans, brings out a crushed packet of cigarettes. He flips the lid, slips one out, then taps its end against the laminated cardboard of the packet. He seems to consider something in the middle distance for several seconds before producing a lighter and sparking his cancer stick into life.

He inhales long and deep, and then puffs out the purple-blue smoke into the darkening afternoon sky.

I observe the plume of smoke rise up.

Gather with the rest of the emissions from the other vessels.

And I wonder when this world will have had enough of us.

What will be the straw which breaks the camel's back.

I look to AA, and, with only a glance, learn that *I'll* be the one explaining the situation.

The captain remains in profile, his foot still resting on the side of the boat. He sucks hard on his cigarette, making the tip burn a bright red.

When I sidle up beside him, I feel as if my calf's going to explode.

And my ribs are starting to ache too.

Maybe they're jealous of all the attention.

"Uh, excuse me?" I say.

The captain glances at me.

His expression is neutral now.

There's no trace of the easy-going smile from before.

"About the payment," I say, "I was wondering if we could, uh . . ." I search for the word for the longest time, then finally stumble across it ". . . send it along later?"

The cigarette dangles from the captain's lips. Smoke continues to coil upwards from the tip. He gently rests his hands on his hips, bunching his fingers into fists. He glances back over me—back to AA. The cigarette slowly burns down, so that there's a large wad of ash on the end.

With a swift gesture, the captain hoiks the cigarette out of his lips and flicks it into the water.

I hear a *hiss* as it hits the surface.

He turns his back to me, busies himself with some aspect of his boat—a tangle of wires nestled behind a removable wooden board.

"Uh," I say, and then flash a glance at AA.

It's then that I see AA's gaze sweeping upwards.

To the top of the port.

I follow his eyes.

See the uniformed soldiers.

Those same blue-grey camos.

Rifles.

And the captain's grandson approaching them at rapid speed.

My eyes cross the soldiers' right as the grandson arrives before them.

My heart chills.

And my calf *aches*.

Six Hours After Landing

<hr />

MY BRAIN RUNS so quickly I almost miss the captain ducking down into the cabin of the boat to avoid the flying bullets.

Despite the acute pain in my calf, I throw myself down.

If the dull *thud* over my shoulder is anything to go by, then AA does the same.

My heart seems to hammer against the back of my teeth as I lie there, my cheek pressed hard up against the wooden bottom of the boat. I feel my skin go cold, and then impossibly warm. I glance up, spot the captain, crawling his way to the prow of the boat.

I wonder if I should feel some sort of anger against him.

It must've been when we were a few minutes out from the dock, when he grabbed his radio, spoke with somebody. I couldn't hear a word he said because of the rumbling engines. And, the second we docked, he sent his grandson out to make sure the militiamen wouldn't miss.

I can't quite shake the feeling that I'll be seeing Grendelin again soon.

And that thought tightens my chest.

Another pump of pain through my ribcage.

It works its way back down to my calf muscle.

Still lying on my front, I manage to stretch my neck back, see AA there.

"What're we going to do?!" I shout at him.

AA's eyes are wide, and his mouth is slightly latched open.

I'm expecting a bullet to fly through the air, right—*thwock!*—into the side of AA's head.

Just like in the movies.

But, as the bullets shoot into the boat, there's nothing but the *thud-thud-thud* of them hitting fibreglass.

I focus on keeping my head down from then on.

It doesn't seem like there's anything sensible I can do for the time being.

When there's a pause in the gunfire, I risk glancing up over the side of the boat. I see the militia men, led by the captain's grandson, heading down the dock.

Towards us.

A chill passes through my blood.

I look to AA—see that he still lies on his front, his hands folded over his head as if he's in some sort of a brace position.

As if his hands might be able to block a headshot.

I know this is our moment.

If there's any chance of getting out of this—*any chance at all*—then we need to get moving right now.

I hop onto my knees.

I'm surprised to notice that it doesn't pain me as much as standing on my two feet.

No strain on my calf—I guess.

On my knees, I head over to AA.

Stare *down* at him.

He continues to cower.

"Hey! Come on!" I say.

He remains in the same position.

I glance up over the side of the boat.

See the soldiers coming closer still.

AA remains motionless.

That's when I believe he *has* been shot.

But when I can't take him playing dead any longer, I grab him by the neck—mumma cat-style—and twist his face up to mine.

His eyes are open, but they're swilling back in their sockets.

Despite everything, I feel a sigh growing and tightening in my chest.

In the end, I blow it out of me, like so much hot air.

"What the hell have you been taking?"

When AA's pupils *finally* find mine, I see that they're dilated. His mouth is latched open so wide that I fancy I could easily slip an apple in it.

It takes all my strength to lug AA over to the other side of the boat.

When I glance back up over the side of the ship, I can't see the soldiers any longer.

They're down to our level of the dock now.

And I know there's no time.

They'll be coming reeling around the corner—*guns blazing*—at any second.

"Help me out, for God's sake!" I say, my words jabbering out of my lips.

AA, though—*thankfully*—from some deeper recess of his soul, hears me.

He deigns to help me.

And that's when I realise that—*really*—I don't have a plan at all.

What're we going to do?

Rush at the soldiers on the dock?

Hope that they don't gun us down?

That'd be *nice*, I guess.

But nice doesn't habitually happen.

At least not to me.

Working on adrenalin, and seeing the first of the soldiers emerging from behind one of the ships docked, I realise there's no other choice.

We need to do *something*.

And so, with a final—*parting*—glance to the captain, hunched over in the prow of the ship, I grab a good hold of AA's shirt, and yank him up, onto his feet.

The pain is blinding for several moments.

I crush my eyelids shut.

Lose myself in the darkness.

But only for a second.

And that's all it takes.

The bullet flies just over my head.

I feel it tussle my hair.

I know there's no choice, then.

Still holding onto AA, I topple us over the side of the boat.

And into the water.

Six Hours And Ten Minutes After Landing

T HE WATER hits me like a concrete floor.
It buffets the side of my head.

I almost lose consciousness.

But I pull myself back.

Silence dominates everything now.

Only dampened, distant echoes of propellers skipping along.

The water is strangely cold.

The pain in my calf dims down to a dull throb.

I sink my teeth into my lip.

Feel me and AA sink down, into the murky depths.

I managed to take a quick lungful of air before unceremoni-ously tossing me and AA over the side of the boat. I hope that AA was equally as quick-thinking . . . but whatever drugs he's dosed himself with suggest that, more than likely, he wasn't.

I keep AA tight to my body.

I'm aware of the rope, tethering our boat to the harbour floor.

I grab hold of it.

Feel its rough texture.

I tug myself and AA upwards, closer to our boat.

Making sure to keep us well below the surface.

I take in a little water:

Petrol.

Oil.

Suffocating.

More than anything else, I want to surface.

Spit it out.

But I know that's really not an option right now.

As I cling to AA, I can feel him vaguely kicking his legs.

Although his motion is a long way from being efficient at keeping us afloat, it might just be keeping the two of us from sinking deeper.

From sinking to the harbour bed.

Up above us—*right above our heads*—I can hear talking.

No doubt the soldiers are thoroughly bamboozled.

Trying to work out where we went.

Or maybe—*surely*—they heard the splash.

I keep me and AA down at the base of the boat, stare out through the filmy surface of the harbour water. Can just about make out the blurred figures. Leaning out over the side of the boat.

Indicating.

Pointing off in completely different directions.

I feel the air puffing up—*expanding*—in my chest.

I know that we need to get moving.

With a kick of my legs, I drag AA along in my wake, away from the base of the boat.

And towards the wooden planks of the dock.

Only when I've positioned us well below the shelter of the dock do I risk surfacing us.

I position us right next to one of the thick wooden struts supporting the dock.

Grab hold of it.

Help AA's hands onto it too.

As I surface, I make a point of turning my attention quickly to AA.

Just as I thought, he comes to the surface with not a little drama.

He puffs out the water he inhaled when he went down.

Splutters a little.

To me—beneath the planks of the wooden dock—it sounds almost deafening.

Impossible for anybody standing nearby to miss.

But then, as I slowly absorb my surroundings, bring it all back, I hear the gentle *thrum* of the ship's engines. The chatter and calls between the ship hands.

Some water got caught in my ears while we were under.

I swallow several times.

Try to bring my hearing back.

But fail.

Only when I shake my head—*vigorously*—from side to side, do I finally get myself shot of the trapped water.

When I look to AA, I see that he's grinning from ear to ear.

I roll my eyes at him and turn my attention back upwards.

My hearing back in working order.

The planks above our heads creak.

My heart lodges in my throat for a long second.

I wait for the bullets to come chomping through the planks.

But they don't come.

I taste the revolting oil on my lips.

All those emissions.

This experience is almost enough to turn me into an eco-activist.

I'd need to cut back on my long-haul travel . . .

Me and AA linger there, on the surface of the water.

Both of us stare upwards.

AA now seems to understand the importance of what's going on.

That not only his life but *mine* is on the line.

More creaking above our heads.

I channel into the voices.

They're speaking a language I don't understand.

If I had to guess, I'd say it's French . . . but to say that I'm not a linguist is like saying that I'm not a gourmet chef of international renown.

As I stare upwards, with AA beside me, all wide-eyed and like a puppy dog that needs a rolled-up newspaper across the noggin, I feel my whole body go stiff.

Almost like I anticipate what's going to happen next.

Bang!

Bang!

My heart stops working for a second.

I gulp at air.

Then bring my hand up, out of the water, and cover my mouth with my palm.

I stare through the gaps in the wooden planks.

See the pair of shadows passing above mine and AA's heads.

Finally, when they've gone—when I *think* they've gone—I

bring my hand back down from my mouth. Allow myself to breathe again.

I glance to AA, see that he's staring right back at me.

Neither one of us can believe it.

But neither one of us has to say it . . .

Six Hours And Thirty-Five Minutes After Landing

"**W**HAT'RE YOU checking that for?" AA says, as we walk along the part of the dock leading back up to dry land.

I turn away from my watch. The images of the captain and his grandson lying dead in their boat are still etched on my mind. I give a shrug. "Dunno, I just set a timer—from when we landed . . . I like to check it—to keep my bearings."

"How long's it been, then?"

I tell him.

He flashes his eyes at me. "Fifteen-hour days, huh? I guess Brian's going to have to pay out some serious overtime."

I don't smile at his attempt at a joke because I'm all too aware of the danger of our situation. That there're—*most likely*—militiamen crawling all over this dock, on the lookout for me and AA . . . the *runaways* . . .

This dock having, as it does, the bigger ships, has a better-developed infrastructure.

A sturdier, less-patchy concrete path leading away from the dock.

But that doesn't make walking with my shot-up calf any better.

And it doesn't seem like I can get much in the way of sympathy from AA, either.

Poor me.

There's a large building—glass windows occupy every one of its walls . . . one of those modern monstrosities.

It seems to be the centre of the port.

The boarding hall for the passengers.

Since, beyond, I can only see a sturdy steel gate—manned by several dozen security personnel—I grab hold of AA's shirt and limp us in the direction of the building.

When we enter, there're no questions asked, although there *are* lots of officials buzzing around the place. Most of the officials, however, are staffing the other side of the turnstiles—seeing to the passengers who're about to set sail.

And that's not me and AA.

Not yet.

Not without a penny between us.

But at least AA's still got his pills . . .

Outside the building, I notice the day growing darker—twilight setting in.

The baking humidity present throughout the middle of the day has been completely replaced now by a fresh breeze. It actually sends a chill through me, despite the fleece I'm wearing. And, from the way that AA rubs at his arms, I can see that it cuts through AA just the same.

Not that he'll admit as much, being a *man*.

The road outside the building is tarmacked, and I steer AA

along the long-grassed verges, trying to keep him out of the way of the traffic.

I could *really* do without getting AA—my only kind of ally on this island—from getting smushed by one of the passing trucks. The trucks lug anything from potatoes to freshly cut flowers. And they squirt exhaust all over us, while scattering dust and dirt onto our clothes too.

Just for good measure.

By the time I've got us a good way along the road, and into a wider stretch, I feel my heart hammering in my chest. Beating against my ribs. Making them ache all the more.

I know that it's my body's way of tapping me on the shoulder, waggling its finger and saying, *Uh-uh-uh, Anna. Go and find a doctor for that leg of yours.*

And, believe me, nothing would make me happier than lying down in some hospital bed, and having a squadron of doctors do their *thang* on my calf:

Patch it up. Make it all better.

But, at the same time, I know those dreams are all in vain.

While me and AA remain on the run.

Fugitives on this island.

Brian Mathewson.

And his *bastard* Mathewson Media.

I take the first lane which leads off the main road, dragging AA along behind me.

The lane leads to a small village, nothing more than a petrol station and about a dozen or so houses. The houses are all —*clearly*—DIY jobs, almost all of them cobbled together out of cinderblocks and mortar. Their roofs are made of corrugated steel—just as rusted up as those warehouses me and AA passed through at the other dock.

Up ahead, an old black woman trudges about her home, a cut-in-half, transparent plastic bottle filled with water in her hand. She's going about watering her plants, all of which stand up against the exterior wall of her home. Her home itself isn't much bigger than a garden shed.

She wears a simple, pink-patterned sundress; a pair of leather-strapped sandals on her calloused feet. Her hair is drawn up into a bun onto the crown of her scalp.

As she ditches the current load of water all over a plant— which I'm fairly sure I identify correctly as a *spider* plant—I speak to her.

"Excuse me?" I say, trying my best to strike a balance between the politeness needed here and the desperation which seeps out of my skin. "May we come in?"

The old woman glances up at me.

I see that she wears a pair of thick, plastic-framed glasses which she pushes back up the bridge of her nose as she takes me and AA in.

I know that the two of us must be *Quite a Sight* . . . our sodden clothes now having dried, and no doubt stinking of all the oil and grease dumped into the harbour.

The old woman cocks her head to one side.

And then she breaks out in the widest smile. "Of course you can," she says, and then flaps her arm at me and AA. "You come right along in now."

I glance to AA.

AA glances to me.

And surely we're thinking the same thing.

Thank *God* for good people.

Seven Hours After Landing

THE OLD LADY'S HOUSE is no larger than a pair of rooms. There's an outhouse a few paces out of the back door. The old lady introduces herself as Sandra and tells us to call her, simply, 'Sandy'.

When I explain that we're broke, and that we're lost, the old lady offers us the use of her phone, so that we might call a hotel.

With a quick glance to AA, I tell the old lady that we're not being put up in a hotel—*a half-truth*—and that I can't recall either the name or the address of where we're staying. I assure her that by daylight, me and AA will quite easily manage to find our way back to where we're staying.

It surprises me that the old woman, Sandy, gives us another easy smile and then offers us the floor of the main room.

The room is a sort of sitting room-kitchen hybrid.

There's a well-beaten, third—*fourth?*—hand sofa where Sandy suggests me and AA lay our heads for the night.

"A veritable matrimonial suite," Sandy says, wishing us a

good night as she slips into the room alongside—her bedroom, I suppose.

I only smile back at her, deciding that now is not the time for me to make some ham-fisted explanation of just what mine and AA's relationship *is*.

Let alone what our occupation is.

I'm comfortable enough with a few cushions from the sofa, and I make my bed near the front door.

When I glance up, across the room, I see the emptied-out, upturned plastic tub where Sandy washed up the dishes.

The little electrical stove, a pair of saucepans:

One saucepan is filled with rice; the other with a thick, well-seasoned, tomato-based stew inside.

I have to admit that Sandy really knows how to lay on the hospitality—I can still taste the rich tomatoey flavour at the back of my throat as I lie myself down.

It might even be enough to take my mind off the blinding pain in my calf muscle.

Thankfully, though, throughout our impromptu dinner, Sandy didn't make any comment about my constant wincing or the sucking of my teeth—only dealing me with a wide smile each time she noticed, apparently taking these reactions of my pain as enjoyment of the food.

Although I usually sleep on my front, that's simply not an option:

My ribs.

And neither is sleeping on my back:

My calf.

So I settle for lying on my side.

I try to ignore the constant flashes of pain.

And AA's snoring.

Fourteen Hours After Landing

W HEN I FEEL THE DAYLIGHT unfurl across my face in the morning, I screw up my eyes to protect myself from the glare. I breathe in the air—already stuffy.

When I glance over to the kitchen area, I see Sandy's already there, at the stove.

Her back to me.

She's heated up some water and she's cleaning something or other in the plastic tub.

I look to my watch.

Can hardly believe I slept seven hours straight.

When I turn to flip a glance at AA, I see that he's still going.

He lies on the sofa, his feet resting on the arm, lips parted, making rasping snoring sounds.

Realising that it's only politeness to do so, I lever myself up onto my elbow, tread over to the sleeping AA and give him a pointed, deliberate jab in the ribs.

AA draws in—*then blows out*—the loudest snore yet before opening his eyes and, immediately, scrabbling about.

Padding the sofa.

As if he might still be back on the boat, floating in the middle of the sea.

When he finally does get his bearings, he looks to me with bleary eyes.

He has dark bags hanging from his eye sockets.

He reaches up and rubs at his temples, then glances at me from out of the corner of his eye. "What time is it?"

To answer that question, I have to look to Sandy.

Who tells us.

Once I've finished updating my watch, I glance to Sandy, around her, and realise that she's now hard at work rolling together some cake type things.

Her hands, all the way up to her forearms, are dusted with flour.

When she drops the first mixture down onto the greased-up frying pan, the smell is damn near impossible to resist.

She finishes up the recipe by cooking us some scrambled eggs too.

She lays the plates down on the coffee table between me and AA before delivering us both some cutlery.

I feel my stomach gurgling away as I set about my breakfast.

And I get it down my gullet almost without fully tasting.

I'm *famished*.

From AA's silence, I can tell that he's similarly occupied.

When we're through with breakfast, I slip AA a glance which says, *We'd better get going*, and he dabs his lips with a paper serviette Sandy gave him.

As Sandy collects up our plates, I offer to help her out with the washing up, and although I expect her to refuse me, she surprises me completely by accepting my help.

"It's good to have another woman 'bout the place," she says. "Another careful, caring touch."

I can only smile at *that* remark.

While AA goes off to 'make use of' the outhouse, I put myself on drying duty, accepting freshly washed plates off Sandy, and then giving them a thorough drying with the tea towel provided. Just standing around sends prickly pains through my calf. I can't say that I'm looking forward all that much to—what promises to be—a long day of walking, and perhaps running, ahead.

Before too long, we've got through the whole lot, aside from a couple of porcelain cups Sandy used for serving coffee.

As I dry up the cups, while Sandy slips out the back, to go pour away the dirty washing-up water, I wonder just what the hell me and AA are going to do next.

We have no money.

We know *nobody* . . . aside from Sandy.

And we're *fugitives* . . . tender prey for the militiamen roaming the island.

Only when Sandy returns, the now-empty plastic washing-up tub dangling from her rubbery fingers, do I remind myself to smile. As Sandy steps past me, sets the now-washed saucepans back down on the stove for use later on, she slips me a quick glance.

"Got something on your mind, child?"

At first, I crush my lips together, not really knowing how I'm supposed to answer the question, but then I turn back to Sandy, smile at her, and say, "Not really—just trying to find the way back to the hotel."

Sandy narrows her gaze. "You told me you weren't staying at no hotel."

My ribcage tightens.

Pain jangles through my body.

All of my nerves seem to fire at once.

I finish up my drying, set the clean-and-dry coffee cup down on the wooden surface. Then I turn to Sandy, look her back in the eye. Almost comically, she rests her knuckles on her hips . . . as if she's a cartoon version of a scorned matron.

"Listen," I say, "those, uh, you know, the *soldiers*."

Sandy's eyes continue to sear holes in my skull.

In the back of my mind, I really hope that AA's going to re-enter the scene sometime soon to take the pressure off. It seems to me that, for pretty much the entirety of this job, the onus has been on *me* to think on my feet. And my feet, or—more precisely—my *calf* is killing me.

Sandy continues to stare at me.

"Well, they're after us—after me and my . . . uh, *boyfriend*."

Sandy keeps up her searing stare for another few seconds and then, with a quick series of blinks, seems to snap out of her daze. She looks away from me, behind me, to the back door.

Perhaps she's worried about AA.

In her outhouse.

Maybe she's thinking about shooting on out there, pinching hold of his ear and leading him off.

Finally, Sandy shifts her gaze back onto me. "You talkin' 'bout Grendelin?"

A buzz runs through my blood—and I can't help but nod

back in reply. "Yes," I say, "that's her name—the name of the leader."

Sandy crushes her lips together and then, behind that closed mouth, grinds her teeth. I can almost see the thoughts firing about her brain as she considers the implications of this . . . of what me and AA are wrapped up in.

Feeling that there's no point holding back now, I say, "We were brought here, by our employer, to this island . . . we don't even know the *name* of the island . . . once we arrived we were apprehended by Grendelin's men, locked up . . . we managed to escape, get a boat out to the port just around the corner."

Sandy continues to stare at me—but not out of disbelief.

More out of severe indifference.

As if she's already heard *far* too much about this Grendelin woman.

The sense that the smallest remark might topple Sandy off the fence, in my favour, leads me to add, "The captain, the man who brought us here, to the port—he and his grandson were killed by Grendelin's soldiers."

Sandy stares back into my eyes.

I try to peer into her soul.

Sandy, finally, turns away from me, makes some minor unnecessary adjustments to the positioning of the saucepans on her stove.

I know I can't rush her.

That I've told her the truth.

That the deception *now* is all out in the open.

"You're soldiers yourselves?" she says, still focussed down on her pots and pans.

I feel my throat tighten. I don't want to lie, but this seems like the easiest way to break the news. "Kind of," I reply.

She gives a nod, in profile, down at her pots and pans. Then she breathes in deeply, taking the air right down to her stomach. She turns on me and, now, I see that there're tears glittering in her eyes. "My son used to serve Grendelin," she says, her voice firm, unshakable, despite the tears dribbling down her cheeks.

Not knowing what to say to this, I only manage a weak smile in response.

Sandy looks beyond me now, and then continues, "He was always a silly boy—a *tearaway*—but I never thought he'd be so *stupid* as to get himself mixed up in all that"—she shakes her head again—"*idiocy*."

"What happened to him?" I say, my throat feeling drier by the second, and that wonderful breakfast threatening to come up at any moment.

Sandy gives a glimmer of a smile, but it soon descends into a frown.

Another tear rolls down her cheek.

"He was killed—*shot*," she adds, looking back to me, snapping her eyes back onto mine.

"I'm sorry," I reply, not knowing what else to say.

Sandy just nods along, to herself, then stares back out the door, out to the sea—twinkling in the early-morning light. "Sure," Sandy says, "I'm sure you're sorry. For you I imagine it'd just be one less of them you have to kill."

"We're not here to kill *anybody*," I say, for the first time in the exchange *surely* able to tell the whole truth without any caveats.

"You said you were soldiers," she replies.

"Not right now," I say. "We're on the run."

There's a long period of silence between the two of us. I have no major urge to break it—it's one of those long-lingering silences where a thousand unsaid words are spoken.

In the end, neither me or Sandy breaks the silence.

It's poor, ignorant AA.

He comes trudging in through the door, fresh from the outhouse; his hair wet from having taken a cold shower. He looks to me, then to Sandy, back to me again, then says, "Well, you got those dishes done in a flash."

08:30 AM

I'M FAIRLY CERTAIN that Sandy will turf us out of her home soon after our conversation, however, instead, she asks me and AA to go out through the back door with her.

Already, I can feel that my calf might give way at any moment.

I force myself not to limp, but have little success.

As I feel the cool breeze coming off the sea against my face— and, on the horizon, muggy clouds looming—I think that Sandy's going to launch some protest about the outhouse. Perhaps she's going to illuminate some sort of discourtesy . . . I mean, another one besides the fact that me and AA *lied* to her . . . tell AA off for leaving the toilet seat up, or something.

However, she paces us past the outhouse, and down a worn-in path which follows the curvature of the downward slope of the hillside.

Heads down towards the beach.

She mumbles to me over her shoulder, in a way which makes

me wonder if she's still thinking straight—if she hasn't begun to lose the plot.

"I have my allotments down here, a little way along now."

And, indeed, Sandy *does* have allotments.

I look to the wooden frame, the neatly dug-out ground, and the sprouting vegetables—or herbs, or whatever they are to my *unculinary* eye.

Sandy halts at the edge of the allotments, casting her eye over them. I wonder if she's going to ask either me or AA to rush back to the house and grab a watering can, or that cut-in-half plastic bottle she was using to water the plants the day before.

I'm not sure my calf would stand up to that.

Standing around is difficult enough without throwing *uphill* into the mix.

But Sandy says nothing.

I slip a glance to AA, who seems to have the same thought on his mind.

That this woman is not—*entirely*—all there.

But, without a word, Sandy shifts away from her allotments, and further down the dirt path leading down the hill. I wonder, a little dizzily, if she's going to take us all the way down to the beach for a morning skinny dip.

That would be hardly appropriate, though, considering the gravity of our previous conversation.

Sandy continues to lead us down the path for another minute or so before we reach a lip.

An edge which simply falls away.

Then my assassin's mind cranks onto the possibility that Sandy has brought me and AA here to *dispose* of us . . . to give us a little prod over the edge and watch us go tumbling.

But that isn't the case either.

Sandy glances back over her shoulder, systematically scanning the hillside above us in a way which will—*surely*—tell anybody watching that we're up to something No Good . . . then again, since I have no idea what Sandy has in mind, I can't really judge whether or not that's the case.

Yet.

"This way," Sandy says, to me and AA, and she sits down on the edge of the earth, indicating for me and AA to do the same.

I've never really been a big fan of heights, but they don't turn me to jelly either.

AA, on the other hand, tends to have more serious issues.

When I glance back to him, see those dim eyes of his, sinking back in their sockets at just the prospect of having to take a tiny leap, I suppose that AA's supplies have run out and he's running on empty now:

Drug-wise.

The path below us is just like the one above.

A simple dirt track.

This one, though, leads off sharply to the left, wrapping back in around the hillside.

Away from the one which Sandy brought us down.

Both me and AA make the jump just fine.

The *crunch* of dirt beneath the soles of our footwear is the only drama.

Oh, that and the *excruciating* pain flashing up my calf.

And, just for good measure, the pinpricks of pain in my ribcage.

I just don't understand how extreme sports people *do it* . . . do they *enjoy* being in pain all the time?

We follow Sandy along the path.

The path remains fairly wide until a point where it becomes *extremely* narrow.

About large enough for us to turn side on and inch our way forward.

Which Sandy ably demonstrates for us.

At the same time, much to AA's concern, the land to our side drops away.

Sharply.

Below, the sea thrashes away against the rocks—a perfect, teal colour, ripped up with white foam. I can't resist glancing back at AA and saying, "Fancy taking a swim?"

He looks very *green* all of a sudden.

Sandy leads us on for another few minutes before she comes to a stop.

At first, observing her looking over the edge, down into the sea below, I believe that she's going to jump. That, for whatever reason, she's brought me and AA out here to *witness* her jump.

Perhaps she sees it as a sort of justice for her son that me and AA—*soldiers, apparently*—might well be implicated in her death.

She doesn't jump, though.

She flashes a quick glance to me and AA, and it's then that I notice the yawning hole in the hillside:

A cave.

Before I can say anything at all, Sandy steps inside.

Me and AA follow soon afterwards.

My heart sticks in my throat for several seconds.

AA might be a fraidy cat when it comes to heights.

But I've never really been one for the dark.

Especially when said darkness involves a likely structurally *unsound* ceiling.

I can almost hear the *rumble* of rocks falling down on us.

It nearly blankets the burning pain in my calf muscle.

Sandy, however, dispels my fear soon after.

She crouches down, and, after a couple of metallic *snicks*, an even, yellow glow emanates out from a gas lamp she holds. It has a glass visor to stop the flame from blowing away in the ocean breeze which sweeps about the cave.

The light brings out the form of the cave around us.

And, at the end, I can already see a large crate.

A crowbar beside it.

She says nothing, she just expects us to follow.

When she arrives at the side of the crate, she lays the gas lamp down, picks up the crowbar and then hands it over to AA. It seems out of place when she shines a smile at the two of us. "Nice to have a big strong man about the place."

AA grips the crowbar, apparently unclear on what to do with it, and then, all at once, he shuffles forwards, jabs the bar in under the lid of the crate, and prises it upwards.

My heart thrums on another couple of beats.

And then it stops altogether.

Although I can only really make out shadows in the cave—in the *crate*—I'm fairly certain of what I'm looking at.

Guns.

Grenades.

Ammunition.

In short, an *armoury*.

Here, in this coastal cave.

I look to AA, and he looks back to me.

Then the two of us look to Sandy for an explanation.

09:37 AM

S ANDY'S SMILE is dimmer now, but still there.

She seems to have a slight twinkle in her eye.

"He never told me 'bout this place, of course, but I knew that whenever he came to see his old mum it wasn't just to have a nice cup of tea." She nods to the crate. "One day, when he came, I followed him along on his merry adventures, and he led me here. To this place. Turns out this was where he kept his *secret* stash . . . at least none of his soldier buddies came to claim it after he died."

AA looks to Sandy, as if asking permission, and then crouches down to the crate. From within, he removes a rifle. He holds it up in his hands, checks to see if it's loaded, then looks back at me confirming that it *is*.

Feeling a little stronger willed, I take my own steps over to the crate.

Peer inside.

There's a few handguns there, for me.

Almost like Christmas has come early.

Like AA before me, I glance to Sandy as if asking for permission.

She just keeps up that same, taking-it-easy smile.

There're even holsters inside.

As me and AA remain shell-shocked at finding this treasure trove, Sandy speaks to us.

"You probably want to know why I brought you down here to see this."

Although neither of us say anything in reply, it's obvious that we do.

Sandy continues, "My son, he never shoulda got himself involved with that Grendelin woman. He shoulda stayed clear. But he never listened to his old mum, that woulda been too uncool, I suppose." She draws in a breath and then goes on, "What I believe of the two of you is that you *are* here to take care of Grendelin, no matter what you say, and that's the only reason why I'm showing you all this here—do you understand me?"

My heart sinks down to my stomach.

I glance to AA.

And I know that, no matter how much we need these weapons, that I simply can't face lying to Sandy again.

It would break my heart.

As if that was the worst of it, I catch Sandy tearing up again.

AA catches my eye, and I give a shake of my head.

But it's too late.

Before I can stop him, AA's blabbing his lips again. "This Grendelin," he says.

Sandy turns her head to him.

"What's she into, here?" AA continues.

Sandy gives him a confused look, screwing up her forehead,

and then shifting a glance off in my direction. Since I can't really say anything *now*, I just give Sandy a smile in return.

Sandy turns back to AA. "Well, she's got just 'bout this entire island all tied up—corrupt, from top to bottom."

Here Sandy's eyes skitter between me and AA, and I get the impression that these are the sorts of things which Sandy wouldn't feel comfortable saying even in her own home.

But we're not in her home now.

We're in this out-of-the-way cave.

Sandy breathes in again, as if it's taking a physical toll on her body to open up to the two of us.

And I have no doubt it *is*.

"There ain't hardly nothing that anybody 'round the island can do with her and her *soldiers*."

If only looks could kill, then I'd be having a *jolly good go* at AA right now.

Who does he think he is?

Dragging up this old woman's memories?

Making her *uncomfortable* . . .

And yet, I can't bring myself to say anything to stop it.

Maybe that's what makes me a bad person.

AA pays me no attention, and turns back to Sandy. "Just out of interest, does Grendelin run any sort of *security* for foreign visitors to the island?"

It's right then that the penny drops with me—when I realise *exactly* where AA is headed with this. He's trying to tie this back to our noble employer.

To Brian Mathewson.

Sandy's eyes widen. She nods her head. "Of course, there's folks who bring their money here—who want to hide it for tax purposes. Those people often need an escort they can rely on."

AA shuts one eye now, really going Columbo on everyone's asses . . . if he keeps up this act then I'll need to give him another well-deserved thump in the arm. "And is there a specific area where those sorts tend to hang out?"

Sandy looks to me, and then back to AA. "Of course," she replies. "There's a part of the island where they all have their residencies." Her features darken for several seconds, and then she says, "Where Grendelin lives, *too*."

AA has the cheek—*here*—to actually give a wide smile, as if he's some sort of shit-hot police officer who's just managed to crack a tough case. "You think you could show us how to get there?"

10:09 AM

A A CAN BE FULL of himself at the best of times.
Now, though, he's positively *bursting* at the seams.

As I bring up the rear, my shot-through calf muscle still causing me serious grief, I can only listen to him chirping away in Sandy's ear.

Questioning her on all the intricacies of the island's geography.

I just concentrate on not screaming out in pain from the gunshot wound to my calf muscle.

From the crate, I grabbed a couple of .45 calibre handguns— holsters too—while AA strapped a rifle to his back and then brought his fleece down over the top.

Subtlety is an underrated virtue.

I think he snagged a couple of hand grenades too.

When we get back up to Sandy's house—but not without a great deal of pain for me—we draw all the curtains and then spread our arms on the floor of the room where we slept the night before.

Sandy, perhaps reasonably, doesn't want anything to do with this, and she disappears into the other room of her house while me and AA see to our weapons.

The firearms are in the condition you might expect from them having been left outside—in the sea air.

It takes me and AA about ten minutes to know what we're dealing with.

Understandably, there's very little in the way of maintenance we can do here, in Sandy's house. There aren't any cans of lubricant lying about the place so we can get things slick and *slidy*.

But we'll just have to make do.

Me and AA stash our respective weapons.

And then I call Sandy back inside once the guns are out of sight.

All of a sudden, Sandy seems somewhat nervous, and I can't really blame her either. But she outlines how we can catch a bus from 'just up the road' . . . it's to be the number seven, and we need to ask the driver to take us to the end of the line. There we'll pick up *another* bus; the number twenty-six.

That'll take us all the way to the beach.

At the end of the beach—and Sandy's very clear on this point—we'll come across an enormous, *towering* cinderblock wall. It's behind that wall where the *affluents* hang out.

All the luxury apartment blocks.

The twisting, twirling exotic gardens.

She points us in the direction of Grendelin's apartment, gives us the address.

The location which, it follows, will lead us to Brian Mathewson.

Or so goes the hope.

As we go about our plotting and planning, Sandy cooks us up *yet another* storm. Me and AA hungrily stuff it down our throats. When me and AA make movements about getting ready to shift off and catch these buses, Sandy stops us.

Tells us that we need to wait a little while.

That it's still too light out.

She suggests that we take a *siesta*.

And, to be honest, I can't see all that much *wrong* with that plan.

17:32 PM

ALTHOUGH IT'S A LONG WAY from being dark outside, Sandy allows me and AA out of her house. But not before she's handed over a piece of paper with her email address on it.

Telling me to write her.

That's perhaps the hardest lie to tell, because I know that it's going to be unlikely that either me—or AA, for that matter—come back alive from this latest of follies.

But there's no other way to do it.

If me and AA *do* catch a boat or—*better*—a flight back home, then it'll only be for us to become entangled with Brian once again . . . and by entangled I mean *killed*.

Out on the road, I feel the gentle throb down in my calf muscle.

When AA sees me limping, he offers me some of his painkillers.

I look at the plastic bottle he holds out to me and then sneer.
"Nah," I say, "wouldn't want to deprive you."

AA gives me a smirk in return. "I'm not taking these anymore
—need my mind sharp, need to be at the top of my game." He
breaks out in a full-hearted *ironic* grin. "Wouldn't want to miss
our stop."

I roll my eyes at him, and we plod on.

Me in intense pain.

AA in intense self-love.

19:18 PM

G ETTING THE BUS is not difficult, and the transitions
go smoothly.

All in all, it takes us just under two hours to arrive.

And, outside, as Sandy informed us, it's already dark.

Only moonlight now.

The perfect cover for the would-be assassin.

Now if only me and AA can sort out all those *other* details.

Like how we're going to deal with this dirty, great big
concrete wall facing us.

I glance along the beach, all pebbles. The waves of the grey
sea wash in gently, stirring the stones, sweeping them in, and then
back out again. On the horizon, I make out the haunted silhou-
ettes of enormous boats—*ocean liners*—looming, making slow
progress.

As my eyes trail along the coastline, I see that the concrete
wall cuts across the beach.

That the wall heads out to the sea.

Keeping the plebs in their place.

I glance to AA, see that he's fiddling away with something on his belt. He has a handgun himself, of course, along with that rifle he has concealed beneath his fleece.

When he meets my eye, I expect him to flick me one of those award-winning smiles of his.

To shoot me a smirk.

Taking the piss out of me for being anxious.

Anxious about killing our employer.

Anxious about killing Brian Mathewson.

But he doesn't.

He only gives me a stern expression.

Then turns back to his waistline.

Up ahead, I can see that there's an opening in the concrete wall—that there's a pair of guards there, occupying a booth illuminated with an orange glow.

A steel barrier on a mechanical arm hangs down in the gap.

Both guards look well-armed.

Try as I might, the thought of killing one of them sends chills through my blood.

Perhaps that's some sort of sign.

Or maybe I'm just getting out of practice.

Once AA's through with his preparations down at his waistline, he gives me a dour nod, and—accordingly with the plan—I reach up and use him as a crutch.

As me and AA trudge towards the concrete wall, I feel my calf muscle burning with pain, despite the support I get from AA. My ribcage feels tight, and my breathing comes slow and shallow. But I warn myself off pity—telling myself that I can't afford to spend so much time thinking about *my own* body . . . beyond keeping it quiet.

I need to get the job done.

What might be my final job.

What might be mine *and* AA's final job.

As the two of us approach the booth, the guards up ahead, I can already feel their eyes upon us.

That they're just *resting* their hands on top of the grips of their handguns.

Just making sure that their weapons are within reach if and when they require them.

And although it feels about as natural as setting a knife blade beneath the surface of my skin, I force a smile onto my lips. Show off some teeth as we get closer to the guards.

I'm aiming for a 'polite grimace'.

An expression which will show off my pain, and yet, at the same time, my British grit at not wanting to show anything *imprudent* to a stranger.

The guards don't smile back at me—or AA.

They stand their ground.

I can smell the bitter scent of exhaust, drifting in with the evening breeze, off the sea.

All mixed up with the salted air.

My mouth feels drier than ever, and the taste of the beans and rice which Sandy prepared for us—and which I pushed about a mile around the periphery of my plate—seems long forgotten.

My stomach stirs.

And my calf muscle *burns* with pain.

"Evenin'," one of the guards says.

I manage to keep up my grimace-cum-smile, and AA keeps up his support, so that I can keep my affected calf muscle from making me *scream*.

The guard who greeted us gives a slight smile—something between amusement and caution.

I can see that his companion has none of the attributes of the former.

He stands on the shoulder of the first guard, his hand now completely wrapped around the grip of the handgun at his belt.

I feel another hot surge through my blood.

"Just heading back to the hotel," AA says.

The unsmiling guard leans into the smiling one.

I can't help but feel that, during the day, it'd be no trouble for two *white* people such as me and AA to stroll right through the gate.

At night, though, it's a different prospect.

Everybody's a potential threat.

I also get the impression that, had the smiling guard been the only one on duty tonight, me and AA would've had little trouble passing through.

However, as it is, the unsmiling guard is here too.

The smiling guard dials down his smile a few notches. "And which hotel's that?"

AA nods to me, as if he's answering the question. "We were down on the beach earlier," he says. "She tripped and fell. Silly cow," he adds, off the cuff.

Despite the situation, I feel a slight sting at AA's little quip.

The smiling guard just keeps on smiling. "Of course," he says. "And soon as you let me know the name of your hotel I'll get you an ambulance."

My stomach suddenly dips down low, because I know there's no other way.

That, if we're going to take care of Brian—*stop* his games once and for all—there's going to be more death.

There's no need for so much as a mumbled word between me and AA.

19:35 PM

S INCE NEITHER me or AA have suppression of any kind for our weapons, there's a pair—a *trio*, actually—of quite loud *bangs*.

My skin tingles all over for a long period.

And my heart bobbles up to the pit of my throat.

I turn my head in the direction of the guard booth, see that there's a radio walkie-talkie sitting up there, on the counter. I can hear it spout static.

After a single look to AA, each of us takes a guard's body each, and we drag them into the booth.

Keeping them concealed for the time being . . . for whatever it's worth.

With AA in the lead, I stumble along behind him—no pretence for me to use him as a crutch any longer. AA still has his gun drawn, and down at his side.

He moves swiftly through the darkened, deserted streets.

I can't help but feel just a shade creeped out.

Something about the streets being all deserted only a little after seven in the evening sends a chilly sensation down my spine. It speaks to me about only one thing—*a fact perhaps* . . . that we're treading on dangerous ground.

Thankfully, some way in the distance, I can hear the gentle *burble* and *grind* of music coming from one of the apartment blocks which towers above.

The storefronts, too: hair salons, mini supermarkets, a café or two, are all just as deserted as the streets themselves.

When AA stops on the corner up ahead, steps into the shadows of a doorway, I arrive at his side.

I take the opportunity to run my hand down the back of my calf, attempting to massage any feeling at all into my aching, torn-up flesh. As if I'm looking for an explanation, AA leans into me and whispers, "Off season. Place is a graveyard this time of year." He taps the side of his nose. "Give it a week, or so, and the place'll be crawling."

I feel more tightness in my chest.

My mind spins back to what the doctor told me.

How I'm supposed to 'avoid stressful or straining situations'.

So that my ribs might heal properly.

I wonder what he'd say about my shot-up calf . . . probably something along the lines of whatever he told AA about his shot-up side.

When I turn to AA now, I see that he's unconsciously stroking his side; that affected part of his body. I have to admit that he's actually been somewhat *quiet* about his own affliction.

He's hardly uttered a word about his injury.

He holds his gun down by his side, and then tilts his head back, indicating the apartment block just ahead. "This's it," he says.

Grendelin's home.

I stare past AA, off towards the apartment block, and I see the sprawling, lush garden, growing a little wild. I get the impression that, no matter how bad the need for clean, drinking water might get on this island at times, that this garden will always be in its same, bristling, *healthy* condition.

Just like all the other buildings in this sector of the island, the lighting is extremely minimal. Maybe a bulb lit—here or there—and a security guard folded up at a desk, leafing through a magazine or newspaper. Or else tapping away at the screen of a mobile phone.

This place *is* just like a graveyard.

Eerie.

With a glance to AA, we move out.

Move in on the target's location.

19:49 PM

O F COURSE we don't go in through the front door of the
block of apartments.

When I peer in through the glass, I can see a light lit somewhere near the back of the reception. No sign of a guard
anywhere, though.

AA leads me around the building, down a side alley, to a
door there.

The service entrance.

No handle on the outside, though.

So maybe more of a service *exit*.

The air smells warm, and stale, of a slightly sweet mixture of
sewage and rotting waste.

This's where all the rich people throw their crap out.

I can feel the pain tingling through my entire body—up from
my calf muscle—and it seems to occupy everything in my mind.
The best I can do to fight the pain, to *control* the pain, is to simply
shove it to the back of my brain.

And that leaves the current task to AA.

Without too much hesitation, though, he appears to come up with a solution. He says nothing to me as he grips hold of a plastic refuse container on wheels, and then hoiks himself up onto it. He glances back at me, and I wonder if he's got another quip prepared—something about me being a liability—but his eyes slip quickly past, almost as if I'm not even there.

His hands reach out.

Dig in around the edges of a hatch.

That's something *both* me and AA are familiar with.

19:54 PM

F OR A DIZZY MOMENT, I believe that AA's going to leave me out in the side alley—with the sweet-smelling rotten waste.

But, just when I feel another flash of pain through my calf muscle, the service door creaks open.

He arrives in the gap, the rifle now over his shoulder.

No need to hide it any longer, apparently.

I step in over the threshold of the service entrance, and into the darkness.

At first it's disorientating. I feel as if the whole world is spinning around me. I take deep breaths, try to ward away the constant pain in my calf muscle. And the ache in my ribs. To make myself feel better, I unclip my holster, bring the handgun out, smoothly.

The darkness seems to wash in over us.

I lean forwards, drop my voice to a whisper in AA's ear. "Where's the guard?" I say.

Without missing a beat, AA replies, "Dead."

Another chill passes through me.

Just how many dead bodies will it take to stop Brian Mathewson?

As we trudge on into the darkness, AA adds, "Only it wasn't me who killed him."

Another tingle of pain passes through my ribcage.

And a fresh *jab* in my calf muscle.

20:03 PM

A A SEEMS TO KNOW where he's going, which, to me, means that he heads straight for the staircase. I tag along at his heels like some sort of faithful dog. I sincerely hope that nobody watches CCTV footage of the two of us at the moment, not only because they'll most likely be an *armed* guard, but also because it'll make it seem as if *I'm* following AA's lead.

As if AA's the one in charge here.

When the truth is far bleaker.

That neither one of us—neither me *or* AA—really knows what we're doing.

I'm thankful for the trainers which Brian Mathewson saw fit to equip us with for the job—for Hell Bird—because they serve me and AA now, by keeping our footsteps totally quiet.

Just as Sandy told us, we go up to the fifth floor of the apartment block.

Nobody stops us . . . but, then again, as AA mentioned, the guard is dead.

I glance up at the etched, brass plaques on the doors, each of them marking out the apartment number. I skim through my mind, picking out the number which Sandy told us would be Grendelin's residence.

I breathe in deeply, and then, off in the shadows of the corridor—the long, *apparently endless*, corridor—I see movement.

Without a word, I reach out, grab hold of AA's sleeve.

Get his attention.

"What?" he says, his voice muffled, his rifle in his hands.

"Over there," I say. "I saw somebody moving."

AA's eyes sketch the dark. He purses his lips.

As the two of us stare out into the darkness, I hear a familiar voice.

"Anna," it says. "It's me."

Amy.

Amy Douglas.

20:08 PM

I LOOK TO AA for what to do, but he remains totally still, continuing to grasp his rifle.

He doesn't yet bring the sight up to his eye.

Aim a shot into the shadows.

From where Amy Douglas spoke to us.

I feel my calf muscle stiff now—the pain dulls to nothing but a distant throb.

Seeing that AA won't do anything, I bring up my own gun.

Aim into the darkness.

Wait to see a *scrap* of movement again.

Something which'll give away Amy's location.

My heart beats at double time.

And my whole body feels numb all of a sudden.

It's then that I know I can't do it.

That I won't *be able* to do it.

Enough killing . . . enough of it . . . now . . .

A shot fires out from beside me.

AA.

Out of surprise, I don't look in the direction of the shot, I look back at AA.

His features are fixed.

Stern.

He grasps his rifle so tight that his knuckles have turned white.

My eyes trace the barrel of the rifle, and then scout off into those shadows.

At the end of the corridor.

There was no reaction.

No dry *thump*.

No falling body.

And—*certainly*—no scream of pain.

Apparently noticing this as well as I do, AA brings the rifle sight back up to his eye. He stares along the barrel. Not thinking, I reach out, grab hold of his arm, tug it hard.

He fires off another shot.

It hits the ceiling.

Brings down a rain of white plaster.

Artificial snow.

To begin with, it's impossible to see anything but the flurry of plaster.

I let go of AA, bring the neck of my shirt up to cover my mouth and nostrils.

Try to get some breaths of air.

Finally, I manage to get hold of myself once more.

To restore some sense of situation and urgency.

Amy—out there—in the dark.

In the falling plaster flakes.

With a quick glance to AA, and seeing that he's done with his shooting for the time being, I turn my attention back to the shadows at the end of the corridor. "Amy?" I say. "Amy, are you okay?"

No reply.

A thousand visions flash through my brain—all those eventualities:

Amy's body all crumpled up, on the hallway carpet.

Limbs sprawled.

Blond hair tousled.

Her chest a crater.

I leave AA behind, stagger off into the shadows.

I almost trip right over her crouching body.

Nothing more than a form in the gloom.

It takes my eyes a moment to adjust.

She still holds her arms up over her head.

Protecting herself from the still-falling debris.

Finally, with a tenderness I never knew I possessed, I reach out for her, touch her lightly on the shoulder. Slowly, gently, she tilts her head up to me.

I see the fright in her eyes—in her *little girl's* eyes.

And then I see it, my gun: *Punisher*, which she cradles in her arms like a baby.

If she'd wanted to, she could've shot the both of us.

She has the skills, no doubt.

But she didn't.

AMY WEARS THE SAME CLOTHES she had on during the flight: the tracksuit top over a pair of jeans. As AA approaches us, comes up on our heels, I can't help spinning around to confront him. "What the *hell* were you doing?" I say, in a strained whisper. "Couldn't you tell it was Amy?"

In the gloom, AA says, "I thought you said she wasn't to be trusted—that she was *lying?*"

"No," I reply, "I said that *one* of you two is lying."

That shuts AA up for the time being and he makes do with shifting the strap of his rifle back over his shoulder, staring off along the corridor, into the shadows:

In the direction of our target's apartment.

Of Grendelin's apartment.

"Come on," I say, reaching a hand out to Amy.

She accepts my offer, and I help her to her feet.

When she's there, she looks me in the eye and says, "He's right, Anna, I lied to you." She takes a sharp breath which makes

280

me think—*for a shocking moment*—that AA might've caught her with a bullet after all. "About getting on the plane." She looks away from me for a second, over my shoulder, back to AA —*apparently*. "I wanted you to think that I'd broken things off with my dad completely, that I wasn't having any more contact with him." She looks me right in the eye. "But that wasn't quite the truth."

"Are you working for him now?" I say, my tone deadpan, my fingertips, almost unconsciously, brushing the grip of my gun.

She gives a vigorous shake of the head. "No," she replies.

I look to AA, see that, already, he's eyeing up the corridor, as if he's thinking about investing in a place here, in this apartment block, when we're through with the job.

"Hey?" I say. "Numbnuts? Are you still on planet Earth?"

AA glances back at me.

Unsmiling.

And—even though it's dark, I'm *sure*—a touch green.

"Why isn't anyone coming?" he says.

Amy, standing beside me, and now turning *my* gun *Punisher* over in her hands, checking that everything's in working order, says, "I killed the guard."

"Yeah," AA says, a slightly sarcastic *twang* to his words, "we *saw* that." He glances back along the corridor, then says, "Why aren't any of the residents coming out?"

"Holiday time," Amy replies. "Most people are out of town —there *aren't* hardly any residents in this building. Grendelin has the entire building on lockdown."

AA paces back towards us, fixes his glare on Amy. "And how come you knew right where to come—that we would be here?"

Amy smirks a touch. "I've been keeping an eye on you—an ear to the ground."

"What does that mean?" AA says, with added venom.

As I watch AA and Amy go about this verbal joust, I can't help but feel slightly glad that, the way they're acting towards one another is either a *great* acting performance, or it's the confirmation I've been looking for which confirms they're very much at odds.

That they're *not* working together.

"You wanted to get to Brian," Amy says, checking over her gun—*my gun*. "And if you want to get to Brian, then you needed to get to Grendelin." She gives a slight yawn, as if this whole episode is boring her somehow. "So I simply staked out this building—Grendelin's home."

"Yeah," I say, seeing the hole in Amy's story, "but that doesn't explain how you *knew* where Grendelin lived."

Amy gives a shrug, then a smile, which seems out of place in the gloomy, deserted corridor. "Listen," she says, "I've been coming here my entire life—my dad's holiday destination of choice . . . for *obvious* reasons. Throughout my childhood, my visits here, I got to know her almost as *Auntie* Grendelin—she was always in and around, invited us here, to her place, more than a dozen times for parties."

I exchange a glance with AA, then turn back to Amy. "And how come you've decided you have no trouble killing her?"

Amy's smile fades completely now. "You don't know what's she's into—I mean, apart from running protection for Brian Mathewson whenever he comes to visit the island."

She gives a slight shake of her head, and glances out a window, down into the deserted street outside.

"She keeps this whole island terrorised—under the radar; apparently *undiscovered*. She goes about recruiting young men and women for her army. I can still remember, even though I was a child, walking about the beach with my father, *Auntie* Grendelin tagging along."

Her features darken.

"Just to think of the expressions on the faces of the street vendors—those trying to make a living—as we passed by, all the free things which they gave us without so much as a word, and often with a *bow*."

Amy gives a shake of her head.

"No, I wasn't so naïve"—she glances up at us again, her sapphire eyes an icy fire—"I knew a bully when I saw one, and I know a bully when I see one *now*."

There's a long pause in the conversation.

I listen hard for any sound in the apartment block.

But the entire place seems dead to the world.

"Care to prove it?" AA puts in, finally breaking the silence.

"Prove *what?*" Amy says.

"That you can *kill* her," AA replies, matter-of-factly.

Amy turns on AA, nostrils flared, teeth bared, in a way which makes me wonder if she's going to tear out his throat. "You know that security guard down in the reception?"

Neither me or AA reply.

"I used to know him as Uncle Roger."

20:29 PM

A MY GOES ON to explain how she's been staked out in this apartment block for the past few hours, waiting for me and AA to show up.

So that she could *kill* 'Uncle Roger'.

She makes a quip about thinking that we were *never* going to show up at all, and I try not to take it too personally. As a declaration of her supreme intelligence over us.

She goes on to say that she took up a vantage point, high up in the apartment block, and that she kept an eye on the gate to the secure section of the island. She saw—*very well*—how me and AA dealt with the security guards there.

Which means, more than likely, somebody else saw us too.

Time, as seems to have been the case all through this 'job', seems to be limited.

I glance along the dead, deserted corridor, and then look back to Amy.

"Grendelin," I say, "is she along here—is that her apartment up there?"

Amy smirks as she shakes her head.

"Seems like you two are dealing with some out-of-date info."

I exchange glances with AA, not really sure what to make of this slight. It seems to me—from *my* perspective—that me and AA have done the very best we possibly could with the information we've been given . . . which, to be honest, has been somewhat *Spartan* . . .

"Tell me she's at least in this building?" I say.

Amy gives a slight smile.

It warms my cold little heart just a touch.

"Oh," Amy says, "of course she is."

"Whereabouts?" AA puts in.

Amy jerks her head upwards, in the direction of the ceiling.

"You probably just went and shot through her floor."

20:33 PM

W HY DOESN'T IT surprise me that Grendelin occupies the penthouse apartment of the building?

. . . I mean, any crime lord—*dame?*—worth her weight in gold would surely make sure they had some decent digs.

Thinking about it from a crime lord's perspective, of course.

Amy goes ahead of us, taking the stairs which lead up to the sixth—and top—floor of the building.

I stay beside AA, using the banister probably as much as someone twice my age.

But, then again, I don't imagine most people twice my age have cracked ribs and a shot-through calf muscle.

I tell myself that I'm going to be playing the backup role here —it's better for me to hang back, and trust in Amy and AA's skills. They can do all the heavy lifting, leaving me to do the extra stuff if and when required.

On the top floor, I find myself almost knocked over by the incredible view.

Windows all around.

Giving a view out onto the surrounding area.

The darkened streets.

I realise now, having had a chance to get my breath back, that only every third streetlamp is lit.

I suppose that—despite the comparative luxury of this cordoned-off section of the island—there's still somebody exercising thriftiness with respect to the electricity bill.

I turn back to AA and Amy, see that they're approaching the walnut double doors to Grendelin's penthouse suite.

I feel my heart stick in my throat.

Something about this just *feels* wrong.

Totally *wrong*.

Amy sidles up to the card scanner beside the door. She digs deep down in her jeans pocket and produces a plastic card. As she grips tight to it, she hesitates.

Finally, she glances back over at me.

Our eyes cross, and then, without a word, she pads over.

Holds out her gun—*my gun*—Punisher, for me to take.

I screw up my eyes. "Backing out after all?" I say.

Amy ignores my comment, and glances down at the gun hanging in the holster at my belt. "Do a swap?" she says.

Not seeing any harm in it—unless this is some sort of a swindle job, Amy having *done* something to my gun—I allow her to slip my gun out of its holster.

She slips *Punisher* into the now-empty holster, and takes the .45 I salvaged from the cave near Sandy's house.

While this exchange takes place, I'm very aware of AA keeping his eyes fixed on Amy at all times. And I know that, if Amy *does* try anything, then AA's got my back.

Just like I told myself when I was climbing the stairs, I'm very much going to be an *extra* here.

A hired gun to fall back on.

With everybody apparently satisfied—*as prepared as they're going to get*—Amy approaches the door once again.

The card in her hand.

She swipes it against the scanner.

The gleaming red light turns green.

And the door slides back into the wall.

20:37 PM

I STAND MY GROUND, allowing AA and Amy to form the frontal assault.

Again, the pain in my calf muscle has subsided, been replaced by a dull ache. But every time I put one foot in front of the other, something within my brain seems to tell my body to expect a bone-shaking pain.

It's a hard thought to get shot of.

As I cross the threshold, several paces behind AA and Amy, I immediately breathe in the thick scent of wilted flowers—that dead, *too-sweet* scent.

On some level, it reminds me of the stink of sewage.

I stalk on into the penthouse, already aware of the windows in the apartment, the ones which also offer a great view of the cordoned-off zone of the island.

And, I notice, the gates.

From here—if Grendelin's even at home—she would've seen

that little trick me and AA pulled on the guards . . . if a pair of headshots can be euphemistically referred to as a 'trick' . . .

I tread forwards, onto a thick, fuzzy carpet: the colour of sand dollars.

I take in the sitting room: flat-screen TV; a long, luxurious sofa; and a hefty oak coffee table with magazines neatly stacked on top.

I breathe in those wilted flowers again, feel them cause the back of my throat to tingle. And my sinuses to well up. I never was much good with pollen, or whatever the hell it is about flowers which brings me out in a rash and a runny nose.

I stand still, in the sitting room, my gun dangling down at my thigh.

I can just about hear the footsteps of AA and Amy off in the distance, can hear them prowling about the bedrooms. Already, though, I've reached the decision that Grendelin's not going to be here.

That we 'just missed her'.

And I wonder what implications that'll have for tracking down Brian Mathewson.

Make it almost impossible, I imagine.

Someone calls out.

AA.

All the hair on my arms stands up straight.

My heart jiggles about in my chest.

Knocks against my ribs.

All of a sudden, my feet feel light, and I bring my gun up, into a ready position.

Ready to kill.

As I pace along the corridor, in the direction of AA's voice, I catch sight of a full-length, gilt-edged mirror. I look at my reflection, see the withered woman staring back at me.

The deep, pitted cheeks.

The saggy bags hanging down from each of my eye sockets.

I wonder, just for a moment, what Mark sees in me.

What *anybody* sees in me.

I look so tired—so *fed up*.

I suppose that's what working for Brian Mathewson does to a girl.

I almost walk right past the bedroom where AA called me from.

All the lights are off—and I can just about make out a pair of shadowy figures.

My mind snaps onto them.

One stands:

AA.

The other sits on the bed:

Grendelin.

As I stand there, in the doorway of the bedroom, I hear footsteps approaching me from the side, and I turn my head to see Amy, stalking through the hallway.

"Clear," she says, to me, her voice near a whisper.

I say nothing in reply, only turning back to the bedroom.

And the shadowy figures.

AA and Grendelin.

I reach out and flip the light switch.

All of a sudden, a bright yellow glow floods the room.

My attention is drawn upwards—to the upturned lightshade, elephants stencilled on around the rim, each using its trunk to hold the one preceding by its tail.

I flip back down.

To Grendelin.

She wears a nightgown: sleek, silvery satin. It shows off her broad, muscular ebony shoulders. She tilts her head in my direction, a slight smile tracing her lips.

"Anna," she says, "nice to see you again."

I exchange glances with AA, and then look back to Amy, usher her into the room.

We all stand around Grendelin.

Waiting for answers.

Since nobody else pitches in, I decide that I should be the one putting the first foot forward, and so I say, "Where's Brian Mathewson?"

Grendelin stays still for a long moment, perched on the edge of the squashy bed.

I look to the bedside table and see that one of the drawers is half open:

A handgun visible within.

AA arrived just in time.

Grendelin gazes up at me with a broad smile. "I was very disappointed that you decided *against* my offer," she says. "It really could've been quite a convenient arrangement."

I think about this cordoned-off area of the island, and get a chill up my spine just to imagine inhabiting one of these long-abandoned apartment complexes . . .

More than I could bear.

Not that I say any of this to Grendelin.

From what I've garnished so far, she's very much my adversary.

The last thing I want to do is play into her hands.

"Where's Brian?" I put to her again, determined not to allow her to throw me off course.

Grendelin gives a slight pout as she stares right back into my eyes—a *searing* gaze.

"What time is it?"

My chest tightens. Pain tingles through my ribs. "What?" I say.

She rolls her eyes. "Look at your watch and tell me."

I DO.

    And this only makes Grendelin smile all the more.

She gives a shake of her head. "Already gone," she says.

"What?" I say, already feeling my hand begin to tremble.

I know that's not a good position to find myself in.

Not while holding a gun.

I need to calm down.

Take deep breaths.

"What'd you *mean* he's gone?" I say.

Grendelin turns her head to look out the window, to the skyline beyond, the sea stretching to the horizon, and the ghostly forms of the ships still trucking along . . . into the night.

"You didn't think he'd arrived here to take up residence, did you?"

Of course I didn't—not that I say so.

Grendelin continues, "By your watch, his flight will've departed about ten minutes ago." She turns back to me, her chocolate-brown eyes meeting mine. "You won't catch him even if you run," she says, with a wry smile.

My heart beats harder still.

I hear the percussive *thump-thump* of my pulse in my temples.

I scold myself—over and over again—all that wasted time, all the time which me and AA spent trying to get here, to Grendelin's apartment.

If only we'd arrived a little before, then we might've made it.

In the end, AA speaks out.

"Don't believe her," he says, and then waves his handgun in her face. "Tell us where Brian Mathewson is or this"—I guess he means the *bullet*—"goes in your eye."

"No, Adam!" Amy pipes up.

Both me and AA look in her direction, almost as if we're surprised she's still here in the room with us.

For a long—*terrible*—second, I'm convinced that Amy's going to take this opportunity to shoot.

To perform her last turncoat act.

But her gun remains down in her grip, pointed at the floor, away from me and AA.

Amy stares long and hard at Grendelin, and I wonder if there's some sort of recognition there—I wonder just how well these two are acquainted these days.

Finally, Amy says, "I know, from my dad, he said he was going to catch a plane tonight. He'll have left with Brian." She looks to AA and Grendelin. "My dad—his loutish friends—they're Brian's security now, they'll be the ones keeping him safe."

My mind wheels and spins at this turnaround.

Although I tell myself that I need to think of a way to turn the situation to my advantage, I also know that I need to *understand* the situation before I can think of that.

And, for me—*right now*—the whole matter is as thick as mud.

AA looks to me for answers, which, under the circumstances, seems *really* the wrong direction entirely. "What'd we do now, Anna?"

20:59 PM

THAT'S THE QUESTION.

And I don't have an answer.

But we can hardly stay here, in this Mexican standoff situation.

I glance to Grendelin's bedside table drawer and, quickly, instruct Amy to remove the gun from within. She does as I say.

I know the gesture is most likely in vain.

That, if Grendelin is anything like me, then she'll have a whole cache of guns scattered around her bedroom so that—like a rat—she'll never be more than a few metres from one.

The next step seems obvious. I gesture for Grendelin to get up off the bed.

She does as I say, stepping into the doorway—awaiting my next order.

I have to think it over first.

Then decide.

"AA," I say, "keep your eye on her—don't let her go running off, okay?"

AA gives me a nod in reply. I can't help feeling a slight warmth knowing that *I'm* in control here. "Amy," I say, turning back to her, "you go out ahead—all right? Make sure the coast's clear."

With a nod, Amy slips past Grendelin in the doorway.

Goes out into the corridor.

That leaves me to bring up the rear.

"All right," I say. "Let's head out."

"Anna?" AA says, cocking his head back to me.

"Yeah?"

"Where're we going?"

I feel that same tightness in my ribs again—the prickle of pain passing through my chest.

But I brush it off.

"Just do as I say."

21:03 PM

S LOWLY, we make our way along the corridor, and towards the exit of the penthouse. I know that we can't simply *slip out* now . . . even if Brian Mathewson is several thousand kilometres up in the air. The second we release Grendelin, the second *any one* of us takes our eyes off her, is the moment we lose control.

When Grendelin—*no doubt*—dials up her oh-so-obedient militiamen and has them come to bear on us.

And, for as long as we can manage, we need to resist that.

We pass by the sitting room. Something seems off.

A little voice at the back of my brain says, *Hey, Anna, take a look over there.*

And, when I do, look out the window of the sitting room, to the building opposite, I'm just about in time to see the flash.

Up in one of the windows of the building.

I hear the *crunch* of breaking glass.

A second later and I tell everyone to get down.

To get *the hell* down.

21:05 PM

_____

W E'RE ALL FLAT on the ground when I hear Amy
cry out.

And then, almost as quickly, stifle her cries.

Maybe she bites into her forearm, but, whatever she does, the cries stop.

Nobody says anything until Grendelin pipes up.

"Guess that the area wasn't as clear as you hoped, huh?"

I busy myself, down on my front, looking out through the windows of the penthouse sitting room.

Staring at the building across from us.

Into one of the windows—_trying_ to get a look at the shooter.

But there's no clue. All the windows are darkened.

Only a scattering of lights, here and there.

The permanent residents.

As I lift myself up onto my knees, I feel a glob of sweat roll down my back—between my shoulder blades.

At any second, as I make my way to the front of the procession, to where Amy lies, quivering on the carpet, obviously in acute pain, I expect to hear another *crunch* of glass, and to feel one last, distant echo about my skull.

But it doesn't come.

When I reach Amy, I lower myself down to her, so that my face is level with hers.

Our eyes meet for a long moment. I look into those blue eyes.

Lose myself in them for a long while.

"What is it?" I say, my voice a husky whisper, though I'm fairly certain the sniper in the building opposite won't overhear me even if I shout.

Amy sinks her teeth into her lower lip, pushing all the blood out. She brings up her hands—clasped together tightly.

I stare, for a long time, at the blood which wells out from between her fingers.

Then I turn my attention down, to the carpet.

I can see the little finger, from the right hand, which the sniper bullet caught.

Lying in a sodden pool of blood.

I look back to Amy, and then to AA and Grendelin.

Amy's complexion looks about as pale as AA's now.

The only one wholly comfortable with this situation seems to be Grendelin.

And why wouldn't she be?

It's her island after all . . .

"I'll be right back," I say, and then, keeping low, and acting before anybody can protest, I make my way into the bathroom I passed by on the way to Grendelin's bedroom.

Although I know it's a risk, I realise that time is of the

essence, so I tug hard on the cord and a fluorescent strip bulb blinks on—joined by the droning hum of an out-of-sight extractor fan.

I turn my attention to the cabinet above the sink.

I snatch open the cabinet's mirror door, and peer inside.

Cotton balls.

Antiseptic.

Everything Amy needs.

I don't think too much—I just *grab*.

Once I have everything in my possession, I return to my downed soldiers—and their hostage—and I set about working with Amy, using the cotton balls to stem the bleeding.

Then, feeling a *truly* icky sensation down deep in my gut, I wrap up the little finger that got blown off by the bullet and collect it together in a bundle.

I use the now-empty little plastic bag the cotton balls came in as an extra layer of protection, enveloping the cotton-balled finger inside.

Then I hand the bundle to Amy.

Wincing hard, I say, "Put it in your pocket, okay?"

Amy does so.

I glance up, back to the window, expecting another shot to come at any moment.

I decide that I need to get some answers fast, and turn my attention to Grendelin.

"How many?" I say. "How many are there in the building across the road?"

Grendelin remains quiet, her gaze seething and sincere. "Why'd I tell you that? Unless you let me go, there's no chance of me calling them off."

I look back to Amy, who's—*understandably*—preoccupied with her swiftly bandaged up little finger.

When she meets my eye, she gives me a shrug, indicates that she has no idea whether or not Grendelin is telling the truth.

Just for good measure, I glance to AA too.

But he's no help either.

I turn back to Grendelin. "I reckon you're bluffing."

"Hmm?" Grendelin says, from her place on the floor. "Wanna try out that theory?"

I stick my head up once again.

Look to the window.

This could either be the most stupid thing I've *ever* done, or it could just tip the scales in our favour. Slowly, not wanting to make a rash move, I work myself back up onto my feet.

Stand up straight.

Already, I can feel my whole body shaking.

The pain in my calf muscle becomes impossible to bear for several seconds.

I sink my teeth down into my tongue, hoping to somehow control it.

It feels as if a bear's caught me from behind and is squeezing my ribs as hard as it possibly can.

As I pace over the sitting room carpet, towards the window, I keep my eyes sharp, looking over the façade of the building opposite, determined to work out the position of the shooter.

It's then that I see the gun:

A sniper rifle.

Up in a window, about three—or four—storeys above our current position.

It sits on its stand, tilted back, pointed up into the clear night sky.

No operator.

Otherwise I wouldn't still be standing.

A quick sweep along the rest of the windows, and I see nothing else.

When I turn my back, it's with confidence.

Even so, as I address the others, I'm certain that a bullet's going to plummet into my back.

Right between the shoulder blades.

"Get her up," I say. "And get her downstairs."

AA and Amy remain where they are for several moments before shifting.

AA grabs hold of Grendelin's arm, making sure he has a firm grip.

There's something a touch surreal about Grendelin wearing that satin nightgown of hers.

And the slippers.

It's only going to look all the more surreal when we get her out in the street.

That's when a thought strikes me.

If we're to have any chance—*any chance at all*—of escaping this island, then we need to keep Grendelin alive.

And to do that we need to make her more inconspicuous.

Believing that I don't have the time to communicate so much to AA and Amy, I shift past them, return to Grendelin's bedroom back down the hall.

I dig through the wardrobe quickly, getting hold of a pair of loose-fitting flannel trousers, and a toggle jacket which, even I find myself thinking, must be absolute blue murder to wear on this island . . . unless people here have a different sense of what 'cold' actually means . . .

Those items in hand, I set about dressing up Grendelin.
Just like playing with a doll as a girl . . . if I'd ever *had* dolls.
I order the others out of the penthouse, and down the stairs.
I give the apartment a final sweep before following them out.

21:18 PM

DOWN ON THE STREET, the air is much more arid than I recall.

I can feel the sweat eking its way out of my pores, turning my clothes damp from the inside-out.

I keep my gun down by my thigh as AA and Amy shepherd Grendelin along the deserted pavement—through the gloom of the evening.

As I limp along behind them, I glance around, knowing to expect a visit from a fellow assassin any second now.

But, for whatever it's worth, it seems like we're clear.

"Anna?"

It's AA.

"What?" I say.

"Where're we going?"

I glance around me, then look to Amy.

Just as she was back in the penthouse, she's preoccupied with her little finger—or *lack* thereof—and I need to call out to get her attention.

I ask about her ability to hotwire a car, and she assures me that she'll have no trouble doing so.

I hope she's right.

I manage to trudge my way to the front of the group again, and lead us along a narrow side street, which emerges into a group of parked cars.

The cars are all held within a steel-fenced paddock, and there's a chain keeping the gate secure.

But, from what I can see, there's no actual physical presence here.

The cars within are all kept beneath tarps—some of them turned green from, apparently, having been left out in the weather. These'll be the cars which belong to long-gone residents.

And we're going to take one of them.

Even before I manage to utter the question, Amy is clambering up the fence.

"What'd we do now?" AA says, looking at me with wide eyes.

"Once Amy busts this car out, we're going to the airport."

AA stares hard at me. "No *passports*, remember? We don't have any cash—*nothing*."

I glance to Grendelin, give her a slight smile. "I'm sure she'll be able to sort out something, don't you think?"

Here Grendelin gives me an indifferent look. "I believe so, yes."

I look back to AA. "There you go."

In the paddock, I can hear Amy fumbling about with one of the cars. Right as I think to turn away, there's the *tinkle* of breaking glass.

I look back at her. The glass has pattered all about her feet. It reflects the dim streetlights.

As if she's self-conscious of what she's doing, she flashes me a glance over her shoulder.

For some reason, I give her a corny thumbs-up in return.

But what am I *meant* to do?

Somehow—*no idea how*—Amy gets herself into one of the cars: a rather sporty-looking model, and red . . . which is about as far as my car knowledge goes.

With a few *chortles*, the engine turns over and begins to purr.

Almost like having my cat Lizzie back in my lap.

Almost.

Amy revs the engine.

It takes me a couple of heartbeats to ascertain what's about to happen.

And to shout for AA and Grendelin to get out of the way.

Once they do, Amy brings the engine to the top of its revs, and ploughs it into the gate.

She gives it enough power to smash through the gates at the first attempt.

21:21 PM

O NCE PILED INTO THE CAR—the gate which Amy crashed through becomes a distant memory. Amy puts her foot down, driving us through the still-life which is the cordoned-off area of the island. When we reach the gateway, the entrance is deserted, of course, so Amy has no choice but to drive right on through the now-static barrier.

To bust us to freedom.

I sit in the passenger seat while Grendelin and AA are in the back—the best place for someone to be held at gunpoint.

Already I'm feeling confident . . . confident that this plan is *somehow* going to work.

All we have to do now is get to the airport, because, once we do, everything becomes much simpler. There'll either be a success story or we'll all go down in flames.

As Amy opens up the car along the seaside road, I feel the throb of the engine passing through my seat, up into my stomach, sending my ribs tingling all over again.

It also sends a quick hum of pain through my calf muscle.

I press my lips tightly together and try not to think about it.

Not *worth* thinking about.

Once I get us out of peril, I can start thinking about how I'm going to patch myself up.

Amy drives us beyond the remit of the streetlights, so that the cordoned-off area of the city has long disappeared behind us, in the rear-view mirror. That's when she slips me a sidelong glance.

"Anna?" she says. "Which way is it—to the airport?"

A little distracted for a second by the darkness which has plunged in over the top of us, I stare out ahead, to the section of road which the car's headlights illuminate.

Although it pains me to admit it, I know the only way we're going to get ourselves onto the right track will be to consult with Grendelin.

I look into the back seat, see her sitting up against the window, chin resting on her fist, staring out at the passing blackness.

AA keeps his gun on her the entire time. He meets my eye for a quarter of a second.

"Which way?" I say, to Grendelin.

Grendelin continues to stare—*casually*—out the window, as if she hasn't heard me at all.

Then she turns to me, a slight smile on her lips as she does so.

"Follow the road ahead," she says, in her easy Caribbean drawl—seemingly so out of place in this situation; *right now*—"then take the next left, the one which heads back into the island."

I give a nod of understanding, then turn my attention back to Amy.

No need to relay the information, of course, she heard Grendelin just fine.

As the car ploughs on into the darkness, I can't help but notice, first in the rear-view mirror—and then in the wing mirror on my side—that there's a single light gleaming through the dark.

On our tail.

I turn in my seat, look back over my shoulder.

See that bright light—*like a moon*—pursuing us.

I look to Grendelin. See that she wears a slight smile.

When I look back again, though, the light has disappeared.

Before I can say anything at all, Grendelin says, "The turn is just up ahead—just here."

Amy slows the car, then brings us around the turn.

She whips the car around a switchback.

I perch on the edge of my seat, feeling the strain at the back of my calf muscle—the ticklish, *annoying* pain in my ribcage.

I spot the light once more.

This time it's in front of us.

Stopped in the road ahead.

I want to tell Amy to slow down, but the snarl of the engine is too loud.

She can't hear me.

Next thing I know—with the *scream* of tyres—the car swivels from side to side.

And then, with one long—*too long*—movement, it rolls.

21:34 PM

T HE WHOLE WORLD spins around me.
Crunching glass.
Crumpling metal.
My brain can't make sense of it for a long time.
I feel my heart kick on a few beats—then stop completely.
The top of my head smashes into the roof of the car.
Bright-purple speckles dot my vision.
My head aches hard within my skull.
I taste blood in my mouth.
And I feel it run—*warm and sticky*—down the side of my face.
The car keeps on rolling.
Glass, like hailstones, strikes me.
The car finally comes to rest.
I blink once—*twice*—and a whole day seems to pass.
When I return to my senses, though, glance at my watch, I
see that no time has passed at all.

I guess I'm going to have to add an MRI scan to my hospital trip . . .

I work quickly, brushing the tiny, glass cubes from the destroyed windscreen off my lap. The pieces are rough against my palms.

That done, I jab the release button for my seatbelt.

The spring-loaded strap spindles away over me.

Returns to its base above.

Or below.

The car engine continues to idle on.

The windscreen has been totally destroyed.

Only frosted glass now.

A warm waft of outside air plumes in through the gap.

I look to my side, see Amy, just coming around from the shock, at the wheel.

"Turn it off," I say, my words hurried, blurring together in my mind.

Amy blinks hard several times, then does as I tell her.

With no engine, the world becomes silent all of a sudden.

And we lose the reflected gleam of the headlights within the car.

It's easier for me to make sense of my surroundings now.

I can tell that the car's flipped over.

That we're all hanging *upside down* within it.

My heart skips another dozen or so beats as my brain comes to terms with *that*.

Then I decide it's time to spark into action.

Enough of this 'coming around' nonsense . . .

"AA?" I say.

No reply.

I turn to look into the back seat, my eyes slowly becoming accustomed to the gloom.

Just like the windscreen, the rear-view window has been almost totally destroyed in the crash.

And, like the windscreen, it now resembles frosted glass.

Even in the gloom, I can make out the sparkle of the broken cubes of glass lying all over the seat.

AA continues to hold the gun in his hand—*gripped tightly*—and he leans up against the window.

Grendelin, too, is motionless.

Not wanting to take any chances, I reach through the gap between the driver and passenger seats, into the back seat, and pry the gun out from his fingers.

I toss it down at my feet, into the floor space.

I glance back to Amy, see that she's still coming around.

Not quite with it.

I look back through what remains of the windscreen.

I can see the light from before.

That single headlight.

Like a full moon.

Ahead of us.

Stopped in the road.

All of a sudden, I feel a tightness settle over my chest.

I can't help wondering if I might've broken yet more ribs in the impact.

But I don't let that bother me right now.

I pad the door, reach for the release catch.

Yank it towards me.

From somewhere, I hear a faint *click*.

Then the door goes loose in my hand.

I push it hard—and *away*.

The door gives a *groan* of protest, but it opens for me.

I stare out at the sky below me, the grassy verge above.

And that shining moon ahead.

I pad my waistline, find my gun—*Punisher*—and slip it from its holster.

Gun in hand, I tumble out of the car.

21:40 PM

T O BEGIN WITH, my brain has a real job to do in terms of figuring out the new lay of the land . . . where exactly the land even *is* for that matter.

When I hurl myself free of the car, I spend a long few seconds, drawing hard breaths, lying sprawled on the grassy verge.

Once I've spent enough time doing that, I roll myself back over onto my belly, and I stare out ahead. That full moon still gleams back at me.

A silhouette approaches.

I tell myself I need to get hidden—otherwise I'll be in *big* trouble.

I just about manage to stagger to my feet.

Waves of pain plough through my calf muscle.

Some sort of punishment, I suppose.

As I get myself upright, I eye the figure.

Impossibly closer now.

The only explanation for me still being alive—for me *not* having been shot down—is that I'm invisible. And that means I have the upper-hand.

I decide that I have to do it—that there's no choice.

I raise my gun, squeeze the trigger.

Nothing happens.

My mind sketches back to when Amy handed me the gun.

I tell myself that I should have known—*should have known!*

Of course Amy was trying to neutralise me.

Of *course* she's a double . . . or *triple* . . . agent.

Why would she *ever* go against her father?

That's when I notice the safety catch still engaged.

I scold myself. Flip it off.

When I try again, the gun works just fine.

21:43 PM

I CATCH THE SILHOUETTE in the upper arm, and the force of the gunshot sends the person keeling over, their limbs flying all over, apparently attempting—and *failing*—to recover their balance.

Despite everything—despite having just rolled over in a car while attempting to flee the country—I allow myself a slight smile.

I stride onwards, along the grassy verge, with my gun down at my thigh.

The pain in my calf muscle is unbearable now, and to call it a 'stride' is really a disrespect to gaits everywhere.

The single headlight—the full moon—comes from a stationary motorbike, parked on the road, set upright on its kickstand.

I can hear the gentle *putter-purr* of its engine clamouring through the otherwise silent night.

With my gun still tight in my hand, I stand over the prostrate body.

Stare down at the face in the glow from the single headlight.

I take in the swirling red hair.

Tanned skin.

The green eyes, half concealed beneath droopy lids.

Tabby.

I suppose that when Grendelin couldn't have me, she decided to go for Tabby.

That'll teach me that nobody's dead until I can give them a nice old kick with the toe of my boot.

Be sure that they're no longer moving.

She looks back up at me, a slight smile on her face, one of those dizzy-with-shock smiles . . . I know those smiles well.

Only then, when I turn my attention to her upper body, to her arm where I shot her, do I realise she's wearing a pretty much identical outfit to the one which Brian Mathewson decided to hand me and AA for the job:

Light fleece over waterproof trousers.

All *black*, of course.

". . . Anna?" she says, her voice faint.

I spot her gun—a *handgun*—lying on the tarmac about ten, fifteen paces away.

Clearly too far for Tabby to grab in her current state.

I suppose, back at the motorbike, she has a rifle all propped up, too.

Guess I'd better make a mental note to sort out those details before fleeing the scene.

Wouldn't want a curious young kid—with even more curious hands—to stumble across any of the above.

I crouch down, at Tabby's side.

I eye the wound, the wet patch on her arm, where I shot her.

"Yeah?" I say, finally replying to Tabby.

". . . Are you . . . are you . . ." Tabby begins, and then her strength seems to fail her.

Her eyes remain open, and although her breathing is shallow, her heartbeat doesn't stop. Her eyes look past me now, over my shoulder. Almost as if she's . . . *distracted*.

I feel my chest clench tight.

Ice runs through my veins.

But, this time, it's not from pain.

I take care to turn slowly, not wanting to set anything off—to make *anybody* jumpy.

When I glance over my shoulder, I see that Grendelin's standing there.

A gun in her hand.

AA's gun.

The one which I tossed into the floor space of the passenger seat.

I stare long and hard into the tiny, black hole of the gun, knowing that I might as well be staring death right back in the eye—just as I have done many times before.

Grendelin herself blurs into the background.

As Grendelin stands there, the gun gripped tightly in her hand, I can only think to utter faint words beneath my breath.

"You won't win," I say. "You *won't* win."

21:48 PM

I T'S ALMOST as if the sound happens on a different plane entirely.

I'm only aware of it seconds afterwards.

The vibration passes across the surface of my skin.

An *aftershock*.

I can almost see the yawning void opening up before my eyes.

Ready to suck me in.

My heart sinks down to my stomach.

And my throat constricts.

I wish myself back home.

Back in my house.

Back with my cat.

Back so that I'll be close to my children . . . no matter how wretched of a mother I am.

I close my eyes.

Waiting.

Hearing my heart tick along in my ears.

The muffled *bum-bum, bum-bum.*

But the end never comes.

No matter how much I wish it would.

Finally, I open my eyes.

Grendelin lies on her front—*dead*—mouth latched open, and eyes agog.

On the tarmac.

The jacket we 'disguised' her in having come open, exposing the satin nightdress she wears underneath.

Dead.

Again, that word rings through my brain.

Makes an echoplex of my skull.

Slowly, I raise my eyes.

They come to meet the figure who stands over Grendelin's dead body.

Amy.

In the headlight from the parked motorbike, her eyes flash like sapphires reflecting a blazing fire.

My heart beats in my throat.

Beneath my tongue.

Gradually, I lift myself up, away from where I crouched at Tabby's side.

It doesn't occur to me to see to Tabby.

My attention is all focussed on Amy now.

The two of us stare at one another.

Amy continues to hold the gun on Grendelin.

As if she might revive.

Leap back up from her dead state.

But she stays still.

A corpse.

In the end, it's Tabby who speaks next. ". . . Anna?"

This time I do turn around—see to her.

I set my gaze on her.

And she sees that she's the focus of attention.

"What . . . what happens now?" Tabby says.

I feel a warmth down deep in my stomach.

And then, almost out of nowhere, a swirling nausea grips me.

I look back to Amy, now holstering her gun, but still hypnotised at having had to kill 'Auntie' Grendelin.

In the distance, I make out the blurred-together composite of AA staggering out of the car. He rubs his head. And, in the glow from the headlight, I can see blood dampening his forehead. He turns in our direction, sleepily, as if he's just risen from his pit after spending an afternoon in bed, recovering from a particularly bad hangover.

If only it'd been a Big Night Out.

If only . . .

00:09 AM

W E REACH THE AIRPORT a couple of hours later, though I don't know quite why we bother.

After all, two of us don't even have passports and, when I ask Tabby whether she has hers, she informs me that she doesn't.

The last time I checked, everybody wishing to travel internationally needs a passport of their own. One passport between four just won't cut it.

I look to Amy, hoping that she has some kind of technological trick she can pull off. That she might be able to go and work her ex-copper's magic on one of the airport officials.

Maybe it's the time of night, or perhaps it's official policy, but Amy finds herself knocked back, over and over, one official after the next.

Nobody wants to speak to her.

Not even when she explains her *police* business.

Even when she flashes a—I'm sure, *one-hundred-per-cent* authentic—badge.

I think back to our trip to the airport, and how we all trudged along the minor road to catch a taxi, after cleaning up the accident site the best we could—leaving Grendelin in a ditch by the side of the road, to be found by the local constabulary . . . or not.

We dug some small holes for the guns in the same ditch as Grendelin—I can still smell the reek of sewage beneath my fingernails.

That should at least keep them concealed before the next big rain storm, and, with any luck, render the guns all useless.

It was a little heart-wrenching to give up *Punisher*, but I reasoned that, since it was going to be so difficult for us to get off the ground in the first place—not having passports or anything—that it was for the best to bury it in the ditch with the other firearms.

The airport, like all airports, smells of body odour and disinfectant. And I can see a bastion of cleaners, all of them with swivel-head mops in hand, making good progress on bringing the beige tiled floor to a brilliant shine.

I can't quite shift the feeling that, in a matter of moments, somebody official—or, worse, one of Grendelin's 'boys', will crop up and recapture us.

I can't imagine they'll take all that well to finding their leader dead and left in a ditch out in the countryside.

Starting to panic that we'll *never* get out of here, I glance to Tabby, who's still pale, but recovered from the initial shock of getting shot.

She seems to have realised that her wound—for the most part —is cosmetic.

From my quick inspection, I noted that the bullet passed cleanly through the skin, and right out the other side.

Tabby, though, just gives me a doleful shake of the head.

Immediately absolving herself of any sort of responsibility.

I glance around the airport, looking for *something* . . . for *some* sort of hope.

It's on the second pass when I notice her.

And, in retrospect, it's no wonder I missed her on the first pass.

How she seems to blend in—*completely*—with the scenery.

Just as she did back at the budget hotel, before this job got started, she wears a long black trench coat. A wide-brimmed hat on top, keeping her blond hair orderly and squashed down on her scalp. She sits up on a barstool beside a shuttered coffee booth. She has a cardboard cup sitting on the ledge before her, apparently long ago finished with.

I look back to the others, to AA, Tabby and Amy.

Then I slip a look back at the blond woman, finally deciding that it *isn't* a mirage.

Or whatever the hell you call it when you see people who aren't there.

Ghosts?

When I meet AA's eye, I realise that he hasn't yet noticed the blond woman.

Without a word to any of the others, I stalk away, pace across the floor of the airport to the blond woman sat on the stool.

Already, I can feel my heart swelling in my throat.

The blond woman has her back to me now.

When I peer over her shoulder, I see she's tapping away at a mobile phone screen. No doubt enraptured by some conversation with Brian Mathewson . . . I'd be so glad never to hear *that* particular name ever again.

"Excuse me," I say to the blond woman.

She feigns not to hear me.

So I reach out, grab her by the shoulder.

Jerk her around to face me.

As I grip her shoulder tightly, she gives a slight sigh and, with her free hand, deposits her mobile phone into the inside pocket of her trench coat.

Finally, she meets my eye.

I can see, like last time, she wears that same brownish-black mixture of heavy eye makeup; the stuff which makes her light-blue eyes really stand out.

That *distinct* perfume she wears:

The one which smells strongly of blackberries and hazelnuts.

"Please, Anna," the woman says, nodding over my shoulder.

Although I know this to be the oldest trick in the book, the old 'look-that-way' move, I do so.

And it's probably for the best, because it's then that I see a pair of soldiers, dressed in that same grey-blue camo, standing by the automatic doors of the airport.

The two of them packing some serious-looking hardware.

More than enough firepower to take care of my impromptu team.

To take care of all four of us.

Already, I can feel a weight dropping down on my shoulders.

It's all been for nothing . . . no, *worse*, we've killed their leader, so there'll be severe repercussions coming.

Why couldn't I just have taken up Grendelin on her offer?

. . . Returned to her office, informed her that I'd have no problem being in her service—in her *debt*—for the better part of eternity?

I turn back to the blond woman. "Do they know?" I say, and then realise that I haven't yet filled in the blond woman on what we've actually done.

That we've *killed* Grendelin.

But the blond woman already seems to know.

She shakes her head.

"Not yet—and they won't until you're a long way from here."

"A long way from here?" I say, shaking my head. "No, there's no way for us to get off the island—three of us don't have passports, we have no money—"

The blond woman draws up a leather handbag from where she kept it previously concealed in her lap. She opens it with a sharp *snap* and digs around within.

After a moment or two, she produces not three, but *four* passports from within.

All that same burgundy-red British-passport shade.

She hands them to me, and I see that an elastic band keeps them stuck together as if they were nothing more than office supplies.

"Here," she says, "that should sort out the first issue."

She continues to dig around in her handbag, and then comes up again, this time producing some neatly folded pieces of paper.

She hands *those* to me.

"That's special permission," she says.

" 'Special permission' for what?" I reply.

The blond woman glances up, then nods off towards an anonymous-looking door on the other side of the airport.

An airport official stands guard, his hands clasped at his waist, clearly with his mind on other matters.

"Just show it over there. And you'll be able to go through."

With the passports clutched in my hand, down at my thigh, I look to the blond woman, the disbelief clearly sketched all over my face. "Who *are* you?" I say.

"Please," the blond woman says, digging through her

handbag again. "There's not much time."

"Time?" I say, feeling a rage building inside me. "What'd you *mean* time?"

The blond woman says nothing in return.

Finally, having apparently gone through the entire contents of her handbag, she comes up with a silvery-blue object. It takes a couple of heartbeats in my throat before my brain catches up with what it is that she holds:

A memory stick . . . no, not quite, *the* memory stick.

The reason why Brian had me and AA go on this whole wild-goose chase.

Like a petulant child, I make a grab for it.

But the blond woman jerks it away.

She gives a slight smile. "Didn't think this existed, did you?"

I say nothing in reply.

She knows that she's got me.

That I *always* like to see a case through.

Finally, the blond woman does pass me the memory stick. "This is an act of trust," she says. "On the part of Brian." She pauses for a second, and then adds, "A parley."

"What?" I say, screwing up my eyes.

"You know," the blond woman says, smiling, "when a pair of pirates decide to down arms, and to have some peace while they work things out. While they lick their wounds."

"I don't follow."

"Brian's giving you this memory stick, Anna, this information which—if shared with certain publications around the world— would bring Brian to his knees. Anything about *anyone* shady Brian has ever employed—has ever even *entertained*—is on this memory stick. And it's up to you to decide when to use it."

" 'When'? " I say.

The blond woman smiles wider. "*If,*" she says, apparently correcting herself.

She looks at her watch, then glances around the terminal.

When I follow her gaze, I see that a white four-by-four with tinted windows has rolled up outside the airport, and that the driver is still running the engine.

"I'd better be off," the blond woman says, gathering her handbag, and slipping the strap over the shoulder of her trench coat. "A few loose ends to wrap up." She glances down at my leg, nods to it. "When you land, there'll be someone present to take a look at your injuries—at *all* of your injuries."

The blond woman makes to leave.

"Wait!" I say, repressing the urge to reach out and grab her this time . . . not really in any mood to get shot by that pair of young upstarts with rifles by the automatic doors.

The blond woman pauses.

Glances back at me.

One of those glances which tells me I have precisely *three seconds* to get my point across, otherwise I'm wasting her time.

"Does this mean it's over?" I say.

"Is *what* over?" she replies.

"Our relationship," I say, feeling my throat constricting again, realising that I'm making the boss-employee dynamic I have going with Brian sound almost *romantic.*

I look over to Amy, AA and Tabby.

The blond woman follows my gaze, looks over the others.

Then she turns back to me.

This time there's no trace of a smile.

"I would've thought that much was implied," she says, and then treads away.

Out to the waiting car.

01:44 AM

I HAVE TO ADMIT, as I sit in my seat on the plane—a window seat, no less—that I'm too tired to summon the energy to be *afraid* of flying.

I feel the engines drone, reaching their high-pitched peak.

The throttle opens up as we soar along the runway.

And I'm not scared.

I glance along the row, to the seats alongside.

AA sits in the seat beside me, an eyeshade already drawn down over his eyes, and his mouth wide open as he snores away.

No surprises there.

Across the aisle, I look to Amy and Tabby, the two of them sitting side by side.

Both dozing, too.

Not quite with their eyes closed, but certainly getting there.

All in all, this has been *quite* a trip.

Some new friendships forged.

Or so it seems.

It does rankle a little to feel that the safety net which is Brian Mathewson has been tugged out from beneath me forever.

And that although Brian Mathewson brought me, Tabby, AA and Amy together, that he's also going to drive us apart again.

But that's just how it goes.

That's *life*.

For the first time ever, I hardly notice the take-off—almost don't even sneak a cursory, suspicious, glance out the window at the sea far below.

Almost.

The plane begins to level out on this *private* service laid on by Brian Mathewson. There was no preamble, not even the pre-flight safety demonstration.

The whole ordeal was—really—just as simple as getting into a very large car.

As I sit in my seat, my stomach strangely obeying, I consider just what it means by Brian giving us the memory stick.

Was this all some sort of a test?

To see just what me, AA and Tabby would be able to manage?

If we could sneak our way out of Death's noose?

It makes me think that the blond woman was sitting by, all the while, keeping score.

Waiting to see whether we would sink or swim.

Are we on a level-pegging now?

If we are, I find it both good news and bad . . .

Because if Brian *does* believe that me and the others are on a level-pegging with him then it follows that he believes us a threat.

But, like all great businessmen, Brian knows that a threat—above all else—must be respected.

That must be what the memory stick is about.

Between us, we have the tool to destroy Brian at will.

Well, I haven't yet told the others . . . haven't got the chance yet . . . or that's what I tell myself.

As I consider all the intricacies of our current situation, I hardly notice that the drinks service has started up.

I glance to AA, see that he's still snoring away.

Like a good lady passenger, I bring my retractable tray down.

And await the cabin crew.

It's only when my eyes skirt the headrests, catch sight of the drinks trolley, that something snicks in my brain—something *deep* and almost out of reach.

But then it strikes me.

My eyes travel over the appearance of the stewardesses.

One blond.

The other brunette.

In their forties—*maybe* fifties.

Smiles stitched onto their faces.

I lose myself for a long while.

Realise that they're the same—*exactly the same*—stewardesses as the ones who came on the flight here . . . on the flight which me and AA 'hijacked'.

A gruff voice breaks me free of my daze.

"Something to drink, madam?"

I glance up.

And then I see him.

Tanned skin.

That slightly accented English.

And the neat—some might say *pristine*—appearance.

Enrique Suarez.

To begin with, I can't speak at all, and when I do, the words are far too quiet.

Suarez busies himself with his drinks trolley, as if he had heard me just fine. He pours out some fizzy water into a transparent cup full of ice. He hands it to me, without another glance. "Here you are, madam," he says, and then heads on, along the aisle, disappearing behind the curtain, into the cabin crew's quarters . . . a place where only *they* can go.

For the longest time, I stare long and hard at the fizzy water sat on the plastic tray in front of me.

I lose myself in the bubbles, clinging to the side of the glass, some of them swilling to the surface where they pop.

AA snores long and hard beside me, his breathing almost in time with the jet engines.

Finally, I reach out for the glass, feel the chill of the contents through the plastic. I grip the glass tight, bring it up to my lips. And then tilt the contents into my mouth—moistening my tongue.

By the time I put the glass down, now half full, I shift a last glance out through the window, down at the silent ocean, illuminated only by the moonlight.

And I know that—*at last*—I'm free.

Truly and completely.

And it terrifies me.

THE END

Author's Note

Thank you for taking the time to read one of my books. If you would like to hear about my latest releases you can sign up for my newsletter here: www.aviain.com

Thanks for reading!

AV Iain

Hell Bird
The Fourth Anna Harris Novel

www.ingramcontent.com/pod-product-compliance
Lightning Source LLC
Chambersburg PA
CBHW030921050726
47498CB00003BA/843